# THE ADVENTURE OF THE PECULIAR PROTOCOLS

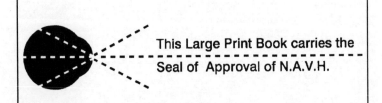

This Large Print Book carries the
Seal of Approval of N.A.V.H.

# THE ADVENTURE OF THE PECULIAR PROTOCOLS

## ADAPTED FROM THE JOURNALS OF JOHN H. WATSON, M.D.

## NICHOLAS MEYER

**THORNDIKE PRESS**

A part of Gale, a Cengage Company

Thorndike Press® Large Print Mystery.
The text of this Large Print edition is unabridged.
Other aspects of the book may vary from the original edition.
Set in 16 pt. Plantin.

LIBRARY OF CONGRESS CIP DATA ON FILE.
CATALOGUING IN PUBLICATION FOR THIS BOOK
IS AVAILABLE FROM THE LIBRARY OF CONGRESS

ISBN-13: 978-1-4328-7621-0 (hardcover alk. paper)

Published in 2020 by arrangement with Macmillan Publishing Group, LLC/St. Martin's Publishing Group

Printed in Mexico
Print Number: 01      Print Year: 2020

For Leslie,
bringer of life

# CONTENTS

# A WORD OF EXPLANATION

For a good portion of my adult life I have been involved with and found myself editing missing, unknown, or unearthed manuscripts alleged to have been authored by Sherlock Holmes's amanuensis, John H. Watson, M.D. It had been years since I had given any thought to this subject when an item in *The New York Times* last September caught my eye.

An auction had taken place at Sotheby's in London at which a diary or journal (the catalogue used both terms) supposedly written by Watson had been purchased for a princely £45 million sterling by an anonymous buyer via phone.

I had no idea what to make of this. Did Watson keep a diary? On first blush, as we've no mention of it, this appears unlikely. On the other hand, Watson refers constantly to his "copious notes" on which his case accounts are based, which may amount to more or less the same thing. I suspect, by whatever name, Watson was a compulsive chronicler, somewhat in the manner of Pepys or Anaïs Nin. He wrote down everything, if only for the sake of writing it down.

Regardless, I did not expect the anonymous diary purchaser to reveal himself — (or herself) — any time soon.

Nor did they.

But last December I was contacted by Greg Prickman, head of Special Collections at the University of Iowa Libraries, where my papers are kept. Greg (who has since become librarian of the Folger Shakespeare Library in Washington, DC) astonished me by saying that the diary in question had been loaned by its purchaser to the university for the period of one year.

"Why in the world would he have done such a thing?" I asked Greg on the phone. "For sure there're places with bigger endowments than my alma mater."

"Hey, this isn't rocket science," the librarian responded. "Can't you guess?"

The first response that came into my head was Holmes's dictum "I never guess: it is an appalling habit, destructive to the logical faculty," but in truth, not being Holmes, I guess all the time. I'm also a sucker for magic acts and can never correctly figure the solution to any mystery stories.

"Well, I can," Greg offered from Iowa City. "The donor — and don't ask who, because I'm not allowed to tell — clearly is aware of your editorial functions on previous Watsonsonia. He knows your papers are held here and is hoping the journal is catnip you'd be tempted to look at and possibly work on."

"But he doesn't want to shell out any more dough."

"Heck, maybe the purchase bankrupted him."

Sure.

Once he'd connected the dots, I suspected Greg was right. I was in the middle of working on *Star Trek: Discovery,* but after the show was up and running, I flew to Iowa City (or rather Cedar Rapids), where Greg met me at the airport.

"What do you think?" I asked him, wasting no time. "Fool's gold or the real McCoy?"

"You're the expert," he said, climbing behind the wheel of his Jeep Cherokee.

"But you must have formed an opinion."

"Yes, I must."

This was all I could get out of him. We checked me into the newish Hilton Garden Inn on Burlington, but only long enough to park my bag. Then it was off to the library, where Greg dialed open the big-ass walk-in, temperature-controlled vault reserved for precious manuscripts. Within was a metal desk and an uncomfortable folding chair.

What Greg showed me was an old date book of sorts, whose brittle red leather binding had almost entirely fragmented. Inside were yellowing, lined pages in what looked to me like Watson's familiar hand. It was some kind of diary, though very hard to make out in places. Truth to tell, the thing was falling apart, and a bunch of pages were altogether AWOL. Some looked like they had been torn out. Greg told me that the document had lain in an airless safety deposit box in a UK bank that had gone under or been swallowed up by a larger bank (he thought Lloyds, but couldn't recall — wherever it was stashed had no humidifier), before it went under the hammer at Sotheby's and was snapped up by . . . who knows? Someone with a lot of kale.

Greg, evidently, but he wasn't talking. Fishy, fishy, fishy. The world of art and artifacts, as we all know, is cluttered with fakes. There are more Renoirs floating around (many of them in prominent museums) than Renoir ever painted. The anonymous donor or buyer, the Rembrandt in the attic, blahblah.

Still, if this was a phony, someone had gone to an awful lot of trouble. And the whole deal was not without what Holmes might term "features of interest." Chief among them is that what I read is the account of a failure. There are, of course, cases in which Holmes failed (one has only to think of the word "Norbury"), but here we have what, if true, amounts to the biggest and most consequential failure of the detective's entire career.

I am — again — in no position to authenticate what follows, and I've done the most editorial work I've ever performed on a manuscript, which was frequently illegible in its original format, mandating much guesswork. There are snatches of dialogue, brief descriptions, cramped marginalia, instructions ("remember!" or "don't forget!"), and occasional words in foreign languages. The writer, whoever he was, used both sides of the paper, which added to my difficulties. There was a lot of bleedthrough. The events chronicled occur at the start of the twentieth century, but there is no evidence that Watson (?), who died in 1940, ever revised or corrected what he'd jotted down at the time. Thus the reader will discover no "prescient" anticipations, rejigged with the benefits of hindsight. The tone, it must be conceded, certainly resembles Watson's. The matter of dates, for once, is indisputable; this was, after all, a journal, and the diarist had been punctilious in specifying them. Moreover, it is easy to confirm these dates when juxtaposing them with events of record, alluded to in the text. I've retained Watson's orthography; he was writing in English, not American. (I note that I've drifted into referring to the writer as Watson, which may reveal a certain willing credulity on my part. I did say I'm a sucker for magic tricks.) As noted above, several pages are inexplicably missing, and another did in fact crumble as I scanned it too hastily. Rather than maintain the diary format (though I've retained his use of entry dates here and there), it was, I confess, easier to recast what I could make out in the form Watson might have used had he seen fit to arrange the case for publication. As will be seen, that idea never occurred to him.

For good reason.

For that same good reason, Watson never appended a title to his notes. "The Adventure of the Peculiar Protocols" has been supplied by me, in addition to occasional explanatory footnotes.

Lastly, it must be stipulated that notwith-standing the foregoing, any errors in what follows are Watson's, not mine.

Nicholas Meyer
Los Angeles, 2019

■ ■ ■ ■

# PART ONE: ENGLAND

■ ■ ■ ■

# 1.
## A REUNION

"My dear Watson, you astonish me," proclaimed a smiling Sherlock Holmes, sitting to my right on a crimson banquette in the newly refurbished Grill Room of the Café Royal. "Baccarat." He tapped the bulbous glass approvingly. "And a more than decent claret within it. To say nothing of a splendid veal chop, Brussels sprouts with chestnuts, and the promise of mince pie to come," he added, "followed no doubt by an excellent coffee, brandy, and cigar. Such largesse! It is inescapable that your practice in Pimlico is thriving. Or can it be that after a mere two years, domesticity has begun to pall?"

Accustomed to his familiar teasing on the subject of my marriage,\* I declined to rise to the bait.

"My bride, as I delight in terming her, is,

\* This would appear to be Watson's mysterious second marriage.

it happens, an excellent chef. I need not dine out for culinary gratification."

"How else then to explain such reckless extravagance in an ex–army surgeon?"

"It is my turn to confess astonishment," I shot back, hardly able to conceal my amusement. "Can you think of no occasion for such a repast?"

"Occasion?" Holmes raised a quizzical eyebrow. His grey eyes twinkled amid the gleam of a dozen gas jets, whose mirrored reflections multiplied their number and gave the place its pleasing ambience, and waved a languid arm with extended fingers in the general direction of the glittering assemblage. I was pleased to see the well-loved establishment had chosen to retain its old-fashioned illumination. Incandescent lights were sure to prove less atmospheric.

"You cannot guess?"

He frowned.

"I never guess."

I sat back, more than pleased with myself.

"Let us marshal the facts," I suggested. "The date, for example."

He frowned once more, twirling the stem of his glass between a thumb and forefinger.

"The date . . ."

"The sixth of January."

"What of it?"

"Come now, Holmes. January sixth is your birthday."

"Oh, that." He swallowed a mouthful of claret with a dismissive expression that belied the vintage.

"Not merely January sixth, *1905.* You are fifty years old today. If that is no occasion for celebration, I cannot imagine what is."

"I'm not at all sure I concur," my singular companion mused. "About being fifty, I mean. As you know, I can never remember the year of my birth. I was doubtless too young to make note of it at the time."

We studied one another after the fashion of friends who've not seen one another recently. I know his eagle eye discerned my *avoirdupois;* it was not that hard to perceive. But I must say, though his jet hair was now agreeably flecked with silver, the detective did not look his age. His eyes remained as bright, his nose as hawklike and imperious, his jawline as firm as ever I knew them.

There was a caesura during our mutual inventory while a silent waiter topped up our glasses. The man was hardly out of earshot when I made so bold as to respond.

"As your biographer, I, on the other hand, am certain of your age. Be that as it may," I rushed on before he could debate me, "here we find ourselves at the dawn of the twenti-

21

eth century, and whether you are fifty or else forty-nine or fifty-one, you are indubitably at the zenith of your capacities and —"

"Ready for retirement, you're about to say."

"I was about to say no such thing!"

"Well, I was. Think, if you will, about 1904," he persisted. "Surely the most boring year on record, and the new one gives no promise of a better."

"Holmes, really."

"From a criminal standpoint, I mean. Oh, for all I know great things are in the works elsewhere, and we have captured Lhasa — which I can tell you from personal experience is nothing to boast of —* but crime, I'm sorry to say, has reached an all-time nadir. There is a positive dearth of imagination amongst the criminal class nowadays. Embezzlement is the best they can manage. Tricks with numbers."

"Does the body found two days ago near London Bridge not arouse your interest? *The Daily Telegraph* says the unfortunate creature had been stabbed. Perhaps," I added, hoping to rouse him, "it is still the

* During the years of the Great Hiatus, Holmes claimed to have visited Lhasa, which the British captured in 1904.

handiwork of Saucy Jack?"

He all but rolled his eyes. "Come, my boy, you can do better than that. Saucy Jack, as you are pleased to call him, added mutilation to his murders, always limited himself to slatterns from the East End, and never disposed of their remains in the Thames. I've no doubt the well-dressed, tallow-haired woman found by the police launch will prove merely the victim of a domestic tragedy. Her husband or lover will shortly be apprehended and the sordid matter speedily brought to its equally sordid conclusion." Here he heaved a sigh. "Ergo, what is left for me, but retirement? Somewhere in the country, I shall rusticate among flora and fauna."

Rather than have him pursue this bucolic if querulous train of thought, I produced the parcel I had hitherto sought to conceal. This time both eyebrows were hoisted aloft.

"What have we here?"

"A gift. Not from me," I hastened to add, knowing his distaste for the sentimental. "My surprise supper was all I dared, but Juliet also wishes you a happy birthday. Go on, man, open it."

With a sigh of what I took to be resignation, Holmes employed the knife he had lately applied to his veal chop to slice the knotted twine and unwrap what proved to be a sizable tome.

"*War and Peace,*" he murmured. "A novel by" — he twisted the volume — "Count Tol-stoy, in a first English translation by Constance — ah." He smiled with a shake of his head. "Garnett. Your wife's sister-in-law, if I am not mistaken?"*

"Constance has cornered the market on the Russians," I conceded. "This one is just published. I know you do not, as a rule, read novels, but —"

"But our friend in Vienna recommends this one highly," Holmes concluded to my consternation.

"How on earth did you know that?"

He chuckled as he idly thumbed the uncut leaves with some skepticism. "You know my methods, Watson, yet when I explain them you are always disappointed. I know you doctors like to keep in touch, though I doubt even our friend, with his keen mind, could keep track of all these Russian names."

"You forget, he endorsed *Crime and Pun-*

* Watson appears to have married the sister of the literary critic Edward Garnett, whose wife, Constance, was the first English translator of Tolstoy et al.

24

*ishment,* by that other Russian with the unpronounceable name, calling it the greatest novel ever written."

Holmes continued perusing the pages. "They *all* have unpronounceable names," he remarked, then looked up, smiling. "But so he did. One day I must give it a try. Please thank Mrs. Watson for her —"

"Well, well, the birthday boy in the flesh."

A large shadow darkened our table, coming between the chandelier and the remains of our meal. The voice behind it sounded as though it emanated from a well.

We looked up in joint surprise to behold a backlit mass of corpulent humanity.

"Mycroft." Holmes looked at me reproachfully. "In the flesh," he echoed quietly.

"Holmes, I give you my word, I had no idea —"

His brother interrupted in a smooth rumble. "And I give you mine, your amanuensis had none, Sherlock. But I have my methods, as you would say, and I could scarcely allow such a momentous occasion to pass unremarked." He surveyed our table. "What a pity your waiter's wife has abandoned him and their two children in favor of a groom in the stables of the Life Guards."

25

"Household Cavalry," Holmes corrected him in a flat tone. "And she only left after he joined the ranks of Italian anarchists. Let us hope our table has not been mined," he added. Mycroft chose to ignore this.

"Ah, presents, to be sure." He fastened his eyes on mine. "When he was a boy, his birthday, coming as it does so soon after Boxing Day, was always experienced as a disappointment. No more gifts, you see. He must content himself with stale New Year's Day trifle and, when he was older, flat champagne."

"Will you join us?" I inquired with some reluctance.

"Mycroft is on his way elsewhere," his younger brother murmured, staring at his plate. "Hence he makes no move to divest himself of his greatcoat."

"Still at your parlour tricks." Mycroft chuckled with what sounded like the reverberations of a volcano. "I will leave you to them — albeit we are far from the parlour. Many happy returns of the day, Sherlock." The Silenus extended an enormous paw, which the detective touched briefly with his fingertips. "Doctor." And with a silent grace for which one would scarcely have given him credit, the great man, if I may so term

26

him, glided from the room.

"How curious of him to trouble about your birthday," I observed, eyeing his retreating form. I was irresistibly reminded of an iceberg on the move.

"My brother had no more idea than I it was my birthday, let alone any thought of celebrating it."

"Whatever can you mean?"

Holmes opened the hand that had recently taken that of his brother. In the palm nestled a crumpled page seemingly torn from an engagement diary. Seeing that he offered it to my inspection, I opened the scrap and read: *Diogenes. Tomorrow. 10:00.*

"Ah."

"Indeed. Perhaps I spoke too soon."

"I'm not sure I follow."

"About 1905 being as dull as its predecessor. As you know, Mycroft never troubles about me unless the Foreign Office is at a loss."

I could see Holmes's spirits lifting.

"And I never understand why, with his own formidable intellect and vaunted powers of deduction, your brother ever turns to you."

The mince pie arrived garnished with ice cream and Holmes tucked into it with a will, declaring it between mouthfuls unsurpassed in his experience. Still constitutionally thin as a musket (another sore point from my perspective), it was remarkable how much his metabolism allowed him to consume with no discernible effects.

He chewed meditatively, evidently still pondering my question.

"*Superior* powers, you tactfully refrain from saying. Ah, but you forget, my dear doctor, how incurably lazy Mycroft can be. Idleness is his métier. If he is allowed to remain in his chair, a vast thinking machine, cross-indexing data and sifting through alternatives, my brother is in his element." He shrugged. "But if it involves any form of exertion, any physical activity, then no, absolutely no. Therefore —" At which point, having inhaled his slice of pie, Holmes turned his attention to the contents of the humidor proffered by our anarchistically inclined waiter and, with the gleeful countenance of a small boy on Christmas morning, selected a slender panatela.

"I take it you will accompany me tomorrow?" he added, his eyes aglow with the twin reflections of his match. "Do come, Watson. When Mycroft sees fit to summon me, the matter is bound to be somewhat *outré,* and you know I am lost without my Boswell." He nudged a fragrant cognac snifter in my direction. "Besides, you will serve as a buffer between us."

What could I do but what I always did and succumb to his Siren lure?

It was after midnight when I reached Pimlico and crawled into bed, trying without success not to wake Juliet.

"How did it go?" she murmured.

"Very well, considering."

"Umm?"

"Considering he'd no recollection it was his birthday. Mycroft put in an appearance," I added for no particular reason.

There was a pause.

"Really. Had you asked him?"

I said I had not. I could almost hear her frown in the darkness.

"How queer. And my gift?"

"I think he was quite touched, actually, though he has difficulty expressing himself along those lines, as I think I've explained. He does not as a rule read novels, but he asked me to thank you."

Juliet patted my arm, yawning.

"It is a stupendous work," she maintained. "Everyone ought to read it, and now, thanks to Constance, everyone will. Including you, my dear."

"I plan to, my love, at the first opportunity. Gracious." I could not suppress a groan.

"Tomorrow I shall have a head. Which reminds me, can you ask Harris to cover for me? I must somehow get myself to Pall Mall by ten."

This intelligence finally served to rouse her.

"Whatever for?"

"I promised Holmes to meet him and his brother at the Diogenes."

My wife was sitting up now, blinking away sleep.

"Diogenes? What on earth's that?"

"Mycroft's club."

"I have never heard of such a club. I've heard of the Reform," she added in a vague tone.

"Yes, I daresay even your Bloomsbury lot knows of the Reform. And certainly the Garrick, come to that. As for the Diogenes, it is altogether fitting you've not heard of it. That is exactly as its members would wish. The Diogenes one might characterize as beyond eccentric. Talking is entirely forbidden."*

* The Diogenes was the original headquarters of what became the British Secret Intelligence Service (SIS). The SIS was formalized as MI-6 in 1920 (the year the old club was razed) and its offices relocated near Piccadilly Circus. It was

I heard a faint gasp at this, accompanied, I was confident, by a moue.

"James,* none of this makes the least sense. Why meet where you are unable to converse? And do you not have a tonsillectomy scheduled for eight thirty at the Royal Marsden? I saw it in the book. The Winslow boy?"

I sighed, subsiding into my pillow.

"The procedure must be rescheduled. I wouldn't trust myself at this juncture to operate on a cadaver."

"But —"

"Please don't press me, dearest. I must go, and I cannot enlighten you."

As my eyes grew accustomed to the dark, I could see her still pouting as she primly drew up her knees beneath her nightgown.

"Cannot or will not?"

I sighed once again. "May not."

We had been married not quite two years, and during that time our pleasant routine had scarcely varied. More properly, I suppose, it may be said that no summons from Holmes had caused me to vary it. Thus it was my sweet wife was put out by my sud-

---

henceforth familiarly dubbed "the Circus" by those who toiled there.

* This is as it appears in Watson's original ms.

den and inexplicable obduracy, but there was no way I could explain. Even had the detective made a concession in the matter of secrecy, I knew that Mycroft was in no position to do any such thing. If I had given the matter any additional thought, I might have wondered what the big man's reaction would be to seeing me alongside his brother at the appointed time in the Diogenes's forbidding precincts.

**7 January.** There was in fact one room at Mycroft's hidey-hole in which talk was permitted, and thither I hastened in a light rain the following morning, with a pounding head. My powers being somewhat under a cloud, I had not thought to bring my umbrella. I debated returning to fetch one but mistakenly assumed I would find a cab before the weather worsened. When one failed to materialize and the other to oblige, I was compelled to trudge to Victoria, which I reached soaked to the bone. I sat in miserable damp from there to Westminster on the Circle Line, then resumed my limping trot through what had become a frigid sleet, my leg now throbbing as painfully as my head, and arrived five minutes late, a sopping mess. An impassive steward in white gloves and sky-blue livery trimmed with gold filigree ushered me into the Strangers' Room, where speech was allowed so long as voices were kept low and conversations brief.

Mycroft was not amused but, to give him credit, evinced no great surprise at my appearance. Later, when I understood more, I reasoned his business was too urgent for him to cavil at my presence. Unsuccessfully concealing his distaste for the task, he assisted me as I shrugged my way out of my sodden greatcoat and handed it to a second steward, who bore it off to the cloakroom at arm's length, as if transporting a carcass. I turned and beheld Holmes sitting before the fire. His garments were dry.

"As intercourse is not encouraged, even here," Mycroft stated without preamble, "I shall forgo banter." Reaching behind a divan, he produced a red dispatch box with a familiar coat of arms emblazoned in gold on the lid. With something like ceremony, he extended a silver key from his fob and unlocked the box, producing from within its recesses a manila envelope of standard dimensions, impressively sealed with red wax. The seal's imprint matched the box's gold escutcheon.

I sensed, rather than saw, Holmes cast a glance in my direction. With precise movements, betraying, I suspected, a certain relish for the task, Mycroft relocked the dispatch box, snapping its clasps with finality, and set it aside, retaining hold of the envelope.

"How is your French, Sherlock?"

Holmes endeavored to conceal his surprise. "Schoolboy at best, as you are aware," he confessed. Mycroft, I knew, spoke at least six languages, claiming it took but eight weeks to master a new tongue, which Holmes sneeringly once asserted in my presence was a sure sign of idiocy.

"It will have to do for now," his brother replied, handing him the envelope.

Here was mystery upon mystery.

"I wish you to take this to the privacy of your rooms," Mycroft went on, "where you may open and inspect the contents at your leisure."

"And then?"

For the first time, the big man hesitated.

"I wish you to tell me what you make of said contents."

"The French contents."

"You'll get the gist, I am confident. In any event, the document is incomplete."

"Incomplete."

"Judging by the pagination numbers, you will see these are random samples from among a total of over three hundred pages. For the present it is only necessary that you see a portion. You'll get the general idea," he concluded dryly.

It was clear that with every question and each unsatisfactory answer he was obliged to supply, Mycroft was becoming increasingly discomfited.

"That is all?"

"For now."

Holmes turned the envelope over, examining it minutely as was his wont.

"Are you quite sure it will be safe? My rooms have been burgled before, as I think you know."

Mycroft ran one of his large hands through his thinning hair.

"The contents of the envelope are already known in certain quarters," he admitted reluctantly. "As I've indicated, what you hold is merely a copy."

This time Holmes's glance met my own.

"Already known? Then why all the secrecy? Why the hugger-mugger? And what do you expect me to make of a mere copy? I cannot fashion bricks without clay, brother."

Mycroft drew an irritated breath and then conceded, "I have in fact included one page of the original."

"One page?"

"Will you kindly do as I ask?" the other cried with exasperation. "The matter at hand is of a delicate and entirely confidential character and of grave concern to . . . members of this establishment."

"Oh, I see." His brother smiled. "This establishment."

"I will call on you this afternoon to hear your views and communicate the wishes of His Majesty's Government."

At which point Mycroft fled the room with waddling alacrity, leaving the detective and myself alone, staring at one another in perplexity.

"You cannot possibly travel home on the Underground in this," Holmes declared after consulting the weather outside the room's enormous window. Tugging the bell pull, he instructed the steward to send for a taxi.

Once ensconced within its agreeable confines, there was no thought of going anywhere but Baker Street. I would telephone my wife from there.

We rode in silence, rain drumming on the roof while the engine puttered reassuringly as we jounced over cobblestones. Holmes fiddled with the envelope in his lap like a boy impatiently fondling a wrapped present, turning it this way and that, tapping it, holding it up to the grey light of the window — all to no avail. The thing stubbornly remained what it was, an ordinary manila envelope, distinguished only by its impressive wax seal.

And then, with an abrupt and decisive gesture, Holmes broke the seal.

"Holmes!"

"My dear boy, do you not despise all brother Mycroft's melodrama? I have already ascertained we are not being followed. Do we imagine our random cabbie to be an agent in league with a foreign power? What is all the fuss about?"

So saying, he withdrew what looked to be twenty typewritten pages and subjected them to a cursory examination.

"Very well. This is French, to be sure, albeit transcribed on an English typing machine, a Hammond 2, if I'm not mistaken, doubtless by some clerk in Whitehall. Hmm . . ."

He held up what appeared to be a title page, pursing his lips as he examined it minutely.

"This is clearly the original page Mycroft was kind enough to include."

"How can you tell?"

"There is dried water on it. And, if I'm

not mistaken, this pinkish tinge is blood."

Unless I was deceived, there was something very near satisfaction in the detective's voice. I watched as he employed his magnifying glass, hovering over the pale stains.

"A woman's blood," he muttered.

"Holmes, that is preposterous. How can you possibly determine what sex the blood came from?"

"See here." He held the page up to the light, by which I was able to perceive a long flaxen strand of hair stuck to the paper.

"Can you make out what it says?"

The detective scowled and finally shrugged, reading aloud, *Les Protocoles des Sages de Sion.*"

"I'm afraid I've less French than you." I blushed to own it.

He frowned.

"Well, roughly, I should translate it as 'The Protocols of the Wise Men of,' no, perhaps better, 'The Protocols of the Learned Elders of Zion.'"

# 2.
## LOST IN TRANSLATION

It had been almost a year since I last visited my old Baker Street digs, and while Holmes laboriously toiled away, jotting down notes and consulting a Larousse★ as he worked through those twenty typed French pages, I prowled the flat, noting changes and improvements here and there. Incandescent light, at 221B as elsewhere, had long since replaced gas. The framed portrait of General Gordon was nowhere in evidence. Holmes's correspondence, I was disappointed to see, was no longer affixed to the mantel with a jackknife. He had become too well known for such a primitive, not to say Bohemian, expedient, and now, supplanting my former workstation, a bulky rolltop desk with pigeonholes had taken over the task, though I noted with a smile that the compartments

★ Holmes must have owned one of the first editions of this invaluable reference.

themselves were bulging with unruly papers, among them invoices, receipts, and the post. I was relieved in addition not to spy, in its habitual location atop the mantel, the fine Moroccan case wherein slept the lethal syringe whose use I had vociferously decried in years past. Holmes might have chosen to conceal it, but I considered this unlikely; he hadn't known I intended to visit. It pleased me to think he appeared to have permanently overthrown his loathsome habit.

"Very repetitive," the detective muttered under his breath as I continued my inventory. "A little of this sort of thing goes a long way."

A telephone was now sandwiched atop the already crowded deal table, with its odiferous chemical apparatus reassuringly more or less as I had known and inhaled it.

Of the Turkish slipper that formerly contained his tobacco, there was no sign, though in truth that item had been giving out long before I quit my rooms. Its place, and Holmes's cheap shag besides, had been usurped by a dark tin of Balkan Sobranie. Success had made some inroads on my friend's personal habits. Some eccentricities had given way to creature comforts.

Doing my best to ignore the detective's snarled expletives, I picked up Juliet's birthday present and tried to make heads or tails of *War and Peace*. I was mildly diverted to see that parts of the first chapter were rendered in French — obviously Count Tolstoy's intention — and realized I'd forgotten my wife's sister-in-law was fluent in that language as well.

"I say, Holmes —"

"Five more minutes, Watson."

Obediently I tried passing that time mouthing some of those Russian names; the task was hopeless. Mercifully, it wasn't quite five minutes before my companion flung his pen across the room with an oath.

"There, that's the best I can do, anyway," he mumbled as we were interrupted by a knock on the door and Mrs. Hudson — her hair now entirely white — appeared to inform us that Mycroft Holmes was below in the entryway. He was certainly wasting no time.

"Dr. Watson," our landlady exclaimed, her face wreathed in smiles, "I had no idea you were here. Did you see? We now have a telephone. Heavens, you are soaked. Give me your coat and I'll hang it by our radiator to dry. Would you gentlemen care for tea?"

I said I would, and she retreated upon that errand, bearing away my poor greatcoat.

Holmes stared meditatively out the bay window at rush-hour traffic as we listened to Mycroft's stentorious panting on the stair. I knew Holmes to be mentally reviewing what he had just managed to extract from the French typescript.

It took his ponderous sibling the better part of two minutes before he had breath to commence conversation.

"Well?" he managed at length.

Holmes turned, his back to the window, hands clasped behind him.

"May I ask how you came upon these curious pages?"

"You may not."

"I will tell you, then." The detective held up the pink-stained title page. "They were retrieved by a police launch from the corpse of a tawny-haired woman whose body was found the day before yesterday floating in the Thames near London Bridge."

Mycroft, it was clear, contemplated an emphatic denial, but gave it up as he looked at the detective. His massive shoulders sagged.

"She called herself Manya Lippman, and she was . . ." Here he hesitated. ". . . in our employ."

"A most dedicated agent. She gave her life for those pages."

"She did." The fact weighed heavily upon him. "Kindly return the page with her blood on it."

Holmes carefully handed over the pink-stained page. With something like reverence, Mycroft folded the paper and slid it into his pocketbook. As he did so, his brother ambled over to the desk, glancing down at his notes.

"If I am reading correctly," he said slowly, "these pages purport to be the minutes of a secret meeting of a conclave of Jews who are plotting to take over the world."

He said this in a studiously neutral tone of voice, as one might remark the regrettable postponement of a test match.★

Before I could ejaculate an astonished response, Mrs. Hudson returned with the tea things and we waited in awkward silence while she poured and distributed the cups, supplying a running commentary as she did so, concerning the inclement weather, my welcome reappearance, and her intention of going to see the latest West End rage, something called *The Scarlet Pimpernel,* at the New Theatre — that is, if she could obtain a ticket. Actually two would be

★ This refers to cricket, a game beyond the comprehension of Americans.

preferable, as her brother★ had expressed a similar desire to attend a —

Mycroft quietly assured her he would procure the two coveted tickets, upon which she withdrew, whereupon I renewed my expostulation.

"A plot to take over the world? Come now. What can that even mean?"

Holmes eyed his brother, who sipped his tea in silence before noting, "I did say the matter was a delicate one. Consider," he went on, before the detective could speak, "the Jews have always exerted a disproportionate influence in relation to their slender numbers. In the arts, in the sciences, and certainly in finance. Even politics. You will recall the late Lord Beaconsfield was in fact a most well regarded prime minister and a great favorite of Her Late Majesty.★★ And Sherlock, I believe you purchased your Stradivarius from a Jew in the Tottenham Court Road? You have at least twice assisted Jewish clients, among them a Viennese physician, who, I believe, aided you in turn,

★ So far as I know, this is the only reference to Martha Hudson's brother.
★★ Lord Beaconsfield, aka Prime Minister Benjamin Disraeli. Queen Victoria liked to call him "Dizzy."

as well as a certain artillery captain in the French high command, accused of treason, no less?"

"As you well know, Captain Dreyfus has been pardoned," Holmes insisted, with evidence of growing impatience.

"But the matter did involve treason," Mycroft reminded him quietly.

The effrontery. His brother was having none of it, returning to the pages before him like a dog worrying a bone.

"Mycroft, who was this Manya Lippman, now unfortunately in the City Morgue? Manya is a Russian name, is it not? I ask again, how did you come by this document? Or rather, how did she?"

"I am not at liberty to say."

Holmes threw up his hands in exasperation. "Watson, we have been gulled."

"Holmes —"

"It was turned over to our agent in Paris," Mycroft conceded in his own tone of exasperation. "Does that satisfy you?"

"It most certainly does not. Who turned it over?"

Mycroft stared stonily at the younger Holmes.

"Mycroft, these pages are arrant nonsense."

"Tell me why," his brother demanded.

Holmes collected himself much like a horse before essaying a series of jumps.

"To begin with, what language do Jews speak? Amongst themselves," he specified. "Hebrew?"

Mycroft emitted a sound, something between a guffaw and a sigh. "Not for five thousand years — except in their liturgy," he informed the detective. "To the degree Jews enjoy a common language, that language is Yiddish, a German polyglot with Hebraic interpolations. I read some Yiddish myself," he added with evident satisfaction.

"Yiddish," Holmes echoed. "Thus a Jew from, say, Turkestan and one from Brazil, or London, for that matter, would be perfectly at ease communicating with one another in that language?"

"They would, yes."

"Yet these pages, which purport to be the minutes of a surreptitious convocation of Jews, are set down not in Yiddish but in French. Why?" He shrugged. "A cabal of Jews writing for other Jews about global domination, in secret, employ *French*? French, which is generally conceded to be the language of *diplomacy*? *Primo,* that fact alone, I would hazard, is, to put it mildly, *suggestive.*"

"But is it not possible the document is a

French translation from the Yiddish?" I interposed. "Perhaps these notes were made by . . . a spy, or someone to whom he later passed on the original Yiddish for translation?"

Mycroft favored me with an expression that was almost gratitude, but the detective shook his head, like one unconvinced.

"It won't do, Watson. *Secondo*," he resumed, now inserting his thumbs in his waistcoat pockets and planting his feet akimbo. "Consider this article from the so-called Protocol labeled number eighteen, and remember, I cannot vouch for every word of my own translation." He hesitated briefly, scanning the sentence before reading it aloud: " *'The time has come for Jews to awaken and seize the reins of control, of industry, currency, and culture, to assert our dormant power to erase Goyim from the earth, to the everlasting glory of the Hebrew race.'* "

We sat in momentary silence, speechless at this chilling manifesto, while Holmes regarded us, passing a hand over his mouth.

"Really?" His attenuated pronunciation of the word dripped with scorn. "A passage that totally incriminates its author, with the subtlety of Richard III forewarning the audience as to his schemes — and set down in a language all Europe can comprehend, at a meeting which is said to be *secret*? *Mirabile dictu.* Come now. It seems rather designed to implicate the fiends who feel conveniently bound to itemize not only their grand designs, but also the very motives which one would imagine had been understood and agreed among the participants long since. For that matter, why is this credo of malice not to be found in the very first Protocol? I remind you of chapter twelve in *Alice in Wonderland.*"

Mycroft was equal to the challenge and quoted from memory: " 'Rule forty-two: All persons more than a mile high to leave the court,' " he supplied with a wary smile, suggesting older times between them, and adding, " 'It's the oldest rule in the book.' "

" 'Then it should have been Rule Number One!' " Holmes concluded the quotation triumphantly, tapping the page. "As this broad announcement of purpose should have been. Furthermore, I must observe, for a lengthy document that purports to be the minutes of a clandestine assembly, one can fully obtain all it has to state in three or four lines, or a page or two at most. The rest is interminable repetition of its improbable thesis, namely, world domination by the Jews. For that matter, why would these same Jews, whoever they might be, trouble to make an incriminating record of their nefarious plans?"

"So you are suggesting this document is fraudulent," Mycroft demanded.

"What I've seen of it, and within my limited powers as a translator, certainly raises one's suspicions. The best forgeries are too agreeable; they are eager to ingratiate themselves with the credulous. Like magic tricks, created for an audience that wishes to believe. This one seems specifically calculated to fulfill the darkest fears and expectations of those who harbor hatred of Jewry. And what of this?" the detective went on, pointing at some of the text in question with an extended little finger. "Here everything is in French except one capitalized word, 'Goyim.' From the sense of the text, it is obviously jargon for 'nonbeliever' or 'gentile.' Am I to believe that an allegedly formal document, such as this purports to be, deliberately if inexplicably composed in French, nonetheless slips into Yiddish when it most wants discretion? Who on earth, wishing to conceal his true meaning from unprivileged eyes, would be so foolhardy as to employ a word that ensures his authorship is identified?" He exhaled like one satisfied with his performance. "There is no cabal, only a canard. I

49

think you may depend upon it there were no secret meetings of Jews. Manya Lippman, whoever she may have been, gave her life for nothing."

Mycroft sat back unhappily. "Ah, you see, but there were."

"Were what?"

"Meetings. Of Jews. In Switzerland."

Holmes, who had resumed his self-satisfied stance at the window, now swiveled back in surprise. "What?"

"Not secret," Mycroft conceded, "but annual meetings nonetheless of Jews from all over the globe. In Basel," he added gloomily.

"Meetings," Holmes repeated, with evident bewilderment.

"Six years' worth. You didn't know? It's hardly secret, Sherlock, but then you never read anything but the agony columns."

I could see the news had rather rocked my friend, though I was obliged to own I had on occasion glanced at something or other about these gatherings in *The Daily Telegraph*.

"Under whose . . ." Holmes groped for the word. ". . . auspices have these Jewish gatherings been convened?"

"They call themselves 'Zionists,' and they have been assembled by a charismatic

Hungarian journalist, one Theodor Herzl. Their avowed purpose is to obtain a Jewish homeland, though what precisely their true aim may be is the issue at hand."

Holmes continued to shake his head.

"I know that elsewhere the good Watson here has listed my knowledge of politics as feeble,★ and perhaps it is, but I find it difficult to believe that some of the most powerful, not to say reputable, citizens of this sceptered isle, financiers and philanthropists — Baron Rothschild, the late Sir Moses Montefiore (formerly High Sheriff of London!), Sir Samuel Montagu, and the like are involved in anything like a global conspiracy. Are you suggesting these men — many of them captains and commodores of finance — are making common cause with the disciples of Karl Marx to somehow upend the world order? Bankers in league with Socialists? Such a Byzantine collaboration can only be the product of a disordered mind."

Mycroft studied his brother before answering.

"I am inclined to agree. Certainly, to our knowledge, none of the men you have

★ In *A Study in Scarlet,* Watson characterizes Holmes's knowledge of politics as "feeble."

named were known to have attended any of these 'congresses,' though we have firm evidence some have contributed financial support. It is a disagreeable situation in which we find ourselves, but we must none-theless understand what is going on and whether it affects the national security. There are unsettling implications outstand-ing," he added after a fraction's hesitation.

"Such as?"

Mycroft withdrew a paper from his breast pocket and unfolded it. "This is the text of remarks recently read into the record by the Right Honorable Member of Parliament for Oldham," he began, and, putting on a pair of horn-rimmed spectacles, read aloud, *"The adherents of this sinister confederacy are mostly men reared up among the unhappy populations of countries where Jews are persecuted on account of their race. Most, if not all, have forsaken the faith of their fore-fathers and divorced from their minds all spiritual hopes of the next world. This move-ment among Jews is not new. From the days of Karl Marx here in London down to Emma Goldman in the United States, this worldwide conspiracy for the overthrow of civilization and for the reconstitution of society on the basis of arrested development, of envious malevo-lence, and impossible equality has been steadily growing. It has been the mainspring of every subversive movement during the nineteenth century, and now at last . . ."* Mycroft's voice trailed off and he removed his spectacles. "Mr. Churchill goes on in that vein for some time."

"Churchill!" I exclaimed. "That publicity hound? Always boasting of his wartime exploits?"* As a veteran myself, with some claim to distinction, I found Churchill's self-promoting antics especially repellant.

"Mr. Churchill may be a publicity hound and his widowed American mother no better than she should be, having just married a man the same age as her son, but that does not alter the fact of young Churchill's frightening eloquence. And that isn't all."

"What more?" Holmes demanded. He sounded tired.

Mycroft resumed that aspect of discomfort

---

* Six years earlier, during the Boer War, a then twenty-five-year-old Winston Churchill had made a daring prison break, whose successful outcome he had cleverly parlayed into a parliamentary career, while Watson, by contrast, badly wounded at the Battle of Maiwand during the Second Afghan War (1880), was invalided out of the service with a mere nine months' soldier's pension.

with which I was growing increasingly familiar. The effects of this peculiar document did not improve upon closer acquaintance.

"As you know, the current . . ." Here he chose his words like one tiptoeing through a minefield. ". . . resident of a large house near the Mall was, in his youth, rather a spendthrift, who ran up considerable debts on both sides of the Channel."

Holmes turned paler than usual.

"Are we speaking of a *very* large house? A large house at the end of the Mall?"

"Just so."

Holmes passed a fretful hand over his mouth. "My understanding is that the obligations of that house's proprietor were settled long since by a friend."

"Yes. A Jewish friend."

"Sir Ernest Cassel is surely a Catholic," I protested. The wealthy banker's long-standing friendship with the house's "occupant" was common knowledge.

"He converted in order to marry,"* My-

---

* Cassel was to become the grandfather of Edwina Ashley, who, as Lady Mountbatten, was the last vicereine of the Raj and as such enjoyed a passionate love affair with India's first Prime Minister, Jawaharlal Nehru.

croft informed me in a tone that suggested that in his taxonomy, conversion didn't signify. "And it is our understanding, Sir Ernest remains in possession of certain additional . . . obligations on the part of His — on the part of the resident of the large house near the Mall," he concluded lamely.

We sat in silence, punctuated by the ticks of a large clock whose sounds I had not noticed earlier. Holmes sat in his accustomed wing chair, whose upholstery, I now observed, was in need of serious repair. Horsehair resembling intestines now leaked from the right arm. Indifferent to the spillage, Holmes threw a lanky leg over a ragged antimacassar and was meditatively packing his charred cherrywood pipe with contents from the tin of Balkan Sobranie.

"Surely the most immediate solution to the problem is to dispatch someone from the Foreign Offi— from the Diogenes to interview Herr Herzl and put these questions to him?" I offered.

Mycroft regarded me unhappily.

"Precisely what we did. Six months ago we dispatched an . . ." Again the careful selection of euphemism. ". . . emissary to interview Herr Herzl, as you term him, in Austria and put those very questions to him."

"And?" Holmes struck a match.

"Alas, Herr Herzl dropped dead before the interview could take place."[*]

"Dropped dead?" Holmes and I exclaimed as one. I could see the detective's interest now fully engaged. Forgetting to light his pipe, Holmes ignored the match until the flame singed his fingers, whereupon he hastily shook it out.

"At the ripe old age of forty-four. They're calling it heart failure," Mycroft added in a tone devoid of inflection.

"Do you suspect foul play?" the detective inquired, adopting the same diffident tone.

"With what conceivable motive?"

"Brother, you astonish me. I am asked to examine a set of documents which purportedly detail a Jewish plot to dominate the world (however amorphous the phrase, but let that pass); these documents are found in possession of one of your own, who died to deliver them; and finally you call my attention to an impassioned Jew who is yoking together annual assemblies of his coreligionists in Switzerland — and you ask me to produce a motive for his assassination?"

"But your theory is that these papers are

[*] In July 1904 in Edlach, a village in Reichenau an der Rax.

false," I struck in.

"No matter," returned the detective, still facing his sibling. "If they serve to prompt the elimination of a forceful figure in Jewish affairs, they will have arguably served the purposes of their creators. It is sufficient for the credulous to learn that Jews have been 'assembling,' for whatever reason, to put Theodor Herzl in their crosshairs. By the same token," he reasoned, "the murder of your intrepid agent may have been less to prevent her delivering these supposedly incriminating 'protocols' to you, than by killing her to convince you of their authenticity. Why else leave them in her possession after she was dead? Let us suppose for a moment," he went on, "the Protocols are authentic, a record of a deadly and gigantic Jewish conspiracy, and somehow your agent manages to procure a copy. Desperate members of the cabal overtake her in London, where she is killed to prevent their infamous scheme from exposure."

"Yes . . ."

"*Then why leave the documents themselves in her possession?* It makes no sense. Unless you grant my hypothesis that the papers are false and the unfortunate woman was slain to make them appear authentic — which the true perpetrators could not accomplish without leaving them on her person for you to recover and draw what mischievous conclusions you will. In Paris, your agent didn't penetrate a Jewish conspiracy; she penetrated a conspiracy to implicate Jews — what for, or by whom, remains to be seen. As for Theodor Herzl —"

"The subject is not Theodor Herzl," his brother reminded him. "It is the Protocols of the Elders of Zion."

"I think they are the same," said Sherlock Holmes. "Regardless of motive: someone was willing to kill for them."

More clock ticks. Mycroft's pudgy fingers drummed an impatient tattoo on the right arm of his chair. I could see my companion mentally regrouping. My tea was now stone cold.

"Surely, Mycroft, if, as you say, Jews from all over the world attended one or more of these meetings, there must be several now here in England who were present?"

"I was just coming to that," Mycroft allowed, clearly pleased to be on firmer ground at last. "A colleague of yours at the University of Manchester was present at several of the annual meetings."

"A colleague of mine? What sort of colleague?"

"A fellow chemist. Born in Russia, educated in Germany — all in all quite cosmopolitan. He took up his post as a lecturer at the university less than two years ago. His Majesty's Government would look with favor on your speaking to him."

Holmes made a face.

"It would be of inestimable help if His Majesty's Government would supply its humble servant with the name of my chemist colleague in Manchester. It would serve to narrow my search, Mycroft."

Notions of dry wit were their specialty.

"Ah, forgive me." Mycroft fumbled for his engagement diary and tore off yet another page, similar in size and shape to that which he'd pressed into the detective's hand the night before. Holmes took it and read —

"Professor Charles Weizmann?"

"Just so. Professor Weizmann will doubtless be able to answer some of your questions."

"*Your* questions," Holmes corrected him in turn. They were forever at it.

Mycroft ignored the gibe and heaved himself with an effort to his feet.

"May I show these pages to my sister-in-law?" I asked as he neared the door.

One hand on the knob, the other collecting his sturdy walking stick, Mycroft turned.

"Mrs. Garnett? Why?"

"Her French is excellent, and we have now mentioned Russia three times in this conversation. It might do to have someone fluent in both tongues examine this. I take it Russian is not one of your six languages?"

Mycroft hesitated. I could see the wheels spinning in that large head.

"A woman's place is in the home," he stated as one who mournfully acknowledged this position was already under assault.

"Manya Lippman wasn't at home," Holmes pointed out mildly. His brother flushed.

"In any event, my sister-in-law works at home," I added, in an attempt to placate him.

"Your sister-in-law's *ménage* is decidedly . . . unorthodox. That Bloomsbury pack." Mycroft remained unconvinced as he remembered to remove and fold his spectacles.

"Constance is an excellent translator. In three languages. Have you anyone at your disposal of whom the same can be said?" Without feeling the need to specify, I knew the thought crossed all our minds that Manya Lippman had been one of whom it could. And she *had* been disposed of.

"Hmmm."

"I will assume full responsibility for them."

Mycroft briefly regarded Holmes, then myself.

"I will retain the original. The rest are not to leave your sight."

"You have my solemn undertaking they will not."

"If you feel them to be in any jeopardy, you will destroy them."

"I shall."*

With no farewell salutation, Mycroft left the room and thudded downstairs.

The detective and I were left alone. Without comment, he finally lit his pipe, tossed the match into the hearth, resumed his chair, and stared into space, emitting smoke puffs as if they were signals.

"What are you thinking?"

"I am wondering which is preferable."

"Preferable?"

"Yes. Is it preferable these atrocious pages prove authentic or fraudulent?"

"Fraudulent, surely," I said. The answer

---

* Things seem to have been a lot more casual back then regarding top-secret stuff. Or were they? Today government officials are always taking home restricted documents, using the wrong email server, or leaking like a sieve. Maybe it hasn't changed at all.

struck me as self-evident.

The detective said nothing.

Mrs. Hudson, anticipating my departure, returned with my coat, now comfortingly dry and warm. Now it was my turn to hesitate, my hand on the knob.

"You will go to Manchester?"

"In the morning. And you will consult Mrs. Garnett?"

"Why not?"

He favored me with a weary smile. "Why not indeed. But first, if I am not mistaken, it behooves us to pay a call on Mr. Brownlow Jr."

Seeing the confusion doubtless stamped on my features, the detective smiled and reminded me.

"The city coroner."

# 3.
## TARADIDDLES GALORE

The cavernous and chilly City Morgue had long been familiar to Holmes and myself over the course of many investigations. The vaulted, white-tiled space always reeked with the pungent odor of carbolic, which nonetheless failed to mask the ever-present scent of putrefaction. Long professional exposure had never inured me to the bilious stench of mortality. The detective and I clasped mufflers to our noses.

Brownlow Jr., the chief coroner, was well known to us both, and we had, as might be termed, guest privileges. Brownlow's father had occupied the post before him, prior to his inexplicable disappearance.* The son now conducted us to the slab upon which the remains of Manya Lippman were dis-

* For details of Brownlow Sr.'s disappearance, the reader is advised to consult an earlier Holmes case, "The West End Horror."

played for our benefit with clinical indifference.

"Her lungs were full of water. And I'm afraid the carp have been at her," Brownlow added in a reluctant undertone, as one who, left to his own inclinations, would never have broached the topic.

The fish had indeed begun a meal of her, though the single gash below her left breast from a blade the size, I should judge, of a butcher's knife clearly accounted for the victim's death, the fatal wound plainly struck by a taller personage who had sliced downward with powerful force. Discounting the carp, there were no other signs of violence upon the body, which was grotesquely bloated and in an advanced state of decomposition. Her hair, the colour and now consistency of straw, splayed about her thin shoulders. Of her features it was impossible to say. Had she been young or elderly, fetching or plain? No evidence remained. Her eyelids, mercifully pulled shut against the liquefaction within, prevented my ever knowing the colour of her eyes, but their remains now leaked onto her shriveled cheeks, like tears.

Bending close, the detective examined her fingernails, using his ever-present magnifier for the purpose.

"What are you looking for, Holmes?"

"Paper. Yes, it is still here. The courageous woman held on 'til the last." He straightened up and addressed the coroner. "How long had she been in the river?"

The little man frowned.

"Less than twenty-four hours by my estimate."

"And let me prophesy: Was the murder weapon left in her body?"

Brownlow regarded the detective with surprise. "Why, yes. We have it here. How did you know?" Unfolding a burlap cloth, the coroner produced a knife of distinctive shape. "It's a kosher butcher's knife," he informed us. There was in fact a Jewish star engraved on the blade, visible through dark bloodstains.

Holmes almost smiled. "They're very good," he murmured. "Damnably good."

"The Jews?"

"Those who would implicate them. Why else leave the weapon and the documents so conspicuously at the scene of the crime? How was she identified?" The detective's questions were, as always in such instances, simple and direct.

The coroner's eyes flickered. "The Yard brought in a gentleman from the Foreign Office."

"Portly?"

The coroner coloured. Both knew to whom Holmes was referring. "Yes."

The detective looked about him. "And her clothing?"

"Nondescript but well made. They took it away and gave us these." Brownlow indicated a pile of fresh but equally unremarkable female garments. "The, uh, portly gentleman indicated she was to be interred at Highgate Cemetery and left funds with my office for that purpose."

"Generous," Holmes murmured. "Highgate is very lovely."*

"And the, uh, gentleman indicated there were funds on deposit at Barings for the lady's child."

Holmes and I glanced at one another.

"Child?"

"A son of twelve, I believe. Presently in the care of his grandmother."

What a world of woe and meaning was furnished by these slight details. There seemed nothing more to be said. Our footsteps echoed spectrally as we left.

* Highgate Cemetery, also a nature preserve in North London, is, among other things, the final resting place of Karl Marx.

"John? Is that you? Where on earth are you?"

"Baker Street. Forgive me, dearest —" I found I was nervously twisting Holmes's telephone wire into a Gordian knot as we spoke.

"Really, John." I could hear my wife's aggrieved tone in Pimlico despite the indifferent connection. "You might have told me you weren't —"

"I know, my love, please forgive me. Did Harris —"

"What?"

"I said, did Harris cover for me?"

"On Grand Rounds, yes, he did. I have his notes, but the Winslow boy —"

"I know, I know. Mea culpa. I'll reschedule."

"John, when are you coming —"

"Juliet, can you meet me in Bloomsbury?"

"What?"

"Bloomsbury. At Constance and Edward's? I'm going there now, and it makes no sense to collect you first."

"Whatever for? I mean, why are you —"

"Please, dearest, just do as I ask. I promise to explain."

Even with a poor connection, I could hear

67

my wife's breathing.

"Juliet?"

"Yes."

"Yes?"

"John, I said yes. I'll see you there as soon as I've told the girl about the marketing."

"You're an angel. Oh, and would you ring Constance and tell her we're stopping by?"

"John, really, I —"

"An angel!"

I rang off to avoid more questions in time to see Holmes, clad in his ulster, clutching a carpetbag, emerge from his bedroom, heading for the door.

"Will you alert Professor Weizmann as to your arrival?"

"You know my methods, Watson. I may learn more if I surprise him. Can we meet here tomorrow afternoon? I should have more data by then."

"Well, I —"

"Excellent! Do you know anything about Manchester? Strange to realize I've never set foot there. Never mind. I've no time if I'm to catch the four-fifteen express from Euston. I'll purchase a Baedeker at the station and learn what I can by nightfall."

"Textiles," I called after him, but couldn't say if he heard.

I reached Bedford Place before Juliet, but

she'd done as I asked and Constance was expecting me. My knock was answered by Nellie Heath, the painter who mysteriously lived under the same roof. She wore an ever-present blue smock, splattered with traces as well as the scent of her calling. We never had much to say to one another, Nellie and I. Frankly, the Garnett *ménage* was an arrangement I found unsettling, and I was grateful my wife was of a more conventional cast than her brother. Having silently granted me entry, Nellie disappeared, her inscrutable countenance replaced by the animated features of Constance Garnett. As always, Constance's reading glasses were perched on the edge of her nose, and her prematurely grey hair lay captured in a haphazard clutch with renegade strands dropping carelessly before and behind her ears.

"And how is the patient?"

She laughed. "Edward hasn't been your patient for years, John."

"I should ask him to write me an encomium, describing his full recovery. Endorsements are all the rage these days. One sees them on the omnibuses."

"I should rather think the shoe is on the other foot; yours is the recovery to proclaim. Would you have met your wife if she hadn't brought her brother to see you? It's for you to thank Edward for his bout of ague."

"*Touché.* I shall do so at once." I looked around. "Where is my brother-in-law?"

"Still at luncheon," she informed me, taking my coat. "The Mont Blanc is his latest haunt, and he's dining with a new writer. Wining and dining," she added.

"New?"

"Someone named Lawrence he thinks is gifted. Edward is always discovering gifted writers, as you know. He reads, I write. Or translate," she amended with a shrug. "I'm infatuated with Turgenev all over again. Knee deep! How I wish I could have met him when he was here."* She gestured to the chaos and led me to her desk, stacked with Cyrillic pages. Pushing aside a toppling pile on a piano stool, she offered me some tea, which I declined.

She lit the stove as if she'd not heard.

"Poor Turgenev. Poor Russia," she lamented, spooning leaves into the pot. "I daresay revolution is in the offing, if not this year then next. Port Arthur has fallen, and Japan is running roughshod in Manchuria. The news is not official, but they say over four hundred thousand Russian troops

* Turgenev visited Oxford in 1879.

are lost. Four hundred thousand men! Can you imagine? And if that isn't enough, yesterday — yesterday! — in St. Petersburg, unarmed demonstrators carrying a petition for the Tsar outside the Winter Palace were fired upon by soldiers of the Imperial Guard, and martial law has been declared." She shook her head. "The Tsar is an imbecile."

"Has Mr. Lawrence written a novel?" I asked in search of a more cheerful topic. She watched the pot, waiting expectantly for it to do what watched pots never do.

"Written and rewritten. Once Edward starts making his 'suggestions,' they never seem to end. I've no idea when he'll be back. Still, Mr. Lawrence, whoever he may be, is lucky to have so perspicacious and attentive a reader."

"In point of fact, it was you I came to see."

"Me?" She shot a surprised glance over the rims of her glasses.

"I'm in need of your professional expertise."

"You don't say," she said, at last settling into her own chair with freshly brewed tea steaming from a Willow pattern cup whose rim was chipped above the handle. "What is the mysterious errand your wife knows nothing about that brings you here in the middle of the week? A patient who speaks only Russian?"

"Not a patient, and not Russian," said I, withdrawing the manila envelope from my Norfolk and setting it before her. "What I'm about to show you cannot remain here and must never be discussed by you with anyone. Including, I'm afraid, Edward."

"Really." Her countenance brightened suddenly. "Oh, it's to do with your Mr. Holmes."

"It's in French, and I should like to know what you make of it." I did my best to adopt Mycroft's oblique delivery.

With a sniff of what might have been resentment at my failure to confirm her intuition, the clever woman adjusted her spectacles and, withdrawing the pages, perused them in silence. Only the pursing of her lips gave any hint as to her reaction.

I sat rigidly on the piano stool, not wishing to distract her. Presently my back began to ache.

"My, my," she mumbled at length and she began flipping through the pages more rapidly. From her expression, I inferred that, like Holmes, she found what she read repetitive.

"Is this genuine?" she inquired without looking up.

"Genuine?"

"Authentic. Are these the secret minutes of a plot to —" Here she cut herself off, aware that completing the sentence aloud would sound ridiculous, concluding instead with "It seems preposterous."

"That is what we are endeavoring to ascertain. Could you make a full and careful translation of the pages? You'd be compensated, of course."

"I am always careful," Constance rejoined tartly.

She sat in silence, never taking her eyes from the text. I awaited her answer, but none was forthcoming.

"What is it?"

"Curious," she said, addressing herself more than me.

"How so?"

She looked up, frowning, then scanned some of the pages a second time, squinting with renewed attention.

"I've seen this before."

"Before?"

"Somewhere."

"Where? Where have you seen this?" I demanded.

She shook her head, and more strands of grey came unpinned. "I can't think. So familiar."

"But you must. It's of vital importance."

Something in my tone caused her to dart me a keen look.

"I don't doubt it."

At that moment, the bell rang and Juliet arrived, all in a dither as I anticipated, with embraces, laughter, and kisses. A quarter of an hour ago, I would have delighted in her presence, but now I own I found it inopportune. I was on fire to know what Constance meant by her cryptic comment regarding what I'd come to think of as the French Protocols.

Constance, remembering my strict injunction, slid the pages into their place of concealment and brewed another pot of tea. This time, in an effort at civility, I accepted a cup and sat in superfluous silence while the two women prattled on regarding family matters. These included Nellie Heath's recent paintings.

"She's done a head of Conrad that is absolutely riveting."*

"And how is my nephew?" my wife demanded. "Tell me about David."

"David is twelve. That should tell you everything. Loathing Harrow but probably

* Conrad? First name? Surname? Not clear.

74

learning something. He is scientifically inclined."

Constance said this with an injured air. The apple had inexplicably fallen far from the Garnett *père* tree.

From time to time during their chatter, she eyed me discreetly. She understood now I had come to her on a truly urgent matter but, having enjoined her to secrecy, saw no way to escape this portion of the afternoon and the banal pleasantries required.

Finally, I could endure no more.

"We must be going, my dear."

"But I've only just got here," Juliet protested, peering in all directions. "Where is Edward? Where is my dear brother?"

"I've booked us a table at the Mont Blanc," I improvised, whereupon she brightened at once.

"What a dear you are, to bring me out for supper. But surely it's rather early?"

"We have tickets to *The Scarlet Pimpernel*," I lied with increasing dexterity. Taradiddle would shortly supplant Hamish as my middle name. I only hoped invoking Mycroft's as our *passe-partout* would suffice at the box office after the fashion he'd promised Mrs. Hudson. If not, I'd raise a commotion and insist on hectoring the management.

Constance slid the envelope back to me.

"What is Edward working on?" Juliet inquired of her sister-in-law as I draped her fox-trimmed cloak across her shoulders.

"Another writer. Another novel. Something called *Mothers and Sons,* or — no, that's not it. Anyway, it's to do with coal mines, as I recollect." She shook her head. At the moment, I knew it to be filled with too many items.

Nellie mysteriously appeared to open the door.

"I should very much like to see your Conrad picture," I told her. She offered a tight smile but no reply as she shut the entryway behind us.

As it devolved, we were early enough at the Mont Blanc to dine without having booked a table but later spurned at the New Theatre, notwithstanding my histrionics and the invocation of Mycroft's name at the ticket window.

"Never heard of him," the agent informed me behind the brass-barred aperture.

"He's a member of the Diogenes!" I protested.

"Never heard of the Diogenes."

At this point a wicked notion occurred to me, but I refrained from asking if the tickets had been left under the name Martha

Hudson. I had not yet sunk that low.

"Next!"

"The impudence," I carried on in the taxi. "I cannot understand it."

Juliet sat in silence for some time.

"John," she finally said, very quietly. "You promised to explain everything. And it must be the truth," she pressed on, lest I contemplated anything else.

Ah, yes, the truth. I knew it would come to this. What truth, jesting Pilate might well ask? Where to begin? Certainly nowhere with any mention of Manya Lippman.

"I can't tell you all of it," I said shamefacedly, "but I can tell you this much."

So saying, I launched into a vague summary of Holmes being asked to verify the authenticity of a French document of importance to the government.

"Where do you come in?" Juliet asked in a blessedly nonjudgmental tone. She was listening attentively.

"I had the bright idea Constance's command of French might prove useful in . . ." "Decoding" struck me as a trifle melodramatic here. ". . . understanding some of the document." Which was close enough.

"And was it?"

"That, my dear, is a question yet to be answered. She needed to think about what

77

she'd read," I temporized, "but as the pages are secret, I could not leave them with her and will be obliged to return."

"How very exciting," she murmured, laying a gloved hand on mine. "Is this rather typical of your Mr. Holmes?"

"You've read some of my accounts, surely."

"Yes, dearest, only forgive me, I did think you might have been . . ." She searched for a tactful description. ". . . embellishing?" Ending on an upturned interrogative.

I had to smile. "Exactly what Holmes always accuses me of doing."

We sat in companionable silence.

Finally she leaned over and whispered through her veil in my ear:

"You never had tickets to *The Scarlet Pimpernel,* did you?"

It was after ten when we returned to Clarendon Street. The girl had sat up, unwilling to retire without bolting the door and reluctant to do so without having heard from us.

"I'm sorry, Maria," my wife apologized. "We should have rung you —"

This made no sense to me, for I am confident the girl would never have made so bold as to answer the telephone.

As if it heard itself being discussed, the wretched device commenced shrilling.

"Who the devil can that be at this hour?" I demanded of no one in particular as the tired girl slowly mounted the stairs to her quarters, yawning loudly, I suspect, for our benefit.

"You're a doctor," Juliet reminded me as I went to reach for the earpiece. "For a doctor the telephone must nowadays be counted an occupational hazard."

"Occupational nuisance. I wish we'd never acquired one. Hullo? Who is speaking?"

"I think I've remembered where I read it."

"Constance?"

"What? Oh, yes, Constance." She seemed surprised not to have identified herself. Her excitement, now evident in her tone of voice, was contagious.

"Where?"

"Where what?"

"Where did you read it?"

"I need to be sure. Could we meet tomorrow in the Reading Room? Say ten?"

"At the British Museum?"

"I need to be sure," she repeated. I looked over at my wife, who was regarding me with an expression that hovered dangerously between curiosity and annoyance.

79

"One moment."

I covered the mouthpiece with my hand.

"It's Constance. She wishes me to meet her at the British Museum tomorrow."

"Say you'll ring her back."

"Constance, can I ring you back directly? Yes, I know it's late. Five minutes." I replaced the receiver in its cradle, and we faced one another.

"John, when you asked me to marry you, you assured me that your . . ." What word did she want this time? ". . . adventures with Mr. Holmes were behind you."

"In the cab just now you found them exciting."

"To read about, yes. But you swore before we wed, those days were over."

"And so they are, my love, so they are!" I insisted, taking both her hands in mine and summoning the most earnest countenance in my repertoire. How to smooth her ruffled feathers? "But earlier tonight you asked for the truth, and I gave it to you. Events beyond my control are unfolding as we speak. There is some question of the national security involved, or you may be sure Mr. Holmes would not have asked my assistance."

This was an evasion at best; at worst, another taradiddle. The larger and plain truth was the game was afoot and the detective's faithful hound was baying at the scent. I had not realized how much I missed the chase.

She bit her lip, lost in thought.

"Juliet?"

"You're not carrying on an intrigue with her, are you?"

"With Constance?" I thought briefly of that disordered pile of grey hair, those steel-rimmed spectacles. "How can you ask such a question?"

She shrugged, disconsolate. Really, sometimes I found Holmes's opinion of women more persuasive than I cared to admit. They baffled me.

"Juliet, this is unworthy of you. I have never given you the slightest cause to question my devotion, and you can't imagine that Constance, of all people —"

She stopped my protestations with a kiss and handed me the telephone. I cranked it vigorously and gave the exchange. It was answered on the first ring.

"Constance? Yes, it's all right. Tomorrow at ten."

"This is Edward Garnett. To whom am I speaking?"

I burst out laughing. "Edward, it's Watson! It's your old GP!"

"John!" The stiffness in the muffled voice on the other end gave way to a good-natured chortle. "I'd heard you'd stopped by. I'm sorry to have missed you. Did you want Constance? Hold the wire. Constance!"

I heard a succession of the indeterminate sounds that telephones seem prone to producing before she came on the line.

"John, yes?"

I was still laughing. "It's all right. I'll be there at ten."

"Bring the pages."

"I will. Good night, Constance."

After which I took my wife in my arms.

Later, with her soft form nestled against mine, I found I was unable to sleep. After years of widowhood followed by a new marriage, a revived practice, and surgical duties at the Royal Marsden, my routine, a train accustomed to running along a familiar and agreeable route, had been abruptly thrown off the metals and was now careering towards a new and unknown destination.

The French Protocols, or, more properly, the Protocols of the Learned Elders of Zion, as Holmes and later Constance had rendered it, proposed, however fantastically, that there was a Jewish plot to take control of the world. The very phrase, so nebulous, made no sense to me, yet Mycroft and, presumably, those whom he served, were sufficiently alarmed to call upon my remarkable friend, who was even now in Manchester (Manchester!) running clues to earth. Was he in danger? Ought I to have let him go there alone?

What was I to think? That the likes of Baron Rothschild, Sir Samuel Montagu, Sir Moses Montefiore, Prime Minister Disraeli(!), and Karl Marx (had any of those imposing personages been alive!), as well as Sir Ernest Joseph Cassel, the Catholic-converted banker to His Majesty, King Edward, the seventh of that name, were all in some dark conspiracy to — what, precisely? Control the price of sterling? The Suez Canal? The stock exchange? The coal mines? Politicians? Railways? The military? What possible combination of capital and labor, left and right, could "control the world"? And what sort of world would it be if they succeeded?

Mycroft had made some remarks about Jewish prowess, and they sparked a vague recollection on my part. I stole quietly from bed and fetched my robe and slippers. In her sleep, behind me, Juliet mumbled something.

"What, dearest?"

"Women shall have the vote."

I left her with this drowsy non sequitur, descended to my waiting room, and switched on the lights. There, for the benefit of patients, I had amassed a collection of magazines and periodicals dating back several years. I always intended culling them but somehow had never got around to it. It was among these that I now rummaged, searching for a back issue of *Harper's* American magazine, which a patient from New Jersey had left behind after I performed an emergency appendectomy.

In short order I found what I was looking for, a piece by the prolific Mark Twain, who, having recently lived in Vienna (he seemed to have lived everywhere at one time or another), had been prompted to write an article about Jews. It concluded with the passage that had somehow pressed itself on my memory:

If the statistics are right, the Jews constitute but one per cent of the human race. It suggests a nebulous dim puff of star-dust lost in the blaze of the Milky Way. Properly the Jew ought hardly to be heard of; but he is heard of, has always been heard of. He is as prominent on the planet as any other people, and his commercial importance is extravagantly out of proportion to the smallness of his bulk. His contributions to the world's list of great names in literature, science, art, music, finance, medicine, and abstruse learning are also far out of proportion to the weakness of his numbers. He has made a marvelous fight in this world, in all the ages; and has done it with his hands tied behind him. He could be vain of himself, and be excused for it. The Egyptian, the Babylonian, and the Persian rose, filled the planet with sound and splendor, then faded to dream-stuff and passed away; the Greek and the Roman followed, and made a vast noise, and they are gone; other peoples have sprung up and held their torch high for a time, but it burned out, and they sit in twilight now, or have vanished. The Jew saw them all, beat them all, and is now what he always was, exhibiting no decadence, no infirmities of age, no weakening of his parts, no slowing of his energies, no dulling of his alert and aggressive mind. All things are mortal but the Jew; all other forces pass, but he remains. What is the secret of his immortality?

How long I stared at this passage I cannot say. Twain's words were evidently conceived as laudatory, but I could not help remembering one of Holmes's dictums, namely, that evidence which on the face of it points in one direction, viewed from a slightly altered perspective, may admit of precisely the opposite interpretation. Having now seen portions of the Protocols, a dark corner of my mind found itself wondering if the Jews were as noble and noteworthy as Twain described them. I confess I have never given Jews much thought. Following my discharge from the Army, I have rubbed shoulders with them daily — as I have with Italians, Frenchmen, Greeks, and other nationalities crammed side by side in our bustling metropolis. I see Jewish patients and never consider them noteworthy because of their race. But now, in the stillness of the night, acknowledging the American's pithy observations, I was mortified to find myself wondering if, despite all logic and probability, there might not be some grain of truth in the Protocols. How *have* the Jews managed to endure where more potent tribes and civilizations failed? What are their secrets? The scurrilous pages had already begun their insidious work, tunneling their way into my poor, addled brain. And if they could manage progress in mine, which was to some degree, armed against them, what might they do to others, who were not?

# 4.
## COMBUSTIBLE

"At Euston, I realized I was being followed," Holmes told me later.* "You know my methods, Watson; observation and inference. Thrice my shadows were masculine. Initially I observed a traveling salesman with a sample case too light to contain any goods. He was succeeded by an effete gentleman with a monocle traveling incongruously in second class, who was in turn replaced by a haberdasher who cared for his bowler with an indifference that belied his alleged profession. And finally — leaving the terminal in Manchester and finding digs for the night — a slattern wove uncertainly in my wake, but I perceived her drunken-

* These notes in the same hand I found on a different sheet of paper slid at this point between the pages of the diary. I'm not sure this is where Watson intended them to go, or even if he inserted them here, but I hesitate to move them elsewhere.

ness to be feigned. Clumsy as they were, from these antics I deduced two points. *Primo,* that, however inept, employing agents in rotation to track my movements indicated a professional operation. *Secondo,* that, unlike Manya Lippman, I was in no present danger. I had nothing they wanted; they were merely supernumeraries, instructed to keep track of my movements. The question remained: Who were they, and what was their purpose in keeping me in their sights? Of course I could easily have given them the slip, but then I would know rather less than before. I might instead have chosen to confront or subdue one of them, but decided it was more prudent to grant them free rein. Were their actions related to my present business or possibly to another issue altogether? Difficult at this juncture to say, but I had no doubt that when they saw fit, they would reveal their intentions, or, if circumstances favored me, our positions might be reversed and I might trace their movements instead."

"And did you?"

He shook his head. "I miscalculated. By the time I left my hotel the following morning, all sign of them had disappeared. Against my own instincts I was inclined to believe these events were unconnected to my present errand. Hubris, Watson. If you should ever discern symptoms of it again on my part, I should be infinitely obliged if you were to merely whisper the word 'Manchester' in my ear."

## The Diary Resumes

**8 January.** As a young chemist living in nearby Montagu Street, Sherlock Holmes had frequented the Reading Room in the British Museum. I, however, could not recall ever having set foot in the place. Surely I would have remembered had I done so. The high-domed chamber with its sky-blue ceiling panels, more reminiscent of heaven than St. Paul's Basilica, larger than Rome's Pantheon but imagined along the same lines, was clearly designed to stupefy any visitor. The vast, vaulted space emitted an echoing, respectful stillness as I entered the following morning. Innumerable readers and researchers were distributed among its concentric rings of desks, each boasting its own green-shaded lamp, the only sound in the place being an occasional sibilance of whispers, the shuffling of papers, or the faint scratching of pens making notes. The room had played host to virtually every English writer with the possible exception of Shakespeare. It took some little time to locate

Constance towards the centre, where she had barricaded herself behind a pile of large, dark blue volumes that almost obscured her from view.

"What have you found?" I inquired, gesturing to the stack of books.

A white-haired gentleman opposite to her, sporting a food-stained yellow cravat and his own supply of texts, glowered in my direction.

With a finger on her lips, Constance signed to me that I must carry the tomes and follow her from the wondrous chamber to one of the adjacent study cubicles, which, for the moment, had her name on the door, indicating the space was presently reserved for her exclusive use.

"Now then," she began, eyes bright with excitement behind those spectacles, when I had set down the load and she had shut the door behind me. "Have you ever heard of a Frenchman named Maurice Joly?"

I said I had not.

"Few have," she acknowledged by way of consolation. "He died about thirty years ago in Paris, an apparent suicide."

"Who was he?"

She gave a dismissive sniff.

"A lawyer."

"Ah," I responded, for lack of anything

intelligent to contribute.

"Also a pamphleteer, a sort of satirist. And a monarchist," she put in as an afterthought, shrugging as much as to say *in toto* an inconsequential figure whose life had counted for little.

If he was indeed a suicide, I reflected, perhaps he had realized this as well.

"And what has Monsieur Joly to do with the Protocols?"

Instead of replying, she opened one of the large volumes and peered at tiny print.

"Joly is most famous — to the degree he is known at all — for his *Dialogue aux enfers entre Machiavel et Montesquieu.*"

"I'm sorry, I don't . . ."

"A pamphlet titled *Dialogue in Hell between Machiavelli and Montesquieu.*"

I blinked uncertainly. "Machiavelli, I remember, was an Italian schemer from the Renaissance, but Montesquieu —"

"Was an eighteenth-century French *philosophe.* Joly's tract was intended as a bitter critique of the so-called Emperor Napoleon III,★ whom Joly despised for a preening tyrant."

★ Louis Napoleon, an unscrupulous adventurer with luxurious tastes, was the self-styled nephew of Napoleon Bonaparte who in 1851 undertook a

92

"He was certainly not alone," I offered. "There were many who felt that emperor had few clothes."

"Many costumes but few clothes," she agreed, running an index finger slowly beneath the French words. "Though he was fond enough of uniforms, Louis Napoleon was no Napoleon." She looked up. "In any event, the emperor was not amused by a conversation fancifully undertaken between a Renaissance pragmatist and a French philosopher. He duly had the book banned and its author clapped in gaol."

"I'm sorry, but I still fail to see what you are getting at."

"May I have the papers?"

I extracted them once more from their manila-envelope home. She placed the first page opposite the page in the large open book.

"As I thought . . ." She trailed off. Without looking up, she threw a backward hand over her shoulder, waggling her fingers, silently commanding me to supply another sheet of the typescript. As I did so, she turned the leaves of the big book before her and set the second page opposite the text.

---

*coup d'etat,* proclaiming himself Napoleon III. Defeated by Prussia, he fell from power in 1870.

"What is it?" I demanded, more than a trifle impatient.

"Stolen," she murmured, glancing briefly in my direction before returning to the pages. "Plagiarized, to be precise. Listen carefully. Here is what Joly wrote in the first of what he calls his 'dialogues.' Machiavelli is speaking."

Translating slowly from the French for my benefit, she read aloud: *"Men must not scruple to use all the vile and odious deceits at their command to combat and overthrow a corrupt emperor and restore the republic to power."*

She regarded me expectantly over the tops of her spectacles.

"Go on."

"Very well." She now picked up one of the Protocol pages. "Here is the so-called Tenth Protocol: *Jews must not hesitate to employ every noxious and terrible deception at their command to fight and overturn a wicked tsar and his goyim and deliver the Jews to power.*"

I stared at the two sets of French words.

"They are certainly similar."

"Similar?" she scoffed. "They are identical save that the word 'Jew' has been inserted in place of 'men' in one instance and 'the republic' in another."

"And *'goyim'* has been squeezed into the Protocols version."

We spent the next two hours pawing through the two texts. In Joly's original, a great deal of talk was spent on the question of modernizing France; in the Protocols, Russia had been substituted. Pages were inexplicably devoted to interest rates. Both proved repetitious, unsurprising since the Protocols so slavishly imitated Joly's interminable jeremiad. Our tedium would have been inevitably quadrupled, were it not for the provoking curiosity of the duplication itself.

In my bored state, something began nagging at me.

"Stop a bit," I said. "Can you go back to the first two passages?"

Without answering, she shuffled the typescript and flipped through the big books.

"Now, please read them both again. Slowly."

Without comment she did as I asked.

"Curious." It was my turn to employ the word.

"Curious, how?"

I stole a look at my watch. It was afternoon. Holmes would be expecting me by now.

"Well, it's not merely the insertion of

'Jews' in place of 'men,' " I observed, "but as you read it again, it becomes clear other words have been substituted as well, though not, apparently, so as to effect any alteration in meaning."

"I'm not sure I follow."

I pointed.

" 'Overturn' in place of 'overthrow.' 'Noxious' instead of 'vile.' 'Terrible' in place of 'odious.' 'Fight' instead of 'combat.' 'Hesitate' where the original says 'scruple.' And so on. It all comes to the same meaning, but why have these irrelevant changes been made?"

She frowned, implicitly conceding my thesis. "Doctor, you scintillate."

I tried not to blush by returning to the question at hand. "Why?" I repeated.

She stared blindly at the words. "In an effort to disguise the plagiarism?"

"A lazy expedient if true. And fruitless. You saw through it handily enough, Constance. Come to that, so have I."

"Why, then?"

We could neither of us imagine.

But I knew there had to be a reason.

It was after two when Mrs. Hudson opened the door for me at Baker Street. I was breathless and frozen, but at least not wet, for the rain had finally let up.

"Is he waiting for me?" I asked as I handed her my coat.

"Yes, he's upstairs and —"

I had no time to hear the rest of the sentence, but hobbled up the seventeen steps to 221B and found the door ajar. Conscious only of my tardiness, I entered, not troubling to ponder this anomaly.

A tall gentleman with what I should describe as a messy Vandyke and the thickest pair of spectacles I had ever seen turned to face me. He peered in my direction through what appeared to be the green-tinted bottoms of Burgundy wine bottles.

"Ah, Dr. Watson." He greeted me with an almost indecipherable accent. It was all I could do to recognize my own name.

I was, however, not taken in. The detective had played this game too often.

"Really, Holmes, at your age, I would think you are beyond this schoolboy practice of theatrical disguises, and your attempt at a Russian accent, if I may say so, is lamentable. Kindly remove that getup and those ridiculous glasses. You'll do yourself an injury sooner or later if you don't discard them."

"Watson, may I present Professor Charles Weizmann, senior lecturer in chemistry from the University of Manchester?" Holmes chuckled behind me.

To say that I was mortified is rather to understate the case, but Professor Weizmann appeared in no way put out. On the contrary, the whole episode seemed to provide him boundless amusement, and he took my error in good part.

"To be mistaken for Sherlock Holmes," said he in his almost impenetrable speech, laughing heartily, "may be the high point of my career. I cannot wait to tell Vera!" By whom I assumed he referred to his wife. The professor held out a large hand, stained with what I took to be the by-products of his laboratory handiwork.

"We were just about to take some sherry," Holmes informed me, walking to the deal table that contained his own odiferous chemical supply and, in addition, his stock of spirits. "Would you care to join us?"

"I think I'd better," said I, attempting to regain my composure and sinking into the green chair with the extruding horsehair.

"I went up to Manchester by train, as you know," Holmes explained, generously pouring out the amber liquid. "A curious place," with a nod to our guest, "if I may say so. Nothing but factories belching smoke to blot out the sun, accompanied by the omnipresent din of steam-driven machinery. I took a room for the night near the university and boned up on Professor Weizmann," to whom he offered a second inclination of the head. "Learning from the porter where he would be lecturing this morning, I attended, sitting in the top tier of the auditorium, introducing myself afterwards and explaining something of my errand.

"As it happened, by happy coincidence, the professor was due to catch a train to town for a conference at the London Polytechnic, and so it made sense to travel back together. I've offered him your old bed for the night to help him economize. I take it you've no objections?"

"None whatever," I was relieved to say, and hoisted my glass in his direction. "What are you working on these days, Professor?" I was eager to make amends for my grotesque blunder and thought to take an interest in his career.

"Acetone," came the heavily accented answer.

I glanced at Holmes, whose eyes twinkled merrily. He was still convulsed by my mistake.

"Acetone?" I repeated, determined to make up lost ground. "Isn't that paint thinner?"

"It has many uses," Weizmann allowed. "The human body produces and disposes of it naturally, but it has agricultural and cosmetic benefits as well. Currently I am working on an acetone-butanol-ethanol fermentation process of my own devising with a view to production on an industrial scale."

He might as well have been speaking Chinese. All I could pluck from it was "Industrial? Whatever for? How much paint thinner do we need?"

The professor shot Holmes a look. The detective nodded, and he turned back to me. "Acetone is required for the creation of cordite."

"Cordite?" I regarded them both with astonishment. "As a substitute for gunpowder? Why on earth are we talking about gunpowder? All Europe is at peace."

"Asia is not," the professor replied, finally seating himself and crossing his legs. "In point of fact, revolution has broken out in Russia."

I stared at Holmes.

"When?"

"Today, in fact," the detective replied equably. "We've had the news via telegraph. It will doubtless be in all the evening papers."

Revolution. Constance had alluded to the possibility yesterday.

"In the port of Odessa." Weizmann took up the story. "Sailors aboard the battleship *Potemkin* apparently have mutinied and murdered their officers.* The latest word is that the citizens of Odessa have gone over to the mutineers, supplying them with food in some manner of small boat brigade. If the rest of the fleet joins the rebellion, it could spread inland and become a full-fledged revolution. Other nations, such as Germany, may attempt to exploit the situation, but Russia, you may know, has entangling alliances with both France and England, so theoretically the thing could soon get out of hand."

"You seem very well versed in politics for a chemistry professor," I noted with confusion.

"And if the revolution does spread," he went on, addressing Holmes, "you may be sure the blame will fall upon the Jews."

"Ah." Suddenly pieces began to fall into place. I couldn't see the picture, but I was starting to make out the frame.

"Why not tell Dr. Watson what you have

* The mutiny appears to have been prompted by maggot-ridden rations.

conveyed to me about Theodor Herzl and the Zionist conferences in Basel?" Holmes suggested, sitting at last and putting up his feet, hands clasped behind his head.

Weizmann took another sip of sherry.

"Anti-Semitism is a familiar aspect of life in Russia, where I was born," he explained. "Jews are natural scapegoats, usually resented for their business acumen, but rather than state this openly, they accuse us instead of ridiculous obscenities such as requiring the blood of a Christian child to celebrate our holy days."

"The blood of — ?"

"Russia is a primitive place," Professor Weizmann continued. "Legends and superstitions take easy root and proliferate. The Tsar in photographs may appear an identical twin to his first cousin, your Prince of Wales — recall they are in fact both grandsons of Queen Victoria — but there the resemblance ceases. The Tsar is ignorant and backward, entirely ruled by his equally uneducated wife, who surrounds herself with mad holy men and allows them to make policy. When the Great Houdini performed for their court a year ago, he stupefied one and all by causing the Kremlin bells to ring, which they had not done in a hundred years. The Tsar, followed by his entourage, genuflected, trembling, and crossed himself, praising Houdini for a saint." Weizmann's amusement was magnified by his glasses. "He would have been appalled to learn the Great Houdini turns out to be another Jew, Ehrich Weiss, a rabbi's son from Budapest," he added, with what I took to be more than a touch of pride. "Nicholas is quite content to let Jews shoulder the blame for Russia's primitive conditions, her lack of contact with the outside world, absence of railways, electricity, paved roads, food supplies, manufactured goods . . ."

The chemist paused for another sip of sherry. Holmes's eyes were closed, not in sleep, I knew. This was his attitude of strictest attention.

"Theodor Herzl, about whom I gather you have already heard, was concerned about the persecution of our race — not just in Russia, but over the centuries and throughout Europe as well. He realized that through an accident of history" — he shrugged — "or perhaps a history of accidents, to be more precise, Jews are a nation without a country."

"A nation in need of a country," Holmes supplied, without opening his eyes.

"Just so. A country of our own. This is the

Zionist goal. Successive congresses have grappled with the mechanics of this question. Where would this country be? How could the territory be obtained? From whom? And of course, who would pay for such a country and who would populate it? Can you imagine the cacophony of a convocation of Jews as they fall to debating such questions?" He eyed us, evidently reconsidering his own query. "No, of course not. It would be like eavesdropping on a rabbinical discussion of the finer points of the Talmud. A Jewish homeland. It was this cause to which Theodor Herzl devoted his life's blood."

"Until his sudden death," Holmes interjected.

"Precisely. Sudden and most regrettable. I have attended all the conferences but one," Weizmann informed us. "Most regrettable — and most mysterious," the professor echoed, swallowing the last of his sherry.

"Have you any reason to suspect his death was . . . unnatural?" the detective inquired softly, eyes still shut.

Unlike Mycroft, Weizmann seemingly did not feel the need to address the question of motive.

"Herzl had already been diagnosed with a heart ailment," he said. "But the two possibilities are not mutually exclusive. As a chemist, I need not tell you there are many ways to make a death look perfectly natural. The fact that a diathesis* had been established might have eased the task. And as you are doubtless aware, the Russians have the reputation of being the most accomplished poisoners since the Borgias."

In the silence that followed, I attempted to digest so much that had been said. A revolution was taking place half a world away. Events were unfolding that, if the nearsighted chemist enjoying Holmes's sherry was correct, could conceivably drag the rest of Europe into a conflagration in which massive quantities of British gunpowder might well be required.

In fact, Holmes and I had been involved years earlier in an effort to prevent such a conflagration. Holmes had remarked at the time that our success had likely merely postponed it.**

Beside these grim realities, the Protocols looked more far-fetched than ever. The Zionist Congresses, if Weizmann was to be

* Diathesis = a preexisting medical condition.
** After the death in 1939 of one of the principals involved, Watson chronicled the case, which he labeled "The Seven-Per-Cent Solution."

believed, had nothing whatever to do with schemes of world domination but rather with the understandable yearning of a long-dispossessed people for a homeland. Had that goal been worth a woman's life?

"Tell Dr. Watson about the prime minister," Holmes prompted the chemist.

I looked from one to the other.

"What prime minister?"

"The present one. Arthur Balfour."

I could not keep the surprise from my voice. "Where does Balfour come into this?"

Weizmann smiled modestly behind those improbable glasses. "In addition to being Prime Minister, Sir Arthur is also the MP for Manchester East, which is how we first became acquainted. I have the honor to call Sir Arthur my friend. Doubtless my current work on behalf of the British government in the possible future mass production of acetone plays some role in this. But I have had occasion to discuss the — what shall we call it? — the Jewish Question more than once with Sir Arthur."

Every word this remarkable man spoke was more intriguing than the last.

"And what is Sir Arthur's view?"

The professor hesitated then tossed his shoulders, as much as to say, *In for a penny . . .*

"He will not state so publicly at present, but Sir Arthur has assured me His Majesty's Government would look with favor on the creation of a Jewish homeland."

"In Palestine," Holmes added quietly.

"He won't say it publicly," the professor repeated. "And of course, not everyone shares this opinion. About Palestine, I mean. Many who have attended the conferences have found the idea of a homeland carved out of the Middle East impractical and are advocating other locations. Madagascar, for example."

"Have you formed an opinion?"

The professor turned to Holmes. "Would you trade London for Saskatchewan?" he inquired, smiling.

Holmes saw that by this point I was reeling.

"Watson, we have flooded your brain with data, but surely you have some information of your own to communicate?"

I confess I was relieved to find myself away from murky world politics and on the firmer ground of my own recent experiences. Methodically, therefore, I laid out what Constance and I had uncovered, showing both men my handwritten copies of the two initial texts Constance and I had compared.

Weizmann listened with gravest attention,

but he was not surprised to learn of the Protocols.

"They were published in a Russian newspaper," he informed us.

Holmes sat up, eyes open and shining at this intelligence.

"Ah, the key!" he exclaimed. "The missing piece. You recall that Cuvier insisted that from a single bone it was possible to infer the entire skeleton."

Holmes picked up the two handwritten passages I had copied and now accorded them serious scrutiny.

"You are learning, Watson! This news explains these seemingly superfluous word changes, so keenly noted by you."

I tried to conceal the pride I felt at this bouquet. For years, Holmes had twitted me that I saw but did not observe. And only this morning (while a revolution was taking place in Russia!) Constance had told me I scintillated. What a day!

"How so?"

"Because, dear man, the French version of the Protocols was not made from Monsieur Joly's original tract about Machiavelli and Montesquieu. Rather it now appears that what Mycroft showed us *was the French translation of a Russian text.* It was a *previous* translator's word choice that accounts for 'noxious' instead of 'odious' and so forth. Professor, what was the name of the newspaper that printed these Protocols?"

Weizmann shrugged apologetically. "It was several years ago, one of many hate sheets that flourish in Russia."

"Which has now appeared in Paris in French," Holmes noted gravely.

"Holmes, this is clever," I allowed, but still feeling duty bound to "scintillate," I had to ask: "But how can you ascertain that the translation Mycroft gave us was made from Russian and not some other tongue?"

"Elementary, Doctor. The proof that you missed is the singular substitution of the word 'tsar' for 'emperor.' Whoever was behind the version you were given was writing the Protocols for a Russian readership. QED."

The professor squinted from one to the other of us. "Was Theodor Herzl assassinated?" he demanded.

Holmes chose not to answer. "May I pose a final question?" the detective asked instead.

The professor took the evasion in stride. "You may pose it." His inflection implied that no answer was guaranteed on his part.

"Your accent, as I hear, is Slavic with an overlay of the Teutonic."

"That is not a question," the other responded, smiling.

"Yet your name is Charles, which is neither Russian nor German."

This time the question was at least implied.

"Very good, Mr. Holmes. Some find my first name difficult to pronounce, so I anglicize it. My first — I do not say Christian — name is Chaim."*

"Chaim," the detective repeated, striving to mimic his guttural pronunciation.

"In Hebrew it means 'life.' "

Outside, searching for a taxi, I wondered aloud how Houdini had caused the silent Kremlin bells to ring for the Tsar.

"Very simply," Holmes replied. "He had a confederate with a silenced Mannlicher carbine and sighting scope shoot at the bells from a place of concealment, perhaps a nearby vacant flat. It had to be a carbine," he added. "They couldn't have taken a larger weapon apart to conceal it in their luggage."

I stared at my companion. "You know this?"

He shrugged. "I deduce it."

* In 1949, Professor Chaim Weizmann became the first president of Israel.

# 5.

## CAIN AND ABEL

Constance Garnett and I toiled the rest of the day in her windowless cubicle in the museum (charitably referred to as an office), wrestling through those interminable tracts, each more tedious than its predecessor, until closing time. At one point, in an effort to jolt myself awake, I began to light a cigarette. "Please don't," my collaborator implored. I sighed, and replaced the tobacco in its pewter case, and we resumed our labors. Joly's *Dialogue* had the dubious merit of being authentic, and one could understand his rage at the cartoonish Louis Napoleon and his Graustarkian* pretensions, but alas, Joly was no writer, and his

---

* Graustark, like Ruritania or Lilliput, is one of those fictitious countries where novelists are pleased to indulge all manner of over-the-top costumes and customs. Napoleon III and his court definitely fall into such comic-operetta territory.

111

prose, so dense and repetitive, made me wonder if anyone beside the emperor's censors could have actually finished reading his screed.

By contrast, the twenty-four Protocols had the defect of not only repeating much of Joly's tendentious ideology (in many instances, word for word), but yoking them to an obnoxious thesis *ad nauseam.* The idea that somewhere in Mycroft's possession were three hundred more pages like these was too dreadful to contemplate — their bile only eclipsed by their invincible dullness.

"And what have we to show for all our exertions?" Constance demanded, pushing ineffectually at the fugitive strands of her unruly hair as the clock inched towards five.

"We have shown beyond a reasonable doubt," I responded, addressing in my mind a phantom jury and employing pleasing legal phraseology, "that in all likelihood the bulk of these wretched Protocols has been, as you so perspicaciously discerned, filched from Maurice Joly with the seemingly random substitution of synonyms strewn higgledy-piggledy throughout. You will be compensated for all your work," I reminded her.

"I can't imagine how," she responded drily.

It was dark by the time the custodial staff watched with ill-concealed impatience as Constance locked her closet — for it was little more than that — and we were herded, along with others equally reluctant to quit the precincts, towards the main entrance. Outside I was accosted by a telegraph boy on his bicycle, who pulled up to the museum gates even as they were being swung shut and locked behind us.

"Watson?" he read off his envelope. "John Watson? Dr. John Watson?"

"Yes," I conceded warily. Was I about to receive a communication from my wife?

The lad handed me the envelope with my name scrawled on it and the British Museum denoted below as the address. With a sudden premonition, I knew before opening it whence it came.

*"Diogenes. Seven"* was all the telegram said. At least it wasn't from Juliet. My shoulders unclenched.

"Are you heading back to Pimlico?" Constance inquired.

"Alas, no. Can I drop you?" I offered, in an effort to make up for the dreary work she had so conscientiously performed. I was searching for transportation, but at this hour neither hansom nor taxi were to be had.

"Don't be silly. It's just around the corner."

She gave me a peck on the cheek and set out for Bedford Place. The weather was cold but bracing after hours of confinement in that airless cell.

As a proper married man, and what is more, a doctor who kept regular hours, I knew where I was supposed to be and where I so clearly wasn't. But by this point I had been so conspicuous a truant, I no longer dared telephone Juliet and took refuge behind a telegram of my own. As the boy was still lurking, hoping for a shilling, and asking if there was any reply, I said there was. I sent to Juliet, promising yet again to explain everything in due course and begging her patience. That bridge would have to be traversed at a later date, and I cannot say I relished the prospect.

At the moment, my chief difficulty was one of transportation. This was unexpectedly solved for me when a taxicab already containing a fare pulled up before me.

"You'll catch your death," cried a gentleman within. "I'm happy to offer you a lift, if you don't mind going halves."

"Thank you, I'm sure I'll manage."

"Nonsense, there's nothing to be had at

114

this hour for love or money. Where are you headed?"

Startled by the abrupt arrival of a Good Samaritan, I chose not to look a gift horse in the mouth and answered, "Pall Mall."

"Splendid," the voice from within replied. "I'm for Trafalgar Square. I can drop you. Do get in, old man."

With no alternative, and attaching no importance to my fortuitous rescue, I gratefully accepted his kind offer and climbed in beside a gentleman of roughly my own age who, from his attire, I judged worked in the City. Which I was pleased to discover proved to be the case. I was learning from Sherlock Holmes.

"West, Cedric West," he introduced himself. "Stockbroker. And you?"

"I'm a doctor," I explained, reluctant to give him my name, which I knew would prompt a conversation about the Great Detective I was too fatigued to indulge.

"A doctor!" he responded with a laugh. "How clever of me to have come to your rescue. Should anything happen between here and . . . ?"

"Pall Mall," I repeated.

"I know I'll be in good hands." There was something in his bearing that suggested military experience at some point in his life.

What I glimpsed of his hair in the dim light and underneath his bowler was the close-cropped grey of iron filings I associate with officers above the rank of major.

We made idle conversation, chatting about the inclement weather, tangled traffic at this hour, and the like. Somewhere I noted the incongruity between his Saxon-sounding name and the slightest trace of an accent I was unable to place, but as I had much else to occupy my mind at the time, I did not trouble myself over this trifling anomaly. At no point, I blush to concede, did it occur to me to question the arrival of my rescuer. And not until much later did the connection between Cedric West and those shadowy personages who had followed Holmes to Manchester make itself known to us. In light of the unpleasant events that shortly followed, the whole episode entirely slipped my mind.

The taxi dropped me off near the Reform Club, which seemed preferable to my true destination. My effort to hew to our agreement and share expenses was now graciously refused. My Good Samaritan had evidently had a change of heart.

"Not a bit of it, Dr. . . . . ?"

"Baskerville," I improvised.

"Baskerville." Did he smile at this? "Perhaps you'll return the favor one day. Drive on!"

The meeting with Mycroft at the Diogenes later that evening did not go well. From the first, the brothers conversing in the privileged "Strangers' Room" were at cross-purposes.

Holmes gave Mycroft assurances that in all likelihood the Protocols of the Elders of Zion was nothing but a clumsy forgery.

"Excellent." Mycroft heaved a sigh of relief and hoisted his bulk out of his chair. "Your estimation is in accord with my own. No secret conclave bent on world domination. That is one crisis off my plate. Thank you, Sherlock, for all your dili—"

"Surely it isn't that simple," the younger man replied, retaining his own seat. "Would it not be prudent to learn who created this forgery and why? You doubtless recall that one of your people gave her life to obtain the document."

"Such courageous folk are more than aware of the risks they are being asked to take on behalf of a grateful nation," Mycroft answered, with, it struck me, little feeling. "They undertake willingly to do so," he went on, adopting — or now affecting to adopt — a cool rationale for Manya Lippman's death.

"This naturally includes funds for the rearing of her orphaned son?" the detective commented, his upper lip curling slightly.

Mycroft scowled in response. "Just so." He was breathing heavily as he leaned down to adjust one of his misaligned spats.

I saw the detective blink, grey eyes agleam with indignation.

"And what of the convenient death of Theodor Herzl, upon the eve of being interviewed by another of your emissaries? Does this not strike you as suggestive?"

"We have been over this before. Theodor Herzl was not a British subject," stated the other firmly.

"But if the man was murdered by a British ally, say the Tsar and his secret police, the Okhrana —"

"Really, Sherlock," Mycroft interrupted with asperity, "you are out of your depth."

"I beg your pardon?"

"The issue is settled. Go back to your little London crimes. Remember: knowledge of politics 'feeble.' Stick to those curious incidents in the night that so absorb your interest and your admirers. Missing papers, purloined jewels, deadly snakes, kidnapped racehorses . . ."

"I wish I could, Mycroft," the detective snapped in reply, "but this is no longer the nineteenth century; it is the twentieth, and crimes, you fail to observe, are getting bigger. It was you, remember, who tasked me with looking into this affair of the Protocols. Sticking your head up — into the sand," he amended, "will avail you nothing. The Russian bear, whose excesses you propose to tolerate, is doubling over as we speak, pulverized by little Japan, her enormous but ill-commanded army slaughtered as revolution has finally taken h—"

"The revolution has failed!" Mycroft fairly shouted. "It has been put down! It's in all the evening papers! Even as we speak, President Roosevelt is negotiating peace between Russia and Japan! The revolution has failed!"

"For now!" Holmes, no longer in control of his own emotions, shouted back. "But do you not imagine the Tsar's other cousin, not our Prince of Wales, but Kaiser Wilhelm of Germany, is not himself closely following events from Berlin? Waiting to seize the advantage should he perceive one? And are you fine gentlemen of the Diogenes, in the meantime, content to dispose of your . . . 'employees' when they have outlived their usefulness, like so much superfluous damage?"

What had begun as a schism now threatened to become a chasm. I had never witnessed such a bitter exchange between the two men. And neither, evidently, had the steward, who hastened into our presence, alerted by raised voices.

"Gentlemen, please!" he protested. "The Diogenes does not permit —"

"Yes, yes, Harcourt," Mycroft assured him with a wave of his large hand. "We are just concluding our business."

After a moment's hesitation, looking searchingly from one to the other brother, the steward withdrew, closing the door softly but firmly behind him.

"We need not pursue this," Mycroft said when we were again alone.

"Why? Because it involves Jews?" The detective's tone was scathing.

Even in the dim light I perceived Mycroft flush, stung by the accusation. "That is unworthy of you, Sherlock. Some of my closest associates —"

"Oh, to be sure," murmured the detective. "But for the record, this is not about Jews —"

"You are one to talk," his brother shot back. "With your Jewish clients."

"Would I do better, in your view, to change my name from Sherlock to Shylock?"

120

"Captain Dreyfus, I remind you, was convicted of high treason!"

"Captain Dreyfus is not, as you would point out, a British subject. What is more, Captain Dreyfus, as you seem reluctant to concede, has been pardoned and brought home from Devil's Island, where he languished unjustly for twelve years in a grotesque miscarriage of justice.* Mycroft, listen to me, I entreat you. This is not about Jews; it is about truth. Which we are bound to seek and to value. These Protocols are almost certainly spurious news, but left unexposed, they will take root and grow in strength and credibility."

"People will believe what they want to believe," I interjected, in an effort to draw their fire. Holmes regarded me almost as if to say, *Et tu, Brute.*

"Watson, you are pleased to say that I do not follow international developments, to which I plead guilty. But as a man of science, surely it did not escape your notice that last year the Nobel Prize in physiology was awarded to Professor Pavlov of Russia, who has demonstrated the conditioned

* The following year, 1906, Captain Alfred Dreyfus was formally exonerated and reinstated with full rank in the French army.

reflex in dogs, who can be trained to salivate at the sound of a bell without the presence of any actual food." He shook his head. "So it is with these pernicious Protocols. If canines can be conditioned to salivate over nonexistent food, may not men one day be likewise taught to salivate at the prospect of nonexistent facts? Is it not possible that men may one day be trained to accept such tripe as your Protocols? Am I not correct, Doctor?"

I shifted uncomfortably in my chair. "To my knowledge such a thing has not yet occurred," was the best I could manage.

Holmes turned back to his brother.

"Mycroft, a lie can travel halfway around the world while truth is putting on its boots. I implore you, let me look into the death of Theodor Herzl. Into the origin of these so-called Protocols . . ."

"Theodor Herzl and a homeland for Jews are not the concern of His Majesty's Government," the other reiterated stubbornly, but I sensed he was weakening.

I knew it was on the tip of Holmes's tongue to invoke Prime Minister Balfour's support for a Jewish homeland and dispute this, but Chaim Weizmann had sworn us to secrecy on that score.

"Let me begin with the Protocols, then.

Send me to Russia."

Mycroft remained maddeningly silent. With a great effort of will, Holmes mastered his temper and spoke quietly.

"Mycroft, you will, I think, allow that in my lifetime I have done some service to the Crown. I asked no reward. But I am asking now for this. Send me to Russia. I am begging you. This business is far from finished. Let us at least justify Manya Lippman's sacrifice."

Mycroft withdrew an enormous handkerchief from his breast pocket and blew a blast like a trumpeting elephant. Then, replacing the handkerchief, an operation that appeared to consume an inordinate amount of time and effort, he stared out the window at nighttime London, his back to us.

In the dim light, Holmes was paler than I had ever beheld him.

"On one condition," Mycroft said finally.

"What condition?"

He turned.

"Interview someone else here who attended those Zionist meetings in Switzerland. So far, all your evidence appears to have been gathered from a single source."

Holmes looked at me briefly. "Very well."

With that, he led me from the room. The

brothers did not even bid one another good night.

Outside, Holmes stared at the pavement, oblivious to the cold.

"We must pay Constance Garnett for her work," I reminded him, in search of a neutral topic.

"To be sure," he murmured, seemingly fascinated by the cracks in the macadam. "It's late," he noted, finally looking about, and insisted on walking all the way back to Baker Street, the temperature notwithstanding. I knew better at such times than to remonstrate, and, after watching his tall, slender form stride briskly down Pall Mall, I flagged a taxi. The driver was just going off duty, but I prevailed upon him. Once within, physically spent from the long day, emotionally drained from the vituperative encounter I had just witnessed, and dreading the possibility of another when I reached home, I fell into a restless slumber. It was as if I were again in the field hospital at Maiwand and had been all day in the operating theatre as they gouged for the bullet in my leg. I had passed out from the pain and was tempted to do so again now.

"Clarendon Street," the cabbie announced over his shoulder. He was obliged to repeat this several times before I started awake and paid him. He wasted no time driving off, barely allowing me to shut the door after I'd stepped heavily onto the curb. I caught a glimpse of my own reflection in the beveled glass by my door. My cravat was askew, I was in want of a razor, and the bags beneath my eyes proclaimed I was yet in need of sleep.

I fumbled for my latchkey and dropped it before letting myself into the darkened entryway. The house was still save for the distant chime of a grandfather clock at the top of the stair. The girl, I knew, had long since retired.

I removed my hat, coat, and muffler, draping them ineffectually on the hall cloak stand before entering the sitting room, which was likewise dark save for the remains of the fire.

Rubbing my hands gratefully before it, I was startled by my wife's voice.

"Have you eaten?"

"Juliet?"

She was seated behind me in one of the wing chairs.

"I've saved you supper. Come."

She rose and, taking my hand in one of hers — hers reassuringly warm and firm — led me to the kitchen, where cutlery and plate awaited me on the table. Silently, I sat while she opened the larder and extracted the remains of a roast chicken and new potatoes.

"Wine?"

I shook my head. "Water, please."

Without comment she ran the tap above the big basin and set a glass before me before seating herself opposite.

"John, you look a sight."

"I know."

"Mustard?"

I nodded dumbly, and she added water to the powder, setting the paste before me.

She sat silent, watching while I ate. I did so waiting for the blow to fall.

"I've been thinking," said she at last.

I looked up.

"Yes?"

"I've been thinking that I owe you an apology, John."

I could not have been more surprised had she informed me she was Chinese.

"Whatever for? Dearest, it is I who must —"

"Please let me finish." She twisted her hands together in what almost appeared a pantomime of washing them as she searched for the right words.

"Yesterday I reproached you for having broken a vow you made me before we married," she began. "I understand now it was unfair of me to exact that promise."

"My dear —"

"I believe you made it in good faith, honestly believing that your days of . . . collaboration with Sherlock Holmes were at an end. Nevertheless, I think neither of us understood what we were about at the time, me in exacting that promise and you providing it. More water?"

"Please." The mustard was strong.

She took my glass and replenished it, resuming her train of thought as she did so.

"What you and Mr. Holmes share is not something that can be turned on and off, like a tap." She gestured to the one she'd just been using as the analogy struck her. "It is, I suppose, innate, an unstoppable reflex on both your parts, which I cannot and ought not attempt to interrupt or interfere with."

"Juliet, you must believe me when I say that it is only because the circumstances are uniquely pressing that I —"

"I was coming to that, John," she said, now offering me a tender smile. "You see, I've had a long time to think these past twenty-four hours, and I realized, as you say, that were the problem not as urgent as you find it, you would not have behaved in the manner you did."

"I would not!" I exclaimed passionately. I knew then I did not deserve such a wife.

"Therefore, rather than assume the role of millstone around your neck, or ball and chain at your feet, at such a time," she concluded, "I hope you will let me help rather than scold you. You may be sure whatever you tell me will go no further. And remember" — she favored me with a broad smile — "a wife cannot be compelled to give testimony against her husband!"

"Why, Mrs. Macbeth!"

"Tell me your secrets." Her smile deepened. "I'll not disclose 'em."

She came over to where I sat then and stood beside me, clasping my head to her waist, and peace was made between us, to our mutual relief. In two years of marriage such a rupture had never occurred before.

Later, sitting again before the restored fire, I told her everything.

"How dreadful," she exclaimed, when I had described the toxic contretemps between the brothers at the Diogenes.

"I expect they'll patch it up," I allowed with more assurance in my voice than I actually felt, finally informing her of the compromise they had reached. "Holmes will unearth someone else who attended those conferences, and what he learns will or won't send him on to Russia."

"And would you accompany him if he goes?" She gave a little yelp. "No! I didn't say that! If he goes to Russia, you will do what you will do, and that's an end of it."

"It may not come to that. If we can talk to someone in England who attended any of those Swiss —"

"I think I might know someone," Juliet said thoughtfully.

"You?"

"Well, not directly, but I am friends with his wife. Do you remember Edith Ayrton?"

"The suffragette?"

"John." She smiled. "John, I, too, am a suffragette."

"Hmm," was the best I could muster. Throughout our courtship and marriage we had playfully agreed to disagree about this topic, and now that I recalled, the name Edith Ayrton had cropped up more than once in our lively discussions.

"Times are changing, dearest," she said, embracing me once more. "And you will have to change with them. It is a certainty women will get the vote. Edith's mother was a doctor, you know. And she herself attended college."

I sniffed. "What in heaven's name can the

author of *Barbarous Babe* — wasn't that the title of her novel? — have to do with Zionist Congresses in Switzerland?"

"I daresay nothing," she replied, "but she is married to the foremost Zionist in England."

"What?"

"Israel Zangwill. Surely you've read him."

Of course I had, along with everyone else. "The Dickens of the Ghetto," as Zangwill had been nicknamed. His prolific writings, his journalism, his essays, his humorous pieces had appeared for years in Jerome's *Idler* magazine, in competition, I had to own, with my accounts of Holmes's exploits in the *Strand.* Somewhere I'd heard that a play of Zangwill's, *The Melting Pot,* was a success in New York, and though I'd not read it, I certainly knew of his novel *Children of the Ghetto.* I understood him to be a pacifist and a champion of the suffragette movement and had, from time to time, chanced to read articles of his on both topics. I seldom subscribed to his politics but confess I enjoyed his wit.

But I had unaccountably missed his Zionism.

"Where does your friend Mrs. Zangwill live?" I asked my wife.

**9 January.** Thus it was that the following morning, Sherlock Holmes and I paid a call on the famous author at his home at 24 Oxford Road, Kilburn, very much in the northern part of the city. As was his custom when in the exercise of his profession, Holmes had given no advance notice of his intention to visit. He sent in his card with the girl, and we waited on the steps, surveying the vicinity to pass the time. The detective looked about and commented, "I see the neighbourhood is slowly being taken over by the Irish."

Without troubling to take the bait and inquire as to how he reached this conclusion, I exclaimed, "Holmes, surely this errand will prove a pointless diversion. We are merely indulging your brother's attempts at procrastination. And he may devise still further excuses in order to delay our departure."

"Possibly," he allowed. "But Mycroft's penchant for methodical preparation is not so easily dismissed. The tortoise has been known to outstrip the hare. And it must be said as well my work is seldom the lightning flashes of inspiration and intuition of which you remain so fond. As I'm sure you've learned by now, much of it involves drudgery, knocking on doors" — here he gestured with slender fingers to the blue portal behind us — "asking many questions, and taking accurate notes."

I took this to be another sly dig at my abilities, and was on the point of saying as much when the girl returned, bobbed a second curtsy, and brought us in to see the great man.

Zangwill was ensconced behind a large antique desk that was in reality little more than an ornate table, having no drawers that I could see. Its surface was covered with foolscap and other papers and situated like an island, almost at the centre of the high-ceilinged room, whose four walls were crammed with all manner of books from top to bottom.

The elegant man rose from his chair and came round to greet us. He was more slender even than my companion.

"Mr. Holmes." He smiled broadly, his intelligent brown eyes magnified behind a pince-nez.

"It is an honor," Holmes began, but the other halted him in mid-salutation with a palm raised outward.

"Not a bit of it," he protested. "Who has

not read of your exploits and longed to meet England's most famous detective? The honor is entirely mine!"

His hair was dark and very curly, and the pince-nez straddled an enormous, beaky nose amid a florid countenance. Yet the total effect was not altogether displeasing. His posture was as sturdily erect as any officer's in the Fifth Northumberland Fusiliers.

Then he turned to me, covering my hand with both of his. "Dr. Watson, I presume." He grinned appreciatively at his own joke. "Behold the competition!"

"Hardly." I was annoyed to find myself simpering.

The writer now gestured expansively to a pair of identical chairs. "I learn our wives are fellow soldiers in the cause of women's equality."

"Well," I harrumphed uncertainly. Seeing this was a topic about which I harbored some ambivalence, he changed the subject.

"And I understand we have both been married for roughly the same length of time. If it is not indiscreet to compare notes," he said with a laugh, "how are you, connubially speaking?"

"Very well."

Our pleasantries, like a well run dry, seemed to have died out. Zangwill looked about in search of another conversational gambit.

"May I offer you gentlemen a morning's refreshment? Some tea? Mr. Holmes, are you about to favor me with any of your deductions?"

"Alas," the detective replied, "they are scanty. Your parents were born overseas, you spent your childhood somewhere in the south of England — Exeter? — later lived in the East End, and were, yes, I think, for a time a schoolteacher. You have a university degree, but not, I think, from either Oxford or Cambridge. And you are a father. Otherwise, I think, your career is a matter of public record."

Zangwill's features widened into a grin. "Plymouth, not Exeter, but otherwise first rate. Splendid. Of course, I must not ask how you know all these things."

"It would be like asking a magician to explain his tricks," Holmes concurred, smiling in turn. "Thank you for seeing us on such short notice. It is certainly a privilege to meet the author from whom I have learned so much about impoverished London."

"I describe what I see, even as you," the other said, volleying the compliment. "Those places in the East End about which

I've written were where, as you surmise, I spent my childhood. I have been fortunate to escape them."

Given his present comfortable surroundings, which included the broad Axminster beneath our feet, this was putting it mildly. Zangwill regarded Holmes expectantly. He was politely waiting to learn our errand.

Perceiving this, the detective took the plunge.

"I believe you were acquainted with the late Theodor Herzl," he began.

If this sentence startled him, Israel Zangwill concealed the fact.

"Unhappy man. His death a senseless tragedy."

"You were close?"

"At one time." Zangwill sighed, and his characteristic good humor seemed to desert him.

"Theodor Herzl changed my life," he went on with feeling. "He turned up on my doorstep, the very same doorstep you gentlemen trod on just now, oh . . ." He cast his eyes towards the ceiling, doing mental arithmetic. ". . . perhaps ten years ago, bursting with dynamism. Possessed of an almost messianic energy and conviction. The man could simply not sit still. One might almost characterize him as a sort of

Jewish Joan of Arc."

"And he spoke to you of the need for a Jewish homeland."

"He said we were a nation without a country, and for many years, I subscribed to this idea. I believe he hardly slept, so consumed was he by the mission he had assigned himself. He was constantly on the move, on and off every conveyance, traveling ceaselessly throughout Europe to Russia to England and back again."

"And you attended Zionist Congresses on that subject, convened by Herr Herzl in Switzerland?"

Zangwill blinked, evidently surprised anew at Holmes's knowledge. "Many. I believe Switzerland was chosen because of its neutral locale. I count his death a great loss, even though we were no longer in accord."

"Oh?"

"What Theodor had in mind was a reconstituted Jewish state — after two thousand years! — to be located where it had originated."

"You are speaking of Palestine?"

"Precisely, yes, Palestine. For a long while I agreed with him. My position, I must own, proceeded from a certain ignorance. I believed Palestine to be largely uninhabited."

"Uninhabited?" Holmes echoed without inflection.

Zangwill made a placatory motion with his hands. "Unoccupied, if that sounds better. I imagined a few scattered Bedouin, some camels, and little more. Believing that, Palestine made perfect sense to me. At the time," he added, now pressing the tips of his fingers together in a gesture I recognized as characteristic of Holmes.

"And later?"

"Over the years and as the result of my reading, I was disabused of this naïve notion. Palestine is home to some six hundred thousand Arabs. Learning this, I proved utterly unable to wrap my mind around the prospect of attempting to displace such a number, as would inevitably be the case, should a vast Jewish migration occur there. If you wish to give a country to a people without a country, it is utter foolishness to allow it to be the country of two peoples. This can only cause trouble. The Jews will suffer, and so will their neighbours."

"I take it Herr Herzl was not of your opinion."

"Quite the contrary. Though successive Zionist Congresses discussed alternatives —

Madagascar was mentioned, among others — Theodor became increasingly wedded to a Palestinian homeland and obdurate regarding alternatives. I myself championed the possibility of another location, one within the British Empire."

"Are you acquainted with Professor Charles Weizmann?" Holmes asked.

Zangwill again seemed to marvel at the detective's knowledge. "Yes, of course. His real first name is Chaim. We encountered one another several times in Basel. He is now at the University of Manchester, I believe. A chemist, as I recall?"

"Just so. And what were the professor's feelings in regard to the location of a Jewish homeland, do you know?"

"He made no secret of it. We had no secrets," Zangwill emphasized. "Chaim Weizmann was all-in-all in agreement with Theodor Herzl. As they saw it, the geographic nation of Israel had to be located in Palestine." He shook his head and jumped up in agitation at the memory. "I, meantime, had arrived at a different conclusion. Assimilation!" Zangwill held up a rigid index finger. "That is the key to human survival! We must all blend or perish. America has the right idea," he continued, "a melting pot of nationalities, mongrel races, and ethnic identities. I wrote a play about it."

"*The Melting Pot,*" I supplied.

"Still running on Broadway in New York!" Zangwill fairly chortled. "Listen to this." His fastidious manner momentarily cast aside, he rummaged excitedly among the clutter on his desk, and shortly flourished a piece of stationery. "From the White House! Received three days ago!" He cleared his throat and read, "*Dear Mr. Zangwill, your play, 'The Melting Pot,' I shall always count among the very strong and real influences upon my thought and life. Sincerely, President Theodore Roosevelt.* I mean to have it framed," he concluded, flourishing the letter.

"You are rightly proud of such an achievement," Holmes said. "But to return for a moment, to Herr Herzl and a Jewish homeland . . ."

"British East Africa, that's what I had in mind. That's what I tried to convince him to consider." Zangwill let the president's letter flutter among the others concealing his desk. "Uganda. But he would hear none of it, and as I could not bring myself any longer to embrace the Palestinian notion, we fell out. Herr Herzl was on fire. He couldn't wait, and he could brook no faltering. I am not wedded to Uganda," he added with a shrug of his shoulders. "But if there is to be a Jewish homeland, it must be somewhere where Jews are not dispossessing an indigenous population."

"It's an old problem," Holmes responded thoughtfully. "Your 'melting pot' has made short work of the American Indian."

"True," the other allowed with a rueful expression.

I did not say so, but it occurred to me Herzl's argument for Palestine might be made on the same basis. Who, after all, had been first in the Holy Land?

Plucking a small cambric handkerchief from his sleeve, Zangwill removed his pince-nez and polished the lenses energetically before replacing the glasses on the bridge of his nose and tucking the cloth back into its accustomed place. "America must be regarded as a work in progress."

"Like all humanity," suggested the detective tactfully. "Can you tell me, or have you any idea, what prompted Herr Herzl's obsession with the creation of a Jewish homeland? Jews, after all, have lived for two thousand years in all countries of the world."

"As it happens, I have a very clear idea of what drove him," Zangwill answered. "It drives many of us, though not perhaps to

an early grave. Have either of you gentlemen ever heard of Kishinev?"

Holmes and I traded glances.

"We have not."

Zangwill hesitated, then rose and drew
from a cupboard beneath the bookshelves
behind him an enormous rolled map, which
he unfurled across his desk.

"Kishinev is a village in Bessarabia, lately
a province of Russia in the Pale of Settlement." He pointed it out on the map of that
country. "It is an unremarkable provincial
town, roughly a hundred miles from glamor-
ous Odessa . . ."

"What an enormous country," I realized.

"Gigantic," Zangwill affirmed. "The
United States boasts four time zones; Russia spans eleven, were they to compute
them."

"Kishinev," Holmes repeated, his finger
under the name. "What does 'the Pale of
___.' "

"Two years ago in Kishinev, a massacre of
Jews took place. The town had a large Jewish population, but over the course of a
mere two days, fifty were killed and over six
hundred raped or wounded. More than a
thousand Jewish homes were ran-sacked

and destroyed."*

"The crimes keep getting bigger," Holmes murmured.

"I beg your pardon?"

"Nothing," the detective assured him, his finger still hovering over the place.

"Did you say six hundred?" I began.

"Raped or wounded. Many burned alive. By their Christian neighbours. The carnage was horrific."

*"Goyim,"* Holmes murmured.

Zangwill's features once more registered surprise. "Just so. Such massacres are not uncommon in Russia. They are referred to as pogroms."

"Po . . ."

"Pogroms. Kishinev was only the most recent and arguably most vicious. The authorities encourage them, using Jewish successes to egg on jealousies they augment with literature calculated to inflame Christians who have otherwise lived in harmony with their Semitic neighbours for generations. Pogroms have become a sort of steam governor for the enraged populace of a failed state."

"The conditioned reflex," I heard Holmes

* As the result of the slaughter and its ensuing notoriety, Kishinev changed its name to Chisinau.

mutter under his breath.

"In this case, the murder of a Christian child was blamed on the Jews, who had allegedly used him in ritual sacrifice, pasting his blood above their door lintels during the ceremony we know as Passover. The blame didn't vanish even when it was discovered the boy had been murdered by his own cousin. Rumors are hard to rectify, and prejudice difficult to undo."

Zangwill rolled up the map and replaced it as we resumed our chairs.

"It was Kishinev that sent Herzl racing to Russia, trying to see the Tsar. He failed. But after the Kishinev pogrom he became ever more frantic on the subject of a homeland for European Jewry. I believe he actually confronted Kaiser Wilhelm personally during a visit to Jerusalem."

"But surely," I said, "his concerns were limited to Russia. Such a thing could never happen in a modern European society."

Zangwill favored me with a penetrating expression.

"You're saying — correct me if I'm mistaken — that such a thing could not happen here?"

Something in his tone gave me pause.

"Yes, I suppose I am," I conceded, beginning to feel uneasy without knowing why.

Zangwill stared pensively into the middle distance.

"You're aware the coronation of Richard the Lionheart was celebrated at the time by massacring all the Jews to be found in England?"

"That was a long time ago," I objected.

He inclined his head, allowing the point.

"Are you gentlemen familiar with Saki?"

"A Japanese rice wine?" Holmes responded.

It seemed to me the writer suppressed a smile. "Saki," he explained, searching his shelves, "is the *nom de plume* of a British writer of amusing, sometimes trenchant short stories, H. H. Munro. Hector Hugh," he filled in the initials.

"Regrettably, my work does not give me much time to read fiction," Holmes explained in turn, a trifle embarrassed, I thought.

Zangwill pulled a slender volume from the shelves and thumbed through it 'til he found what he was looking for. "This is a story by Saki called 'The Unrest-Cure.' In it Saki's mischievous hero, Clovis, is playing a practical joke on a middle-aged couple named Huddle, whose complacency he wishes to . . ." He searched for the words. ". . . wishes to shake up."

144

Zangwill then read aloud from the book:

"This very night is going to be a great night in the history of Christendom," said Clovis. "We are going to massacre every Jew in the neighbourhood!" "But there aren't thirty Jews in the whole neighbourhood!" protested Huddle. "We have twenty-six on our list," said Clovis, referring to a bundle of notes. "Do you mean to tell me you are meditating violence against a man like Sir Leon Birberry?" stammered Huddle. "He's down on our list," said Clovis carelessly. "We've got some Boy Scouts helping us as auxiliaries." "This thing will be a blot on the twentieth century!" exclaimed Huddle. "And your house will be the blotting pad. Have you realized that half the papers of Europe and the United States will publish pictures of it?"

Zangwill gently shut the book. "It's played for laughs," he reminded us. "But beneath the laughter lurks another possibility, would you not agree?"

"The possibility that under adverse economic conditions," suggested Holmes, "and prompted by sufficiently persuasive propaganda masquerading as truth, ignorant folk might be brought to turn on neighbours

145

with whom they have never quarreled before."

"Precisely."

I knew the detective was looking at me. Holmes and I had recently seen such propaganda.

"May I ask," the detective inquired, as if reading my thoughts, "whether you are familiar with the Protocols of the Learned Elders of Zion?"

The other raised his eyebrows. "I am not."

Holmes rose to his feet. "Watson, let us thank Mr. Zangwill for his time and for a most enlightening interview. We must be off."

Zangwill rose, as well. "Where do you gentlemen go next?" he inquired.

Holmes turned to me.

"Russia," I informed him.

# 6.

## MR. AND MRS. WALLING

They seek him here, they seek him there,
Those Frenchies seek him everywhere.
Is he in heaven, is he in hell?
That damned elusive Pimpernel!

That insistent jingle lodged annoyingly in
my brain throughout the first act of Baroness Orczy's play concerning the secret
identity of a foppish eighteenth-century lord
who doubled on the sly as a daring adventurer, bent on liberating doomed French
aristocrats across the Channel from the guill-
otine.

I had better things with which to occupy
my mind and, looking at him sitting next to
me, suspected Holmes was of the same
opinion. Juliet, to my left, was clearly enjoying the play, but I knew she, too, was preoccupied. I had related the substance of our
meeting with her friend's famous husband.
It was the least I could do in view of the

fact that it was through her offices that Holmes and I had made the connection with Israel Zangwill in the first place. Taking in what I told her of the encounter, she sensed events were likely to accelerate, but, true to her word, no remonstrance escaped her lips.

We found ourselves at the performance of the highly touted *Scarlet Pimpernel* because Mycroft had chosen the New Theatre in St. Martin's Lane for our latest assignation. Memories of the recent debacle at the Diogenes had rendered all of us skittish, and we agreed to reconvene on neutral turf.

At the first interval, our trio congregated as arranged in the white-and-gold foyer, jammed amid playgoers, all chatting enthusiastically about the piece, with special emphasis devoted to the horses that galloped convincingly across the stage on treadmills. Many were happily reciting that cloying rhyme. I overheard talk to the effect that the Baroness was even now turning her play into a novel.

"Brilliant choice of venue," Holmes commented sourly. "Did our Irish friend review this claptrap? I can imagine his notice."

"Holmes, Shaw no longer reviews plays. Nowadays he writes them."

The detective grunted noncommittally at

this news. Music, not theatre, was his passion. Notices for the play, I knew, were indifferent ("claptrap," one critic had indeed written), but audiences evidently felt otherwise.

"The safest place to keep a secret is in a crowd," Mycroft remarked, as he succeeded in joining us. We jostled one another, trying to keep our drinks from spilling.

"I'm going to collect my ice," Juliet tactfully informed us. After she was out of earshot, Mycroft produced a bulky envelope and passed it to his brother.

"Very well, you've convinced me," he said. "Here are your passports and visas for France, Germany, Austro-Hungary, Bulgaria, Romania, and Russia. You will travel as Mr. Gideon Altmont, and you, Doctor, as Colonel Rupert Morcar."

"Picturesque," Holmes said.

"You are journeying to Bessarabia to study the polyphonic motets of the Greek Orthodox liturgy at the Monastery of St. Basil."

"You've been reading Watson's inflated accounts of my doings," Holmes chuckled. "*All* motets are polyphonic, my dear Mycroft."

Mycroft looked briefly over his shoulder before resuming. "Your itinerary as far as Varna has been drawn up by Thomas Cook.

At Varna you will change trains and proceed to Odessa in the Pale of Settlement — the Russian landmass to which Jews are restricted. From Odessa, there are no trains and precious few roads to Kishinev. You will be obliged to make your own way. Funds are on deposit at Rothschild's. Kindly keep track of your expenses, and be mindful that His Majesty's Government does not provide *carte blanche.* You are traveling second class. Such incidentals as tobacco and *aperitifs* will not be reimbursed."

"Typical," the detective murmured. His tone suggested that he had anticipated such caveats, though the other affected not to hear this.

"It may be cold even in warm-water ports like Odessa. Dress accordingly. And have your Mrs. Garnett send her invoice to me, *poste restante,*" he added, sensing I was on the point of broaching the topic, then went on, precluding any possibility of interruption, addressing his brother, "And remember this above all." Here he lowered his voice, though in this throng there was hardly a need. I was mordantly expecting something from Polonius, but instead he whispered, "Should anything untoward befall either of you, His Majesty's Government is unaware of your existence. They

150

know of no Gideon Altmont or Colonel Morcar."

"And thus, I take it, our chances of paid interment in Highgate Cemetery, should the worst befall, you would characterize as remote."

Mycroft glared at his brother. "I find that remark in the worst possible taste."

"Anything else?"

"Yes. Before you leave, I wish you to take tea tomorrow at the Savoy."

Yet another procrastination? I knew the thought occurred to both of us.

"I never go there," Holmes protested. "It's always filled with Americans."

"You may well visit America one day," his brother mused. "Doctor, did you not practice medicine in San Francisco once upon a time?"

How he came to know this, I could not imagine.

"In any case," Mycroft Holmes said, ignoring my look of surprise, "it is Americans I am sending you to take tea with."

"We'll never be able to book a table at this late date."

"I've taken the liberty of doing it for you. The D'Oyly Carte family was only too happy to oblige, in memory of your past services to their father."[*]

Holmes lodged a final objection. "We have a great deal to do before we depart."

"I promise you will find the conversation useful. They are a married couple, recently back from an extensive Russian tour."

"Oh?" We both perked up at this.

"Mr. and Mrs. William English Walling. He is, I believe, a native of Kentucky."

Holmes frowned at this intelligence. "And why have the Wallings, so impressively named, visited Russia?"

"Mr. Walling and his Russian-born, Jewish wife, one Anna Strunsky, are American radicals, much concerned with the plight of Russian Jews. Mrs. Walling, I am given to understand, is most becoming. We keep them under close observation."

"Is there anyone you don't keep under close observation?" Holmes inquired.

"No one, in fact. Here is their dossier." He handed the detective a second, smaller envelope.

I wondered at that point if there was also a dossier with my name on it. Was that how Mycroft knew of my American sojourn?

Juliet returned with her ice. "I've wan-

[*] Richard D'Oyly Carte, who built the Savoy Hotel and adjacent opera house of the same name.

dered about as long as an unescorted woman decently could," she informed us, ignoring our sour expressions as the bells recalled us for the second act.

"I really see no need to remain here," Holmes declared bluntly, and threaded his way to the lobby. I knew from Juliet's look that she would be dismayed not to see the rest of the piece and offered her my arm. When I turned around, Mycroft, too, had vanished, no mean feat in his case.

Juliet and I sat through another two hours of Sir Percy Blakeney captivating the audience, who tittered every time the baronet said, "Demme!" in his best blue-blooded drawl. All agreed that Fred Terry was splendid in the role and that the *piéce de résistance* was when the Pimpernel, trapped by the evil Chauvelin in a lonely Normandy farmhouse, brilliantly escaped capture at the last moment by flinging a fistful of pepper in that monster's face, reducing him to a helpless sneezing fit, during which our unhindered hero sauntered out the door to freedom and wild applause. I had no wish to spoil Juliet's enjoyment by pointing out the absurdity of such a stratagem.

**10 January.** This morning I spent at the Royal Marsden, ordering my affairs and ensuring my surgical practice was seen to during my absence. Harris, always obliging (and no doubt hoping to purchase the practice on my retirement), undertook to see my general patients, and Mr. Brattler, a rising star in the department, would assume my duties in the operating theatre.* The Winslow boy's tonsillectomy was now on the books for next Monday at eight. I sent his mother a note, apologizing for the abrupt shift in our arrangements, claiming my own indisposition as the reason.

The night after the theatre had been a somber one. Juliet and I had by now achieved that special intimacy where words seemed unnecessary; looks and caresses sufficed. We knew the pattern of our marriage was about to undergo a significant alteration, but felt confident that neither time nor distance would fundamentally change our relations.

When I left the hospital I traveled to Baker Street, where Holmes, in the act of packing — a surprisingly chaotic task, given his otherwise logical brain — broke off long enough to hand me the Walling-Strunsky dossier.

* In England, civilian surgeons are typically titled Mr., not Dr.

"Tell me what you make of it," said he offhandedly.

"I am curious to know what a gentleman from Kentucky is doing in Russia," I owned. "Peddling bourbon to the Cossacks?"

Receiving no answer as the detective flung clothing about, I resumed my old chair, lit my pipe, and perused the file, marveling at Mycroft's thoroughness.

William English Walling proved to be a labor reformer and Socialist Republican (the designation was unfamiliar to me), from a wealthy Louisville family. He had been graduated from the University of Chicago, followed by Harvard Law School, after which he had moved to New York, where, in 1903, he had founded the National Women's Trade Union League, whatever that was, but I had my suspicions. I couldn't seem to escape the suffragist movement, I reflected dourly.

About the woman called Anna Strunsky, far fewer facts appeared to be known. Born in Russia, she'd spent her childhood in New York before moving to San Francisco. Where and when or even if she'd married Walling were not specified. "Novelist" was the only other note attached to her file.

"It seems straightforward enough," I commented. "What there is of it."

"You surprise me." Holmes sat on his battered valise to close it. "I've not been to America, but surely it excites one's curiosity to learn that a gentleman of that Southern stamp has contracted a liaison with a foreigner? And a Jewess? And has uprooted himself so far out of his orbit as New York? Aren't members of the Old South, as they clannishly term themselves, prone to clinging to their ancestral turf, their Mississippi châteaux? Does all this not occasion remark and proclaim Mr. Walling a most unusual specimen?"

It nettled me that Holmes — Holmes, who had never set foot in America and might never do so (notwithstanding his brother's offhand speculation*) — should think himself qualified to comment on the customs of that country's population. It irritated me still more to think that he might well be onto something. The Wallings, on paper, at least, seemed a most unusual pairing. "Suggestive," as the detective might term it.

"Holmes, have you read anything about

---

* Mycroft was prescient. Holmes would eventually spend two years in America, working undercover for his brother in the run-up to World War I.

this part of the world except *Uncle Tom's Cabin*?"

His silence, punctuated by grunts to close the bag, intimated I had scored a point.

The Savoy, crowded as always, when we reached it, elicited a host of memories. I knew why Holmes had objected to meeting there. It was at the adjacent eponymous theatre, built to accommodate the genius of Gilbert and Sullivan, that a promising young soprano had had her throat cut in one of the most sensational cases Holmes had ever been called upon to solve. I mean to set down the details someday, but Holmes has consistently refused permission to do so.*

Sir Arthur Sullivan, alas, has left us, but for all I knew, we could bump into his prickly collaborator at any moment. The hotel itself appeared a monument to Victorian stolidity while at the same time seeming effortlessly to embody a streamlined opulence. More sophisticated or knowledgeable critics than myself might have caviled at the mixture, but hoi polloi, especially the Americans, adored the place, intoxicated by its luxurious fittings and easy ambience,

* Those details may be found in the aforementioned "The West End Horror."

regularly crowding out the English who struggled to stop there.

Tea was served in an atrium overflowing with floral arrangements and walled with mirrors, which had the effect of multiplying its opulence. We had arrived early and were shown to a pair of yellow silk divans with a low table of pink Carrara between them at the best location in the agreeable room.

"Compliments of the management," the smiling *maître d'hôtel* informed us. Part of the Savoy's charm in the face of its splendor was the affability of its staff. Quite simply, they knew they were the finest, had nothing to prove, and were content to go about their business without affectation. The atrium fairly vibrated with animated chatter.

Having ordered our tea, Holmes looked about him. "Three couples from Liverpool, two from New Mexico, one from Carlisle, that older pair from Brittany, a lone Italian widow from Umbria, and one gaucho from the Pampas, if I am not mistaken."

"Really, Holmes, you have outdone yourself! How on earth can you —"

He chuckled.

"My little joke, Watson. I've not the least idea. Except for the Americans," he added. "Their loud voices give them away."

"Have I the honuh of addressin' Mistuh

Sherlock Holmes and Doctuh Watson?"

The voice that posed this question was not particularly vociferous; quite the contrary, it was subdued, one might say "honeyed," but definitely laced with an accent that proclaimed the speaker to be from the southern portion of the United States.

Preoccupied by Holmes's little prank, we had failed to notice the approach of a strikingly handsome couple. We scrambled to our feet to greet what we instantly understood to be Mr. and Mrs. William English Walling.

"How do you do?" Holmes extended a hand, first to the lady and then her husband.

Neither could be thirty years of age. Walling brought to mind the most dashing leading man imaginable in a West End melodrama. Well but not ostentatiously kitted out in Savile Row togs, the man was slender, erect, immaculately groomed, clean-shaven, and pale, with chiseled cheekbones, a firm mouth, and piercing dark eyes. He exuded a confident but not overbearing intelligence, like one who is accustomed to his own virtues but, like the staff of the Savoy, sees no need to trumpet them.

His wife was an altogether different proposition. Mycroft had not erred in describing Anna Strunsky as "becoming." I cannot remember how Scott described Rebecca in *Ivanhoe,* but this creature irresistibly put me in mind of that heroine. Simply put, Anna Strunsky was the most breathtaking woman I had ever seen. As I have no plans to share these memoranda, I need not censor my reaction. She was slender, but not so tall as her husband; her skin, in contrast to his pallor, was a dusky satin, denoting, perhaps, her Levantine origins. But it was her face that struck all who beheld it dumb with wonder. Patrons in the atrium could not help breaking off their talk and staring. Her chief features were large, luminous eyes of an unprecedented violet that gazed candidly at all within her field of vision. Like her husband's, her hair was jet and lustrous, glistening as if jewels were embedded in her tresses. The contrast between that glorious dark crown and those radiant, heliotrope eyes, once seen, I feel certain, was never to be forgotten. Her nose likewise suggested the perfection of an Attic sculpture, perhaps the Venus de Milo, whose features I vaguely recalled from a picture postcard. Her vermillion lips completed the statue; bowlike, they were thick, with the lower drooped in a sensual pout.

Holmes, towards whom I directed a side-long glance, though avowedly unsusceptible to the charms of the female sex (with one notable exception*), seemed not immune in this instance. This I inferred from his reluctance to gaze at the lady too directly or too long, like one who fears staring at the sun.

It was only when Anna Strunsky spoke that the spell was broken, for while the timbre of her voice was agreeably low, her speech was marked (marred is perhaps too strong a word) by a thick Russian accent that challenged all Olympian associations.

"So pleased to meet you," she said, offering me her hand.

"Likewise, suh," added her husband, facing me with a slight bow.

Holmes gestured to the divans and asked if they preferred muffins or scones.

"Muffins, if you please," Walling answered for them.

"Oh, English, dahlink," his wife remonstrated, "I like better scones." She then broke into a rapid patter which I judged to be Russian and which he seemed perfectly to comprehend. His middle name, I inferred, was his wife's term of endearment

* That would be Irene Adler, referred to by Holmes as "the" woman in the case Watson dubbed "A Scandal in Bohemia."

for him.

He answered her fluently in the same tongue, though his pronunciation still smacked of Kentucky rather than the Steppes of Central Asia. He was pleased to indulge her preference, and the order was changed.

Holmes, having his own timetable, thanked them for agreeing to see us on such short notice.

"I understand you all are goin' to Russia," Walling said, crossing his long legs. "We have just spent the better part of a year there."

"A year?" I could not help remarking.

"We sail home the day after tomorrow on *The Majestic.*" Walling seemed pleased by the prospect.

"He will write book," his wife explained, daintily tearing off a fragment of scone. "Is called *Revolution in Russia.*"

Walling smiled again and took her hand. What a strange pair they were. "We don't yet know what it will be called,"[*] he temporized. "Events in Russia are still playin' out."

"May I ask," said Holmes, studiously stirring honey into his teacup, "how you, from

[*] The book, published in 1908, was titled *Russia's Message.*

America's southern regions, come to be so interested in Russia? A year is such a long time," he added. "Can it have anything to do," he wondered aloud, "with the plight of Negroes in the United States?"

Walling flushed uncomfortably, confirming Holmes's intuition.

"The plight of Jews in Russia, to which my wife first brought my attention (we met working at the Hull Settlement House in New York)," he inserted parenthetically, "is grotesquely similar to that of the American Negro. My family, as you have deduced, formerly owned slaves."

His clouded countenance gave evidence of tortured guilt. "Cossacks or members of the Klan make little difference. All victims of injustice suffer alike."

Holmes and I exchanged glances.

"*Da*. Oh, yes," Anna Strunsky said, following our look. "Is true. In America, Negro is treated like Jew in Russia. Hang. Burn. Slave. Rape."

I could feel myself turning scarlet at her blunt use of the word.

"In America, we have 'race riot,' " she added, ignoring my blush. "Is no different."

Holmes, I knew, seldom read any international news. On the other hand, I could not pretend ignorance of the phrase.

163

"Are you familiar with the journalist Theodor Herzl and his writings?" the detective inquired.

"Herzl?" Their eyebrows arched in unison.

"Are you Zionists?"

The question took both by surprise.

"Not at all," Walling responded, as though irritated with us for having failed to grasp his meaning. His wife leaned forward to clarify.

"We are Socialist," she said proudly.

"Capitalism will be the death of democracy," her husband added.

"Who said that?" I wondered.

He appeared puzzled. "I did."

His wife, seeing things becoming confused, struck in. "English and me, we study conditions in Russia to understand solution in America." She broke off to say something to her husband again in Russian then turned brightly back to us. "Now we understand how to do."

"Fortunately in America there is no Tsar to stop us." Walling smiled.

Their faces radiated a youthful idealism that struck a pang. When I first set out for Afghanistan, had I, too, been a believer?

"Stop you from — ?" Holmes was conscientiously applying butter to his muffin, but I knew he was registering their every word.

"We are formin' a new organization with Mr. Du Bose* to help American Negroes protect and defend their rights," Walling said.

"Will be called" — Mrs. Walling took a portentous breath — "National Association for Advancement of Coloured Peoples."** Her husband smiled indulgently.

"It's a bit long," he chided her.

"If *I* can say!" Anna Strunsky exclaimed, at which point they broke into companionable laughter. In that moment I perceived that more than ideology bound them. Holmes, however, was not to be dissuaded. He set aside his muffin.

"When you were in Russia, learning about the plight of Jews there," he asked casually, "did you visit Odessa?"

"Of course. We were also in Moscow, St. Petersburg, Kiev . . ."

"We meet Count Tolstoy!" Mrs. Walling

* Watson, I believe, is noting what he heard phonetically. I think Walling was referring to W. E. B. Du Bois, American civil rights activist and author.
** The NAACP was founded in the New York apartment of William English Walling and his wife, Anna Strunsky, in 1909. W. E. B. Du Bois was among the founders.

smiled at the recollection. "Count Tolstoy very great man. He tell us, 'Read Emerson! Read "Civil Disobedience"'! I say, 'We know Emerson! Emerson American!' "

"He does not wish us to use his title," Walling corrected her. "We were always to address him as simply Lev Nikolaevich."

She shrugged indifferently. "Count Tolstoy say, 'Lead simple life,' but in Yasnaya Polyana life not so simple."

"His plantation,"* Walling explained, a trifle self-conscious and perhaps, it did not escape my notice, amused. "When we sat down to luncheon, a butler announced, 'Plowing is served.' " Holmes reached into his pocket and withdrew some papers familiar to me.

"Have either of you ever seen anything like this in a Russian newspaper?" he inquired, lowering his voice.

Sitting beside one another and leaning so their temples almost touched, the couple scanned the pages. Anna Strunsky extracted a pair of glasses, rendering her yet more mortal. She evidently had no difficulty reading English, for she frowned in recognition at what she saw on the page.

Walling looked up almost at once.

* Yasnaya Polyana today is a museum.

"We did see something like this in a news-paper, almost a year ago. It was in Russian, not English, of course. I speak some Russian, as you hear, but don't read it." He cast a fond glance at his wife. "Mrs. Walling translated it for me."

"Was it titled 'The Protocols of the Wise Elders of Zion'?" the detective prompted.

"That's right. I remember now. The hateful thing was serialized, day after day." He shook his head at the memory and translated for the benefit of his wife, but she was having no difficulty following our discussion. His words produced an agitated expostulation from the lady in Russian, to which he responded, *"Da, da,"* several times, which I took to mean yes.

"Do you remember where you read them?" Holmes asked, then held up a hand. "No, don't tell me. Was it in Kishinev? Did you stop in Kishinev?"

The couple's mood darkened instantly.

"We did. How did you guess?"

Holmes chose to ignore the temptation to dilate on the subject of guessing.

"Please think very carefully now. It is of the utmost moment. What was the name of the newspaper that printed the Protocols?"

They conferred in an undertone, then brightened. Anna Strunsky Walling addressed us in firm tones. "Newspaper was *Bessarabets.* Published in Kishinev," she added emphatically.

Holmes gazed at her directly now.

"Mrs. Walling, I cannot begin to tell you how helpful you have been."

**11 January.** The following morning, in a driving rain, Juliet accompanied me the short distance to Victoria Station. There seems scarcely any point in describing our melancholy final evening together. At supper we made desultory conversation, and later, while I packed, she sat and watched from the day bed. Her eyes widened but she said nothing when she saw I included in my luggage my Webley Bulldog and a box of .422 cartridges. I judged my old Adams .450 calibre centre-fire service revolver too bulky for the occasion, and the Bulldog I oiled regularly.

"At least pack the cartridges separately," was her only remark. It was a good suggestion, and I took it, shaking out the bullets before stuffing the revolver in the toe of one boot and concealing my supply of ammunition in several rolled socks. If I was stopped at a frontier with a weapon in my possession, I could always point out that it was unloaded.

Sleep was a restless affair, with much turning and tossing, but at last we drifted off. In the morning the smell of coffee in the kitchen helped wake us. Maria had made a proper breakfast for my leave-taking. By daylight, Juliet and I chatted brightly and inconsequentially. It was clear neither of us relished the prospect of a maudlin parting.

"I shall miss you and your omelets, Maria," said I, folding my serviette and inserting it into its ring.

"Come back soon, sir. I'll look after the missus while you're away."

"Thank you, Maria."

Following breakfast, as I was slipping on my greatcoat in the entryway, Juliet surprised me with a gift.

"My dear," I began.

"Try it on, John." She did her best to smile.

I put on my new hat, a lovely grey homburg. It fit wonderfully.

"John, it is most becoming!"

"Dearest, how thoughtful."

"Stay warm in Russia, John."

At the station Mycroft was waiting with further instructions concerning our route and more paperwork to facilitate it. Like a nervous mother sending her youngest off to

Eton, he fussed and showed me our itinerary with stops scored with thick pencil.

"When you reach Paris, you have a layover before you catch the Orient Express. You are at the Hotel Esmeralda."

"I know, Mycroft."

"Rue Saint-Julien-le-Pauvre."

"Mycroft —"

"There are stops at Strasbourg, Munich, Vienna, Budapest, then Bucharest. Don't disembark at Bucharest whatever you do. The pickpockets there are legendary. Stay aboard all the way to Varna. And remember: your return is booked on the second of February. If you miss that connection you must wait another ten days for the train's return."

Holmes joined us in time to hear this advice. He was fumbling with two suitcases, his violin, and Constance Garnett's translation of *War and Peace* given him by my Juliet.

Mycroft looked around. Daylight did not agree with him. "I'm off," he informed us. "Sherlock, take good care. And good hunting."

To my astonishment, the burly fellow caught his brother up in an awkward but fervent embrace before walking briskly away, instinctively losing himself in the throng. I don't think I quite grasped the danger into which we might be placing ourselves until I beheld that ursine hug.

Whistles were shrieking, announcements being made. Travelers were scrambling aboard.

"Now, boys," said Juliet, putting on a bright face. "Remember you are no longer boys. No larking about. Be careful." .

"We will," Holmes and I dutifully chorused, though under his breath I distinctly heard Holmes murmur, "But boys *will* be boys." Aloud he said only, "We're in *wagon-lit* number four, compartments twelve and fourteen. I'll see you there, Watson."

He made as if to offer my wife a kiss on the cheek but evidently thinking better of it, snapped her a smart shake of her gloved hand before boarding the train.

Juliet and I faced each other. We both knew communication between us from this point would be problematic, at best. It had been arranged I would write c/o *poste restante,* but there was no way she could answer.

"Come back," she said simply.

"I promise."

I gathered her in my arms and then, fumbling with my bags, took refuge aboard *wagon-lit* number four. Almost at once the

Continental Boat Express squealed to life. Vaguely, as I made my way down the narrow passageway, I wondered why Holmes had secured two compartments when we typically required but one.

Instead of entering compartment twelve, I stayed at the window, watching Juliet as she walked alongside.

"Take care!" she repeated. "Stay warm!"

"Stay dry!" It was all I could think of to say.

The train now moved faster than she could keep pace, and I saw her figure diminishing as we left the platform behind. There was nothing for it but to drag my bags into the compartment and heave them up on the racks.

It wasn't until I had completed the task that I turned and beheld Anna Strunsky seated on one of the green cushions at the window, facing forward.

"You will need a translator," said the stunning woman.

She now had only the trace of a Slavic accent.

Behind me, I heard Sherlock Holmes offer a low chuckle.

■ ■ ■ ■

# PART TWO:
# RUSSIA

■ ■ ■ ■

# 7.

## OKHRANA

"This is monstrous!"

"Now, Watson —"

"Holmes, have you taken leave of your senses?"

My companion could not conceal his amusement as he shrugged off his coat.

"Come, you will admit we require the services of a translator. Even Mycroft acknowledged as much."

I bit my lip to prevent commenting on just how easy I imagined it must have been for that chilly dispenser of "superfluous damage" to consign Anna Walling to sacrifice herself for a "grateful nation" — notwithstanding that nation was not hers.

"But we can't just —" I turned to the lady, who was watching us with the disinterested expression of an impartial observer at a tennis match. "And what has become of your accent, madame?"

Anna Strunsky Walling offered an enigmatic smile, feline in a way that put me queasily in mind of the Cheshire cat. It was the first of many queasy moments to come.

"I exaggerate it from time to time. It has proved useful." The accent may have diminished, yet her throaty purr remained.

She wore a becoming dark blue travel ensemble with something white at the throat and, as I watched, calmly unpinned her rakishly brimmed hat and set it on her lap. I swung back to the detective. Given his lifelong mistrust of her sex, I could not fathom this unprecedented *volte-face*.

"It took some doing," he admitted, evidently anticipating my confusion, "but in the end Mrs. Walling was the logical choice. Her Russian is fluent, her visas already in order, and her . . ." He paused for the word. ". . . credentials, unique."

"And my bags were already packed," the lady pointed out.

"And Mr. Walling?"

"Is presently on the high seas, bound for New York. When the situation was explained to him by no less a personage than" — here she cast a look at Holmes — "a member of the Diogenes, he was . . . content to approve my . . . participation. Mr. Walling and I . . ." She paused. ". . . respect and make allowances for one another as individuals."

Seeing what must have been a look of consternation on my face, she added simply, "I am accustomed to making my way in the world." As if to emphasize this point, she fished a cigarette from her purse and lit it with practiced gestures.

I confess I could not understand much of what she said, but there was no mistaking the confident manner in which she said it.

Indifferent to the pelting rain, the train was now rattling at a goodly clip, and I was obliged to grasp a handhold to remain upright. It was easier to grasp a handhold than the situation. There seemed little I could say and less point attempting to say it. I spared a thought for Juliet, wincing to think of her response should Anna Strunsky's role in this business ever come to light.

Holmes, who had settled on the opposite side of the window, facing backward (and incidentally in the direction of Mrs. Walling), now packed Balkan Sobranie into a black briar with which I was unfamiliar.

"Let us review the data," he suggested, shaking out his match. At a loss, I subsided onto the seat nearest the compartment door. "In the town of Kishinev a newspaper called — ?" Here he addressed Mrs. Walling.

"*Bessarabets,*" she reminded him.

"Just so. This *Bessarabets* publishes, in serial form, the alleged minutes of a secret conclave of Jews conspiring to take over the world, a French copy of which makes its way to London at a frightful cost, where it falls into Mycroft's hands." Before giving Anna Walling the opportunity to pursue this cryptic reference, Holmes withdrew one of the now crumpled pages translated by Constance Garnett and read aloud from what he found there: "*We will not permit any religion espousing a sole God except our own. As we are the Chosen People, we are destined to rule.* Etcetera." He shrugged and blew aromatic smoke, whose familiarity, I acknowledge, had a calming effect on me. "Upon closer examination, these Protocols reveal themselves to have been slavishly copied in Russian from a French pamphlet written forty years earlier by one Maurice Joly, during the reign of the Emperor Napoleon III and directed at him rather than against any so-called gentile oppression. But as we may reasonably infer, whoever translated the version my brother entrusted to Mrs. Garnett and myself had no knowledge of Joly's tract. 'Our' French translation came from the series of Russian newspaper articles read by you and your husband, Mrs.

Walling, while in Russia. Whoever was behind 'our' translation, the one Watson shared with Mrs. Garnett, clearly had no idea the Russian text from which he'd worked had been plagiarized from an obscure tract written by another Frenchman on another topic in another age. It was Mrs. Garnett who fortuitously recognized the theft. And it was you, Doctor, who distinguished the translations by noting what appeared to be the superfluous substitution of meaningless alternate language in what we may term the 'Russian version.' "

"With its references to 'tsar' instead of 'emperor,' etcetera," Mrs. Walling noted.

"Translation is a tricky business," Holmes observed, placing the tips of his fingers together in his accustomed fashion. "Cervantes once said that reading something in translation is like looking at a Flemish tapestry wrong side out. The image may be there, but is obscured by a great many dangling threads. How many different equivalent combinations of words may various translators working in different eras in different languages have recourse to in order to produce an approximation of the original sentence? In the present instance, we have a French original translated and plagiarized into Russian and then translated back into

French again by someone else. In our case, the change of wording from 'noxious' to 'odious,' from 'overturn' to 'overthrow,' etcetera, proves to be merely the caprice of a different translator."

With a determined effort, I shook off my lethargy of shock, finally getting into the spirit of the thing and recalling the purpose of our journey.

"But events prove there *were* in fact regular meetings of Jews in Switzerland over the last five years, though they were by no means secret," said I. "Again, on closer examination, these congresses appear to have been devoted not to a conspiracy of world domination, of whatever definition, but rather the more prosaic search for a Jewish homeland. Yet the architect of these meetings, a passionate Zionist, drops prematurely dead from what may or may not have been a heart ailment just before being interviewed by . . . an employee of the Diogenes."

"Splendid, Watson. I am reminded anew of your narrative abilities. If only you wouldn't embellish," he added, his eyes twinkling mischievously. On the chase, the detective was obviously in high spirits.

"I don't embellish," I insisted, annoyed at this charge he always laid at my door. "I include colour."

I leaned over both of them and slid open the transom above the window. The air was frigid and wet, but the aperture did serve quickly to rid the compartment of smoke.

"You write very well, Doctor," Mrs. Walling interjected, stubbing out her cigarette in the ashtray. "Don't let him get under your skin."

I could not make her out. Still less could I understand her husband's willingness to allow his wife to venture alone back into the mouth of the Russian bear in what very possibly were its death throes. The thought of allowing Juliet to do any such thing, no matter how worthy or urgent the cause, was beyond my capacity to envision.

Holmes blew more smoke.

"On the working hypothesis, then, that the Protocols are a forgery, we are left with the following questions: *Primo:* Who created them? *Secondo:* For what purpose? And finally: What was the true fate of Theodor Herzl? If he was assassinated, who was his assassin, and what were his motives?"

"Why did you not begin your investigations with the dead man?" Mrs. Walling inquired coolly.

"Watson?" Holmes turned to me. It was clear he did not wish to acknowledge Mycroft's prohibitions regarding Theodor Herzl. Neither, I inferred, did he feel it wise to reveal the existence of a second, more recent (and female) corpse. Having concluded we had need of Mrs. Walling, Holmes saw no point in alarming her.

"Such details may prove distressing," I improvised, "but by this time, the decomposition of the Zionist's body has doubtless so far advanced, trace amounts of poison would be difficult, if not impossible, to detect, much less prove."*

"Depend upon it, if the man was murdered, those responsible have long since quitted the vicinity," the detective added. "At the moment it must be termed a cold trail."

Anna Walling sat back, wrinkling her nose at this information.

"But if Theodor Herzl's entire purpose was to concentrate Jews in a country of our own, why trouble to assassinate him in the first place? Surely ridding the world of Jews was what they wished."

* It was not until 1964 that the University of Glasgow developed a test of human hair to detect the presence of excess arsenic in the body, suggesting, among other possibilities, the poisoning of Napoleon on St. Helena.

Holmes's hawklike features bespoke his appreciation of her intelligence.

"If the Protocols were believed, Herzl's purposes may have been perceived by his murderers as a screen to conceal his true ambitions."

"Besides which," I struck in, "Jews have always been convenient scapegoats. Take them away and whom can people blame?"

"Bravo, Watson." Holmes nodded, emitting another puff of Balkan Sobranie. "You continue to astonish me."

I had astonished myself. Thanks to these malignant Protocols, things that lurked unexpressed in the dark recesses of my mind I now found myself voicing aloud for the first time in my life.

Satisfied with the detective's reasoning, Anna Walling returned to the less odiferous problem of the translations.

"One thing must also be the case," she suggested. "Whoever published the Protocols in *Bessarabets* must also be fluent in French in order to have copied from it."

"Someone with a catholic knowledge of arcane political literature, to know of Joly," Holmes shrewdly added. "One must also wonder: Were these Protocols published before or after the good citizenry of Kishinev turned on their Jewish neighbours? If before, they might be argued to have catalyzed the slaughter."

"And if after?" Mrs. Walling wondered, her violet eyes, as always, unblinking.

"To have justified it."

"There is an additional possibility," said she. Holmes favored her with a quizzical look.

"To terrify the Tsar."

"Ah."

"He is easily frightened."

"Oh?"

"A credulous, superstitious man. A year ago his son was born. The Tsarevitch is hemophiliac."

Holmes frowned; his knowledge of chemistry and anatomy were profound. "He bleeds?"

She nodded. "At the slightest touch. It is not generally known. The Tsar and Tsarina are first cousins, which may be responsible for the boy's condition. Their majesties are desperate to find a cure. They make no distinctions between doctors and faith healers. Lacking a cure, they seek scapegoats."

"Ah," repeated Holmes. "The Protocols would serve to legitimize his encouragement of these pogroms."

It required no great act of imagination to connect the dots between a document such as the Protocols and Nicholas II's attitude towards Jews. Such a document, which, by now, had surely been brought to his attention by zealous ministers (if not created by them), could only serve such a purpose.

I recalled, yet again, the distended body of Manya Lippman, lying on its slab in the City Morgue. True or false, the Protocols of the Elders of Zion were proving to be lethal in all directions.

"Our only hope of containing their damage," Holmes concluded, "is to expose them as a hoax. And the only way to do that is to uncover the perpetrators. We are in a race against time. Even now the contagion is spreading. If the Russian version appeared almost a year ago, there may be any number of foreign translations in circulation by now."

Silence fell upon the compartment, and to my surprise the detective drew forth his copy of *War and Peace,* found his place in the book, and was soon absorbed in it.

Mrs. Walling closed her eyes.

Still recovering from the shock of her presence, I scarcely knew how to occupy myself. I made some effort to arrange these notes but soon fell into a light slumber, comfortingly rocked by the agreeable motion of the train.

At Dover, we were delayed by the weather. It had begun to snow, and the wind whipped fiercely into a gale. Our Channel crossing, when it was at last under way, proved a vertiginous ordeal. Dubiously christened *The Flounder,* our ferry slewed and yawed for all she was worth, her stern scouring troughs while her nose ascended vertically, only to plunge downward again. I am no mariner under the best of circumstances, and it is well known that the passage from Folkestone to Calais traverses what is generally conceded to be the roughest body of water in the world. The entire ghastly experience recalled to my mind the interminable weeks I had spent, years before, traveling on a troop ship to Bombay, prior to taking up my duties in Afghanistan. The seas were nothing to this in my recollection, and yet I remember little else of my voyage to India save my *mal de mer.*

It was almost eight when *The Flounder* hove into Calais. In an effort to recover lost time, still-trembling passengers were bundled onto the Paris train for the final leg of the route. Thoroughly seasick by now, I was no longer soothed by the rhythmic oscillations of the railway carriage. Several times I was obliged to excuse myself.

It was close on midnight when we stepped

off the train at the *Gare du Nord.* After the smoke-filled confines of our compartment, the bracing air of Paris was welcome to this traveler, but the city was entirely shrouded in a mantle of glistening snow, and there were few taxis to be seen. Shivering, we finally located one stoic hack, whose horse was mercifully protected by a thick blanket. For a sizable inducement, the driver undertook to take us across the silent city, traversing the Seine at the *Pont Neuf* and so fetching up at the *Rue Saint-Julien-le-Pauvre.* At this hour and under these conditions, there was scarcely a pedestrian, omnibus, or motorcar to be seen, giving Paris the look of a veritable ghost city. Even the footfalls of our poor horse were not to be heard.

The Hotel Esmeralda, when we were informed we'd finally reached our destination, proved to be diagonally across from Notre Dame on the *Ile de la Cité.* The cathedral's massive form could just be made out in the darkness, through vast swirling flurries of white powder, stirred upwards by a night breeze. In my exhausted fancy, the flurries took on the aspect of white locusts, undulating in endless configurations.

"Watson, come."

Under different circumstances, I might have found the Hotel Esmeralda charming.

Built in the seventeenth century, the *auberge* proved irritatingly cramped. Our late arrival obliged us to rouse the concierge, and the impossibly narrow, turning staircase created havoc as we struggled with our luggage. There were no bellmen.

"This, I expect, is the Foreign Office's notion of economy," Holmes grumbled as we clattered aloft. Mycroft had thoughtfully procured a room for Mrs. Walling, but Holmes and I were obliged to share a narrow bed.

"Any better?" he inquired from the window as I tugged off my boots.

"I will be. What are you looking at, Holmes?"

"Come see."

As I rose to obey his instructions, Mrs. Walling entered without knocking.

"Have you seen?"

"Yes."

All three of us now crowded the mullioned fenestration and gazed into the medieval lane. There, beneath a solitary lamppost, two figures huddled in astrakhan greatcoats and Persian lamb's-wool hats, clapping their gloved hands and stamping their feet in a futile effort to promote circulation. One bearded face was briefly revealed as its owner, retaining his thick gloves, awkwardly attempted to light a cigarette.

"Okhrana," Mrs. Walling informed us in a quiet tone which admitted of no doubt.

"I thought as much," Holmes concurred. "I was wondering if they'd put in an appearance."

"Which is Okhrana?"

"What," corrected Holmes.

"Okhrana is the Tsar's secret police, Doctor." It was Mrs. Walling who answered my question, never taking her gaze from the two figures below.

"But how did they know?"

"They followed me to Manchester, that much is now clear," the detective admitted, "but they had no way of knowing what my business there was." He turned to face Mrs. Walling, who shrugged.

"They could not have learned from me," said she. "Officially, Anna Strunsky Walling sailed for New York two days ago with her husband from Southampton on *The Majestic*. I" — here she gestured to herself with a gloved forefinger — "am Miss Sophie Hunter, music copyist, currently traveling on a British passport with that name, supplied by your brother."

Holmes stared at the two men below. One could almost feel sorry for them.

"How, then?" I repeated.

"When you eliminate the impossible," the detective murmured, "whatever remains, however improbable, must be the truth." He faced me. "It's your Mrs. Garnett."

"What? Holmes, you are absurd. My wife's family —"

"And you, my dear doctor. It's you."

I felt my jaw sag.

"Me?"

I was uncomfortably aware Mrs. Walling had turned her wide violet eyes in my direction. I felt myself pinned by their beam of unalloyed interest.

"Not on purpose, my boy. I'm not suggesting either of you is in league with the Okhrana —"

"I should think not! Constance, that Bloomsbury bunch . . . they're all . . . bluestockings, 'artistes', intellectuals . . ."

"But one of them is a translator of Russian," the detective reminded me. "That fact alone had doubtless long since drawn their attention." He rummaged on the bed and held up his copy of *War and Peace.* "Count Tolstoy and his civil disobedience terrifies them, but they daren't arrest him. The fact that your sister-in-law was disseminating his writings to a wider readership was by itself cause for a certain level of interest, but when you brought her the Protocols . . ."

"Dear God. Cedric West!"

"Who?"

It now all came back to me in a rush: the propitious arrival of the stockbroker in the taxi, with his vaguely unplaceable accent, offering me a lift.

"That was when they chose to transfer their attentions from Mrs. Garnett and fasten them on you," Mrs. Walling concluded.

"I didn't give him my true name," I now remembered with relief, "as I hadn't wished to get into conversation about my writings."

"Excellent, Watson," Holmes murmured. I knew he was trying to put the best light on my blunder but it had been mere impulse, not cleverness, that prompted my deception.

"He wasn't by chance carrying a box camera and proposing to take your photograph?"

"Certainly not." With a shudder, I wondered if Cedric West, my kindly cab-sharer, concealed a kosher butcher's knife on his pinstriped person.

"Then at the least he has no confirmation of your true identity."

"I told him my name was Baskerville," I now recalled, whereat the detective laughed and Mrs. Walling appeared confused.

Holmes shook his head. "No matter," he declared. "I will explain it another time."

The idea of Russian agents operating freely in London, knifing women in the heart of what I thought of as civilization and throwing their bodies into the Thames, was a notion I would have ridiculed less than a fortnight since. After all, weren't England and Russia allies, bound by treaty? What need had they to spy upon one another?

"Allies spy on each other all the time." Holmes was reading my mind. "The nature of espionage is such that once commenced, it never knows where or how to stop. Secrets are addictive. Knowledge confers power."

"She was the right person for the job," I protested. "If it weren't for Constance, we'd never even have learned about the Joly plagiarism."

"No one is blaming either of you," Holmes again assured me. "The question is, what do we do about these gentlemen now?"

The room was freezing.

"To elude them would only excite their suspicions," Mrs. Walling argued.

Holmes made no remark in response, but I knew he was turning over the problem in his agile brain. It was clear this unusual woman had some experience in these matters. This could hardly be surprising; if she and her husband had been traveling in Russia for a year, poking their noses into a Jewish hornets' nest, they could not have failed to attract official notice.

"Will they follow us on the train tomorrow, do you think, or simply telegraph ahead, Holmes?"

"The latter, more likely," the lady theorized before he could answer. "These are most probably agents in place."

"As were those who trailed me to Manchester," Holmes concurred. "The resources of the Okhrana following Russia's recent defeat at the hands of the Japanese cannot be unlimited. The likelihood is our watchers are mere 'day hires' who will hand us off to others, like a relay baton. This, however, still leaves us in a quandary regarding our own doings."

I took a turn about the small room.

"Why do anything?"

They regarded me.

"We are Mr. Altmont, Colonel Morcar, and Miss Hunter. We are traveling to St. Basil's Monastery to study Greek Orthodox liturgical music. What contradicts that?"

"These." Holmes held up a sheaf of the crumpled Protocols.

"Then we must destroy them."

"Not destroy," Holmes mused, warming to my idea. "They were acquired, after all, at great cost. Not destroy," he repeated. "Conceal."

"But these are merely copies," I protested. "Your brother has the originals. Why trouble to retain them? If they are discovered, we will be hard put to account for ourselves."

This was a sobering thought.

"True," the detective conceded, "and yet retaining them may prove useful in ways we cannot presently anticipate."

"Give them to me."

It was Anna Walling who spoke, extending a slender gloved hand.

"You?"

"Mr. Holmes, surely you know what devious creatures we women are. You have said so often enough in print. Give the pages to me."

After a flicker of hesitation, he did as she asked.

Later, as Holmes and I lay exhausted side by side on our flaccid mattress, each struggling for a share of that flimsy coverlet, the detective allowed himself a rare moment of introspection.

"I hope I've done the right thing."

"So do I."

At that time, I suspect neither of us was

sure what thing we were referring to. Or even if it was the same thing.

But after this exchange, neither of us seemed capable of keeping our eyes open.

When we looked out our window again, it was morning. The blizzard had stopped, and our two watchers had vanished.

"They left hours ago," Holmes declared, vigorously rubbing his thin upper arms.

"How can you be sure?"

"Their footprints are entirely obscured by fresh snow."

So they were.

Meeting Mrs. Walling half an hour later in the confining vestibule of the Esmeralda, a cab was summoned, but Holmes waved it off, first paying the driver and ordering him to proceed to the Gare de Lyon, with neither fares nor luggage. His action appeared to baffle Anna Walling, but I knew from experience what this dodge was meant to accomplish.

Sure enough, as we watched from within the hotel, two ruffians emerged from behind the corner at the bottom of the road and hastened after the cab, shrieking for another as they kicked up the fresh snow.

"Never take the first cab," Holmes explained.

Mrs. Walling, I could see, was impressed.

Our hack, when it arrived, brought us instead to the *Gare de l'Est,* where we boarded the Orient Express, *première classe,* entirely undetected, so far as I could determine, by our pursuers.

*"Première classe?"* I asked the detective. "Isn't this rather rich for our blood? I understood Mycroft to say we were traveling second class."

As we stepped aboard, Holmes allowed himself the gleeful smile of one sibling who has outwitted another.

"An oversight, surely. The man is so terribly busy. I had Cook & Son correct our booking."

Smartly uniformed porters adroitly handling our bags were a welcome change from the Esmeralda.

"We have certainly earned it," I allowed.

"By the by, Watson, I infer from your new hat that your marriage is flourishing."

The train in question was simply enormous, stretching over fourteen hundred handcrafted feet and comprising no fewer than eleven sleeping carriages, many with individual names such as Perseus, Minerva, Ibis, Ione, and so forth mounted in raised brass on their vestibules and painted in gilt on their sides as if they were ships. There were in addition several so-called "Continental" Pullmans that could only boast numbers. In addition to the sleeping carriages, there were three restaurant cars, two "parlour" or bar cars, and a new innovation, a "business car," boasting ten typists on call at the push of a button, day or night, ready to transcribe important communications on diverse typing machines in as many languages for whichever diplomats, royalty, or titans of industry had need of their services.*

"How convenient for you, Watson," Holmes remarked. "Your memoranda can be transcribed en route."

"Holmes, I —"

EDITOR'S NOTE: IT IS AT THIS POINT THAT THE DIARY PAGES HAVE MADDENINGLY GONE MISSING, SEVERAL EVIDENTLY TORN OUT. THE NARRATIVE, AS WE SHALL SEE, RESUMES OUTSIDE VARNA, AND SO WE MUST CONTENT OURSELVES WITH LISTING

* The "business car" (car number 3557) was short-lived, being discontinued in 1908. The staff, originally male, was quickly changed to female typists, who appeared more amenable when summoned at odd hours.

THE KNOWN STOPS MADE AT THAT TIME BY THE CELEBRATED TRAIN. FROM PARIS, THE ORIENT EXPRESS STOPPED IN MUNICH AND THEN VIENNA, BEFORE WENDING ITS WAY SOUTH TO GIURGIU IN ROMANIA AND FROM THERE STILL FURTHER SOUTH TO VARNA, ON THE BLACK SEA.* NORMALLY THE JOURNEY TOOK FIVE DAYS, WITH OCCASIONAL STOPS TO REPLENISH THE ENGINE'S COAL AND BOILER WATER, AS WELL AS RESTOCKING THE DINING CARS' LAVISH GUSTATORY REQUIREMENTS. I THINK WE MAY ASSUME THIS PASSAGE WAS NO DIFFERENT.

THE NARRATIVE RESUMES MIDSENTENCE:

. . . arguably as exhausted by this time as its occupants, finally squealed to a panting stop, punctuated by an unending belch of steam, at Varna's gloriously sunlit station. Though we had availed ourselves of every amenity and convenience along the way (though carefully refraining from doing so in Bucharest, as Mycroft advised), we were

* The route of the fabled train varied over the years. Some versions later went to Constantinople, aka Istanbul, while others finished up in Athens.

nonetheless travel weary, our bones rattled from a journey that had crossed all Europe.

I descended first, limping awkwardly, followed by Holmes, who handed Mrs. Walling down behind us.

"Thank you, Sherlock."

"Mrs. Walling, aren't you warm?"

The fact that suddenly we all experienced the rise in temperature served to distract me from this exchange. Had it not done so, I would certainly have noted Mrs. Walling's familiar use of the detective's Christian name. Neither, at the time, was I conscious of the fact that Holmes and the lady never looked at one another throughout these banalities. It was only later that this was brought to mind.*

Holmes helped Mrs. Walling shed her heavy traveling cloak, slid out of his own ulster, and turned to me.

"Watson, we are overdressed."

"I'm fine," I insisted testily, but, ignoring me, he tugged at my greatcoat with his surprisingly powerful hands, then handed off our wraps to a shabbily attired porter, who addressed him rapidly in a foreign tongue.

"Romanian," Mrs. Walling explained. "Or

* Holy cow. Where are those missing pages??

Bulgarian. No matter. They all speak Russian. In the Balkans," she informed us in a neutral tone, "frontiers and languages are fluid."

"Can you ask when our train leaves for Odessa?"

She posed the question to the porter, who jabbered back with much gesticulating while we waited. Why is it, I wonder, that when such seemingly simple exchanges occur in a foreign tongue they always appear to consume inordinate amounts of time?

Finally she turned. "Maybe tomorrow."

"Maybe?"

"Tomorrow?"

Holmes and I had spoken simultaneously. This information differed from our itinerary.

She turned back to the porter, and more rapid-fire talk and gesticulation ensued.

"Most likely tomorrow. We will need rooms for the night."

This at least was easily accomplished. A large, if undistinguished, Hotel Terminus was situated within two minutes of the station. Two minutes toting several pieces of bulky luggage on a warm day is not the most difficult task, but not the pleasantest, either. We were surrounded by packs of chattering children, palms extended, some offering to carry our luggage (which I was convinced we should never see again), others simply begging. They settled about and traveled with us like a squadron of houseflies.

"Watch your pockets," Anna Walling cautioned us. I was indeed obliged to slap away an importunate hand reaching for the notebook bulging in my pocket.

At the hotel, while Holmes booked rooms, I located the concierge and obtained a postcard, on the back of which I drew a heart before posting it to Juliet c/o *poste restante* in London. After depositing our belongings in adjoining rooms on the third floor, we gathered in the foyer for a stroll through the city. We were all, I think, eager for some diversion after days of confinement aboard the train.

From the first, we could not escape the impression that we had somehow contrived to journey backward in time. Regardless of its attractions, this part of the world appeared not merely impoverished, but fifty years behind the conveniences we in England take for granted. Such streetlamps as we observed were still illumined by gas; roads were largely unpaved, and motorcars were nowhere to be seen. The port of Varna on the Black Sea was obviously famous for its sun-drenched situation. The shingle, even in January, boasted hardy sun worshippers and was fronted by an esplanade up and down which visitors and holiday-makers promenaded, taking their ease.

The local population appeared a polyglot of Bulgars, Greeks, Armenians, Turks, Romanians, also Macedonians, more than a smattering of Russians, Magyars, and, of course, ubiquitous Jews. There was a large cathedral topped with various silver-gilt, onion-shaped domes, and the sea air was pungent with competing aromas, ranging from the cooking fires of differing cuisines to the not unpleasant scent of fish wafting from nearby trawlers.

The sun was soon setting behind several white-and-pink stone public buildings, the most modern features of this provincial metropolis. In this part of the world it was accounted far too early for supper, but a waterside bistro with a name in Greek lettering above its shutters afforded us a respectable charcuterie, dominated by lamb.

"It makes a refreshing change after days of *cordon bleu*," Holmes admitted.

We ordered a bottle of the local white we found undrinkable.

"Ouzo," Mrs. Walling informed us, smiling. "It is an acquired taste."

I declined to acquire it.

"Holmes, what are you looking at?"

"Those curious tourists."

I twisted in my chair in the direction of his gaze.

Two gentlemen, attired in identical straw boaters and seersucker jackets, were using binoculars to scrutinize the horizon. All the fishing craft had long since put into port.

"What can they be looking at, Holmes? There's nothing to see."

"That is what makes them curious."

"They're looking at us, Doctor." It was Mrs. Walling who grasped the detective's meaning.

Holmes resumed his meal.

"It was to be expected," he conceded. "When we failed to appear at the Gare de Lyon, they realized their mistake."

"What will they do?"

Holmes tried the wine again and made a face. "They are unsure."

"Unsure of what?"

"Are we Mr. Holmes and party, poking our noses into sensitive Jewish issues . . ."

"Or?"

"Or are we, as our passports and visas proclaim, the Altmont party, bound for St. Basil's Monastery? In a word, have they been trailing the wrong troika?"

"But in London," I objected, "they saw me. They saw Mrs. Garnett . . ."

"Yes, you were seen in London," the detective agreed, "and a description has certainly been circulated, but if what you report of your encounter with your spurious stockbroker is accurate —"

"It is," I insisted vehemently.

"— and no actual photograph has been transmitted, they cannot be sure. Very likely they will not take chances. Tomorrow, we will give them their answer."

"How will we do that?" Even the knowledgeable Mrs. Walling was at a loss.

"By visiting the Monastery of St. Basil and studying the motets of the Orthodox liturgy. The metropolitan★ is expecting us."

Tomorrow, however, would prove too late. Returning to our hotel, we ascended to the third floor where Mrs. Walling unlocked her door while Holmes and I repaired to our room, only to be startled by what we beheld there. The place had been turned topsyturvy, suitcases flung open, linings slit, mattresses gutted, goosedown like snow everywhere, the huge wooden wardrobe tipped

★ An ecclesiastical title in the Greek Orthodox Church. A metropolitan typically ranks above an archbishop and below a patriarch.

on its side and our clothing strewn about pell-mell. I searched frantically and was relieved to find my Webley where I had wedged it in the toe of a boot. My rolled socks, as it proved, were deemed unworthy of their attention, and thus my cartridges were likewise safe. Had they found bullets, doubtless they would have redoubled their efforts to locate my weapon.

Holmes's copy of *War and Peace* had been torn in half and his cherished violin smashed to bits. It was perhaps the only time I ever beheld the detective stupefied. I don't believe I understood fully the fiddle's importance to him until this instant. He sat as one turned to stone, holding the instrument's fragments in his open hands, staring with unseeing eyes at the shards as they slid from his fingers.*

More fortunately, my journal had escaped their clutches. I always carry it with me.

It was at that moment we heard the muffled cry.

"Sherlock!"

"Anna!" Holmes exclaimed, and we ran

---

* Holmes's violin was allegedly a Stradivarius. Watson, whose judgment in such matters is questionable, deemed the detective an accomplished player.

back to Mrs. Walling's room.

Clothing, including articles of intimate apparel, as well as toiletries and miscellaneous items of no conceivable interest or value, had been torn to shreds and flung about as though by a madman. Mrs. Walling did not own (or at any rate, did not travel with) much in the way of jewelry, but such as she had remained conspicuously untouched.

She was sitting motionless on the bed, facing the window, her back to us.

"Mrs. Walling, are you all right?" I asked.

She turned, displaying an ashen face. Unable to speak, she could only stare, those violet eyes displaying an emotion I had yet to behold: fear.

"The Protocols!" shouted Holmes. "Where are the Protocols?"

# 8.
## TEA

"Your first thought was of the Protocols!"

Lying on the remains of the mattress in our demolished room, I could clearly hear the unhappy woman's voice through the wall we shared with hers.

Holmes's reassuring murmur was incomprehensible, but I could guess its substance. He'd seen she was unharmed.

"But still — !" And then, as another thought struck her, expressed so I could hear it distinctly: "What was the 'frightful cost' you alluded to in obtaining them?"

"They are my responsibility." His voice was a trifle louder now as he evaded her question. "Surely you can see that. Anna, we are struggling to contain a genie in a bottle that is threatening to burst at any moment. The pusillanimous thing already exists in three languages —"

"Two!" she sullenly corrected.

"Three," he gently insisted, "if we count

the English translation you are carrying. Where is it?"

"Safe."

"Give it to me."

"No."

"Anna."

There was the sound of shuffling and, as I thought, the rustling of clothing unfastened.

"Thank you."

Then silence.

"What now?"

Holmes heaved a sigh.

"We must go through the motions."

"Sherlock —"

"Gideon. We must play our parts, Miss Hunter."

Another silence, followed by —

"Do me up."

"Mr. Gideon Altmont," the police captain read in hesitant English, leafing through Holmes's passport. Then, taking up the second, he savored, "Colonel Rupert Morcar," glancing briefly in my direction before perusing the third. "Miss Sophie Hunter," he intoned with evident relish, allowing his frank gaze to rest on the exquisite Mrs. Walling for an uncomfortable length of time before returning his attention to our other papers. She took the occasion to put on her reading glasses. If she thought by this action to nullify or dilute the effect of her beauty, I am not at all certain she succeeded.

As he scanned our documents, the official made no further comment, granting us time to examine our surroundings and interlocutor. We were in a high-ceilinged room in one of those imposing pink-and-white stone buildings I had previously had occasion to remark. The desk and our chairs, squeezed into one corner, were the only furnishings (aside from a massive filing cabinet) in the gigantic place, which was big enough to host a ball and for all I knew had originally served that purpose. Electric lights in wall sconces flickered intermittently, the result, I judged, of a primitive power apparatus, while above the desk, a wafting fan of the kind in India we termed a punkah was propelled by a small boy seated cross-legged on the marble floor, his back to the wall. He tugged continuously at the rope which controlled its pendulous swing. Throughout the interview that followed, I cast looks now and again in the punkah wallah's direction. Neither the little fellow's expression nor his mechanical gestures betrayed the least variation. In my estimation the ceiling was too far above us for the device's sway to confer any benefit on the room or its occupants.

"I am Captain Valerian," the man behind the desk informed us without elaboration. His Armenian name seemed in no way at odds with his Bulgarian rank or the tarboosh he chose not to remove throughout our interview. "You say you have been robbed?" His hair beneath the fez was brilliantined black and, I suspected, dyed. A monocle in his right eye seemed to have taken up residence there from birth. Across his upper lip ran the thinnest possible dark moustache. It might almost have been applied with a bit of charcoal. Something in his aspect suggested his health was not robust.

"Our rooms at the Hotel Terminus were broken into and vandalized. Clothing and property have been damaged or taken, my violin destroyed," Holmes informed him.

Mrs. Walling relayed this in Russian, explaining her role as our translator.

"Violin?" The policeman coughed, politely covering his mouth with the back of a white-gloved hand. He, too, spoke Russian.

"We are on our way to St. Basil's, outside Odessa, to study liturgical motets."

Captain Valerian cupped a hand to his ear. "Liturgical — ?"

"Anthems. Music of the Greek Orthodox Church. We are endeavoring to preserve such music for posterity, lest it perish from —"

The policeman interrupted her translation in accented English: "Western ears?" Clearly he understood more than we'd supposed. The question was put in a neutral tone, but I nonetheless sensed a lurking hostility. It was followed by another cough and the introduction of a handkerchief. From the blood flecks visible on the cloth and now on his glove, I suspected the man had contracted phthisis.*

"I believe in the value of preserving history and art," Holmes stated sententiously. "This is what I do."

"What you do," the other echoed, again in English. His cough racked him again, and he had recourse to a carafe of what I hoped was water.

"I beg your pardon."

We waited 'til the fit subsided and the policeman returned to meditatively thumbing our passports.

"If you wish to satisfy yourself regarding my credentials," Holmes suggested, "please feel free to look up the entries attributed to me in *Grove's Dictionary of Music and Musicians,* published by the Oxford University

___

* Consumption or tuberculosis.

Press. You will find articles under my name regarding Gregorian Chants, the music of Hildegarde of Bingen, and songs from the Benediktbeuern Abbey of Bavaria."

Valerian, who clearly understood, nonetheless allowed Mrs. Walling the formality of repeating the detective's words in Russian.

I confess I marveled at Holmes's assurance in manufacturing this pack of lies. It was certainly the case that he knew and had written about medieval music, but never a word for *Grove's* that I knew of. And certainly nothing under the byline of his present alias. No doubt he gambled the odds of the celebrated reference work lying about were remote.

Valerian turned to Anna Walling.

"I am a music copyist," she explained from behind her spectacles. "We are expected at St. Basil's."

"And you?" He coughed anew and addressed me. I had had time to think of my reply.

"An enthusiastic amateur," I explained, smiling. "I've been helping defray the costs of the trip for the privilege of viewing the manuscripts."

"Very good of you," Holmes murmured.

The policeman sat back, tapping his lips

with a gloved forefinger.

"It is fortunate you kept your travel documents with you," Valerian observed. Were his words intended to convey suspicion? From his bland expression, it was impossible to say.

"Surely that is a sensible traveler's precaution. Captain, what is to be done regarding our burglary?" Holmes's tone became a trifle peremptory. Anna Walling strove to echo his tone in her translation. Her English, I was now aware, had resumed its original thick Slavic inflection.

Taking his time, the policeman removed his monocle, breathed on it several times, then polished the lens with the bloodstained handkerchief before rescrewing it in front of his eye, after which he favored us with a wintry regard.

"We will fill out a report."

"A report."

"Yes. You will please to make lists of all damaged or missing property."

"Captain," I interposed, "where is the British consulate?"

"In Sofia. Three hundred and eighty kilometers inland." I believe it gave him some pleasure to say this. Before I could expostulate, Valerian brandished our itinerary. "Tomorrow you go to Odessa. There

213

you stay — ?"

"At the Grand Hotel," Mrs. Walling replied, reaching for our documents.

After a moment's hesitation, he shrugged, handing them back to her and rattling off a passage in Russian, followed by a smirk of the pencil-thin moustache.

"He says if they recover any of our property or apprehend the thieves, we will be contacted in Odessa."

"He said something else," Holmes intuited.

She coloured. "He did."

**17 January.** A greater contrast between the Orient Express and the dilatory milk train that bore us northward paralleling the coast to Odessa could hardly be imagined.

While the Orient Express was a virtual hotel on wheels, furnished with every modern amenity, the "Odessa Flyer," as Holmes snidely dubbed it, had nothing in the way of a dining car, let alone food. We were obliged to sit among a very different class of traveler, hard workers who seldom had the opportunity or perhaps inclination to bathe, wedged beside us on crammed wooden benches without cushions. The windows, minus shades or glass, admitted all kinds of dust and agricultural odors along with the occasional welcome gust of sea air. According to the map, the distance between the two cities was less than three hundred miles. In Europe such a distance might have taken six hours in a proper train; crossing the Bulgarian border into Romania and then across the Romanian frontier into Russia, it consumed the better part of twelve. Every now and again we were treated to tantalizing glimpses of the Black Sea. The rest of the time the train meandered as though unsure of its route, through endless fields populated by a seemingly inexhaustible population of toiling peasantry. Our fellow passengers, I must own, were a genial sort and kind enough to offer us some suspicious cheese, which we thought wise to decline.

In the event, the barriers proved no impediment. The customs officials and guardians of three countries appeared to be bored old men, and our arrival on the train occasioned no more than indifferent yawns, illegible signatures, and perfunctory stamps.

But it wasn't the boredom or the lack of stimulation that had dampened our spirits. Being robbed is a peculiarly depressing experience. It wasn't merely the destruction and loss of our possessions (though Mrs. Walling bemoaned the shredding of a pink chemise given her by her husband); it was the sense of personal violation that left one in a state of impotent fury.

And though he did not allude to it, I knew that Holmes suffered the loss of his beloved Stradivarius keenly. My singular friend was an intensely civilized man. Nothing more surely represented this aspect of his nature than his affection for and reliance upon music. The wanton destruction of his violin, cherished as much for its pleasing contours as its historic value, to say nothing of the agreeable sounds it produced, had shaken him to the core. He could not, I suspect, wrap his head around the idea that human beings were capable of such pointless destruction.

Added to which, the fact the thieves had contemptuously expressed no interest in Mrs. Walling's jewelry made clear beyond all doubt that the robbery was as much a warning as a theft. "This is what we can do if we choose," the Okhrana seemed to be saying.

I wondered if Mrs. Walling was now regretting her decision to accompany us.

"What was the point?" she demanded, as if reading my thoughts. "Had they any idea what they were looking for or why?"

"They were seeking to protect their secret,

the secret of the Protocols," Holmes explained. "They want to know what we know and to prevent our telling what we know."

"We don't know everything."

"We know enough to worry them. We know the Protocols are a hoax. We don't yet know who perpetrated the hoax. And they are intent on preventing us from finding out and revealing it."

"Why stop at robbery, then? We're in Russia. Why not simply kill us? People disappear in Russia all the time. Just look what happened in Kishinev."

Holmes might have dismayed her by informing her it had recently happened in London as well, but smiled instead. "It's a very pretty problem they're faced with. They're confronted with too many imponderables. What good would disposing of us do if we've already passed on our knowledge? They've no way of knowing how far we've let the cat out of the bag. Worse, if the celebrated Sherlock Holmes and his almost equally admired (forgive me, Doctor!) Boswell were to . . . disappear while inside Russia! — His Majesty's Government would raise the very devil with our Romanov ally. And at present, Nicholas Romanov can't afford to lose an ally."

"But Holmes, you forget: Mycroft said if

anything untoward were to happen, London would deny all knowledge of us."

"Ah, but these creatures don't know that. They can only guess. And worry. Can they circulate this lie in every possible language before we expose its author?" The detective shook his head, like one amused by the symmetry of the equation. "No, they can't harm us without harming themselves. For the present they can only hope to frighten or intimidate us."

With this cheerful thought, he closed his eyes.

Odessa, had it not been crawling with tsarist troops that gave it every appearance of an armed camp, was inarguably the most beautiful city I had ever seen. The architecture of this warm-water port was emphatically European, not to say Mediterranean, in character, with lovely seaside villas and public buildings that would not have been out of place in Paris. Only the diversity of its population, which easily eclipsed that of Varna, informed visitors they were not in Nice. In addition to the many residents of the Balkans and Ukraine, in Odessa were to be found innumerable Germans, French, Italians, and Scandinavians. At one point I am sure I also heard a smattering of Spanish.

Beggars were nowhere in evidence. Either the presence of armed men or the city's prosperity discouraged them.

It was clear that Anna Strunsky Walling knew Odessa well, but her previous affection for the place was confounded by the vastly altered circumstances in which we discovered it. Normally a municipality that prided itself on welcoming travelers and tourists, there were now clusters of soldiers at every street corner and crossing. People were arbitrarily stopped and their papers inspected. Before leaving the station, we were obliged to stand in winding queues, waiting to be interrogated by suspicious and exhausted civil servants, all too aware of uniformed troops peering over their shoulders as they filled out interminable paperwork. The abortive revolution that had begun in Odessa was fresh in the minds of citizens and constabulary alike, and the government was taking no chances.

Finally confronted by a diminutive bureaucrat in a dark green coat whose hem descended to his ankles, we were quizzed extensively as to our plans, our place of residence within the city, and our intention to visit St. Basil's on our way to Kishinev.

"Why do you go to Kishinev?" the harried commissionaire demanded in what I could easily detect as a peevish tone.

"It's closer to St. Basil's," Holmes explained through Mrs. Walling. "And less expensive for scholars."

The man scowled at each of us lingeringly through tiny hexagonal spectacles, sniffed and grunted, then finally scribbled our information in one of countless ledgers no one would ever inspect and affixed stamps to our documents with what I judged to be perfunctory motions. Whatever he'd been told to look for, he was satisfied it wasn't us.

The Grand Hotel near the Square de Richelieu was all that could be advertised and more. Our rooms were, as the Baedeker put it, "sumptuously appointed." We might as well have been at the newly opened Ritz in Paris. Or still aboard the Orient Express.

"All we lack is proper clothes," Mrs. Walling observed. Having been robbed, with many items of apparel torn to shreds — particularly hers — this was indeed the case.

Making sure that our important papers (and my notebook) were again carried on our persons, we set forth to make some purchases, during the course of which Mrs. Walling delivered an impromptu tour.

The city's magnificent physical high point was the Square de Richelieu, from which, leading to the waterfront below, descended the longest series of steps I had ever seen. From below it must have appeared a veritable stairway to heaven.

Mrs. Walling gestured to the bay beyond. "That is where the battleship *Potemkin* was anchored when the mutiny occurred," she informed us, lowering her voice. "All the small craft from shore set out to feed the starving sailors."

"And here the troops marched down the steps, shooting?" Holmes inquired.

"Not here," she corrected him.

"But the newspapers all said —" I began, but she cut me off.

"The newspapers got it wrong." She had lived most of her life in the United States and sometimes spoke bluntly like an American. "The shooting was over there." She gestured. With a shudder I was unable to suppress, I beheld the nearby yellow stone parapet hideously besmirched by brown stains.

Mrs. Walling followed my look. "Many were killed. Shot. Slashed with sabers. Men, women, children, babies. The streets ran red. They've tried to expunge the blood," she explained, "but the stone absorbs the colour. It will not allow them to erase their crime."*

We moved on, eager to quit the site of that silent witness, but I found it hard to escape the queer impression we were being followed wherever we went by a trail of blood.

Dawdling later through a colourful souk near a park called the City Garden, we soon acquired a motley assortment of clothing. Mrs. Walling, seemingly at home in such a place, bargained furiously and was soon exotically clad in native sartorial splendor. Odessa was widely celebrated for its beautiful women, and one would have had to be blind not to count Mrs. Edward English Walling now among their number.

"There are many Jews," Holmes observed. The Jews we saw were typically distinguished by round hats, some trimmed with enormous fur brims, and long strands of curled hair which fell before their ears. Unlike the rest of Odessa's colourful population, Jews proclaimed their uniqueness by wearing black gabardine, the only variation being their curious white aprons with dangling strings.

* In his 1925 epic, *Battleship Potemkin,* director Sergei Eisenstein staged the slaughter on the unending steps, one of the most famous sequences in all cinema.

"A third of the city's population," Mrs. Walling assured him, following his look. "They are slaughtered periodically."

"The Protocols?"

She gave a small shrug. "There are many pretexts."

"Our friends have arrived," I pointed out.

Secure now on Russian soil, and making no attempt to disguise their interest, instead of staring pointlessly out to sea, the two gentlemen in straw boaters and seersucker jackets from Varna had become three. All pretense of furtiveness cast aside, they regarded us with blank expressions.

"First my violin and now this," declared Sherlock Holmes. "Watson, my dear fellow, would you be so kind as to let me have several sheets of blank paper from your journal, and have you a pencil I might borrow?"

Knowing better than to question the bright gleam in his eye, I gave him the materials for which he asked. Motioning us to join him at a nearby café near the self-same interminable steps, Holmes busied himself for several minutes while Anna Walling and I exchanged self-conscious pleasantries, avoiding fruitless speculation regarding our observers or the detective's activities. While Holmes appeared to be sketching something, I asked her where she had lived in San Francisco. "One sixteen Cherry Street," she answered with a smile. I confessed I was unfamiliar with Cherry Street.

Holmes was now writing on a separate sheet of paper. I was on the point of giving Mrs. Walling my own San Francisco address and youthful memories of the place when he finished whatever had occupied him. He stood and handed Mrs. Walling two slips of paper, one of them blank, along with my pencil.

"Would you kindly render this in Russian and then, without being seen to do so, drop it where the authorities will be sure to find it?"

Mrs. Walling glanced at the paper. Her violet eyes widened, but when she looked up, Holmes had already patted me on the shoulder.

"I'll return directly, Watson," said he, and, stuffing the remainder of the papers into his pocket, he ambled over in the direction of our unwelcome watchers while Mrs. Walling left in the direction of a nearby police kiosk.

I saw the detective approach the three men, with amiable aspect and expansive gestures. At first they appeared worried he intended a confrontation of some sort, but their fears were quickly allayed and they were suitably mystified by the detective's efforts to communicate. Holmes laughed heartily, pointed, shrugged as if he had not a care in the world. His pantomime implied his hope they might provide a stranger with directions, which, from their reciprocal gestures and expressions, they were endeavoring to supply.

Grateful, he practically hugged one of the startled men, eagerly pumped hands with the other two, and returned to our table, barely concealing his hilarity.

"I think I'll have some Russian tea," he announced. "I believe the word is *tchai. Puzhalsta* means please, and *spasiba* thank you. Incidentally, in Russian they have no word for 'foot.' Which may explain a great deal. Mrs. Walling has been educating me," he explained, still in the grip of his own amusement.

I refrained from commenting on his education or its source, contenting myself instead with wondering what was going on.

"Do you enjoy theatre?" he responded to my surprise, having successfully given his order to our waiter.

"Are we discussing *The Scarlet Pimpernel*?" I asked, utterly bewildered by now.

"By no means. One might call this 'living theatre.' We have front row stalls," he added with a smirk.

"Oh? And when does the curtain go up?"

"Any minute now, Watson. Any minute."

Our trio of watchers, satisfied we were going nowhere, had seated themselves under an umbrella in an adjacent establishment and were in the act of ordering drinks of their own.

At which point the very devil broke loose. The air was rent with the shrieks of police whistles and a horde of soldiers with fixed bayonets descended on the square, trailed by a squad of Cossacks on horseback who clattered past them, knocking over tables and diners as they surrounded the three astonished men. Panicked Odessans and visitors created chaos as they fled in every direction. Several pistol shots were fired into the air, adding to the confusion.

For several hair-raising minutes I had a glimpse of what Odessa must have looked like on the fatal day not a fortnight before when these same troops had systematically mowed down the citizens of Odessa on more or less the same spot.

Holmes calmly sipped his tea as a furious altercation erupted between the soldiery and our nemeses, loudly protesting their innocence in language that required no translation.

It was then that one of the soldiers, to the consternation of its owner, plunged a hand into the seersucker pocket of the man Holmes had hugged, triumphantly extracting several papers and waving them aloft. I recognized the pages as having been torn from my book. What had Holmes drawn on them?

Mrs. Walling returned in time to see the play's finale, the men dragged off, raging against the incompetence of the constabulary, one of whom responded with the cry, *"Espion!"*

"Bravo, Sherlock," said she admiringly.

"Well done, Mrs. Walling," he returned equably, affecting not to be as pleased with himself as I very well knew he was.

"What did they find?" I demanded.

"Incriminating drawings of the city's harbor defenses and fortifications, including the Vorontsov Lighthouse, accompanied by various mysterious symbols, letters, and numerals. A few strategically placed arrows, indicating I've no idea what, but not the sort of thing it would do to carry about in one's pocket at this time and place. Personally I would regard the entire production as rather less than trustworthy, but the city is jumpy enough just now that I suspect my sketches will serve our purpose."

I, too, was impressed but felt bound to point out it was unlikely the men would be held for very long.

"I'm not sure I'm with you there, Watson," said he. "It will take them some time before they persuade themselves my indecipherable code is in fact gibberish, and I don't see them releasing these villains before that occurs. Would you care for some tea, Mrs. Walling?"

# 9.
## TARGET PRACTICE

**21 January.** The town of Kishinev, when we finally reached it by horse-drawn wagon — there being no other access from St. Basil's, or indeed anywhere else — was remarkable only for its ordinariness. Mrs. Walling likened the sleepy Bessarabian backwater to the San Fernando Valley in Southern California, which she had known from the time she dwelt in that state. Flat fields of fruit trees and other crops stretched out from the city centre, whose few public buildings contrasted with primitive adjacent streets and one-story houses, some more closely resembling hovels. On those dusty, dried-mud side streets one could not help observing vacant lots where homes once stood, their owners fled or dead. The charred ruins were gone, but square patches of ground remained ominously black.

Yet I must count the town, however drab and uninviting, a welcome distraction from the tedium I experienced after three days within the Monastery of St. Basil, situated roughly two-thirds of the way from Odessa on the nonexistent road. Instead of miles, distances here were reckoned in *versts,* which, if I understood correctly, roughly correspond to kilometers. For three days I was once more obliged to sit on unforgiving benches, more properly designated as pews, this time beneath domed ceilings, emblazoned by enormous shimmering gold icons and vibrant frescoes, many displaying the Greek cross peculiar to the faith (though in some ways reminiscent of the Celtic), and feign total absorption as I listened to the black-clad choir, their tall headpieces resembling toques in mourning, intoning the chants we had purportedly come to study. In the queerest contrast to the singing, the monks spent the rest of their time in resolute and total silence. They held their missals or breviaries before them and mutely recited whatever version of the rosary their liturgy prescribed, but never spoke to one another under any circumstances. Their most common orison, as I later learned, was the ceaseless repetition of the phrase *Lord Jesus, have mercy upon me.* Otherwise, you might accompany one of them from matins to vespers and never be acknowledged. It was worse than the Diogenes, which I had not thought possible. Conferring with Mrs. Walling, who was not allowed within the sacred precincts but had to wait outside the chapel, Holmes took what I hoped were convincing notes about the notes.

The main thoroughfare of Kishinev was an impressive boulevard called Alexandrova Street, shaded by splendid trees, but one could not escape the impression that it was a road that led nowhere.

"Pushkin lived here," Mrs. Walling informed us. "And despised the place."

"The poet?" I vaguely knew the name. "Why then did he choose to do so?"

"He was exiled here."

"Exiled," I echoed stupidly. Yes, in this strange place people could be exiled.

"The town is more prosperous nowadays than in Pushkin's time. It is a big agricultural centre. The land hereabouts is very fertile."

"With no roads, how do they export their goods?" Holmes wondered.

"The River Bic is close by, and waterways ferry crops and merchandise to market. It's a very effective system."

Yet her civic boosterism — if that was what it was — failed to dispel a more sinister impression. The somnolence of the town I judged deceptive. As Israel Zangwill had informed us, terrible events had taken place here not two years before, and it seemed to me the quiet that pervaded its dusty streets had taken on the surreal aspect of a dream (or nightmare, to be more precise), its residents mere zombies, as though all were still stunned by the convulsion that had occurred.

Of course, dreadful events had occurred mere weeks ago in Odessa, and the city trembled with the tension of those events, but here, with the passage of time, the convulsions had subsided into a collective stupor.

"It's changed in the year since English and I were here," Anna Walling commented.

"How so?"

She considered, looking about her.

"Ten months ago they were still reeling from the massacre. Burnt-out homes and ruined shops were everywhere. You could scarcely see any people on the streets amid the rubble. It was as though the survivors were hiding."

"From shame?" I inquired.

"Hiding," she repeated without embellishment.

"There are still Jews," Holmes observed.

"There will always be Jews," Mrs. Walling

answered. She regarded us intently, making up her mind. "Let me introduce you to some."

What followed next I can scarcely bring myself to write. Anna Strunsky Walling led us to the hut (it can only be termed thus) where a formerly prosperous wool merchant named Nussbaum now lived with his daughter. His once agreeable home had been burned to the ground in the pogrom. On that occasion, Rebecca, his wife of twenty-one years, had her throat cut, and their child, Rivka, now sitting before us, was violated that same night, according to her father, no fewer than six times by rampaging townsmen. She had been thirteen. The girl, in a rigid posture, gaped blindly into space, curled fists grasping the arms of the chair in which she sat, while her torso rocked imperceptibly to and fro, causing the furniture to creak rhythmically, almost as if there were a clock in the small room. Her red hair was tightly curled as well, as if clenching itself in response to what had happened. Her pale, freckled face seemed almost separate from her taut jaw, her yellowed teeth in a kind of perpetual snarl. But most disturbing were her wide, unblinking eyes, the pupils dilated beyond the promptings of the semidarkness, as if they had been dipped in belladonna. Those eyes had beheld too much, and yet now they refused to close. When I struck a vesta and passed it before them, the pupils refused to contract, or indeed follow the flame. In the aftermath of her experience, she remained catatonic, endlessly swaying. In the darkened single room, with odorous sheepskins hanging from rafters, and dust motes floating in shafts of sunlight from holes in the roof above her, I attempted a cursory examination while Mrs. Walling endeavored to explain our presence to the bereaved father and widowed husband. He responded in monosyllables that required no translation.

"Why don't they leave?" I found myself asking. The girl's pulse was astonishingly strong and regular.

"Jews are not allowed to travel."

"And go where?" the wool merchant added when my question had been relayed. His own affect and presentation were little different, from a medical standpoint, than those of his child.

"How do they manage?" the detective, who had remained silent, now asked in a voice I had never heard before.

Mrs. Walling sighed. "They don't. They exist without living."

Sherlock Holmes, a man who seldom allowed himself to express emotion of any kind, made to lay his slender fingers gently on top of Rivka Nussbaum's. With a whimper, her hands recoiled from his as from an electric shock or scalding iron — but her tremulous oscillations never ceased.

"She cannot bear to be touched," the father explained.

As hard as it is to describe my own reaction to this excruciating interview, the response of the detective I found more unsettling. Judging from his pallor and twitching cheek muscles, I saw a man who had been poleaxed. Always excepting the murder of Manya Lippman, until now the Protocols of the Elders of Zion had been an abstract outrage; now Holmes had encountered its effects in the flesh. It was now plain that men who would not scruple to crush a violin were equally untroubled doing the same to human beings. Holmes had earlier theorized that crimes in the twentieth century were getting bigger. In Kishinev we were both confronted by an example of unparalleled malice.

After endeavoring to extend our condolences to Nussbaum — and how pitiful and insufficient our mumbled words sounded in our own ears — we left the pathetic residence of the wool merchant and his ruined daughter, wincing at the daylight as we, as if fleeing a dream, returned to a reassuringly familiar sunlit world. The detective shook himself in an apparent effort to escape the effects of our visit. I knew him well enough by this time to know that such efforts would prove futile. Though he liked to present himself to the public as a reasoning machine, nothing more, I knew at present he was seething. We both were.

"Where can we obtain a copy of *Bessarabets?*" he asked in the same eerily strangled voice.

Mrs. Walling pointed to an impressive stone building, constructed in the late second empire style. I might have mistaken it for a substantial train station or opera house, save that I knew this part of the Russian empire possessed neither.

"What on earth is that?"

"Kogan's pharmacy and general store. Much of it was destroyed in the pogrom, but now it is back in operation. They should have local newspapers."

Her prediction proved accurate, and we shortly thereafter found ourselves silently consuming a very sweet tea in a shop down the street, where Anna Walling, at Holmes's insistence, once again donned her glasses and translated the broadsheet from front to back.

There were only six pages, and as she read, Holmes's brows knit in consternation.

"That is all?" he said, frowning, when she had closed the paper. "Farm news, crop yields, animal obituaries, and a weather almanac?"

She removed her glasses.

"I have read you everything except market prices. Should I — ?"

Sherlock Holmes shook his head, reaching for the paper, which he examined minutely, going so far as to view portions of it through his pocket magnifying glass. Unable to read Russian, he only succeeded in smudging his hands with inferior ink.

"You're certain this is the same periodical that ran the Protocols?"

"Quite certain," she answered a trifle frostily. "This is their usual fare, but anti-Semitic tirades are regular features, typically inserted among the rest."

Holmes reopened the paper and searched for the masthead, then refolded it and handed it back. "Who is the publisher?"

She replaced her glasses and squinted at the small Cyrillic typeface. "His name is Pavel Krushenev." She sat back. "I seem to recall he's well known in Kishinev. Something of a local personality."

"Pavel Krushenev," the detective repeated, looking about him. At such times, when his wheels were turning, he bore an uncanny resemblance to his brother. "What we need," he proclaimed finally, "is a drink."

"We've just had tea," Anna Walling protested.

"Holmes means a *drink*," I explained. "What is the local specialty?"

She laughed at this. "Colonel Morcar, you must be joking. In this part of the world there is only one drink. It is made from potatoes."

"And where might one sample this elixir?" Holmes asked.

She puzzled briefly over this; then her countenance assumed an expression of amusement.

"Do you wish a *goyische* or *yidische* establishment?"

The detective pondered the question.

*"Goyische."* Then, as an afterthought, "Will they admit you?"

She smiled. "Everywhere."

Ruminsky's *pab,* or *taverna,* when we entered it, was a large, smoke-filled, low-ceilinged affair, crowded with peasantry, all in a semi-intoxicated state, the result of the

238

potent vodka they consumed in astonishing quantities, whose fumes, mingled with perspiration, permeated and characterized the foetid air. Originally and perhaps optimistically called Pushkin's, the place bore as much resemblance to an English pub as a horse-drawn carriage to a motorcar. In contrast to the somnambulant behavior of the citizens by day, night and drink had released their inhibitions, unleashing a boisterous bonhomie, accompanied by a pleasant-sounding instrument whose twanging I confess I enjoyed more than Sarasate's violin. Mrs. Walling informed us it was called a *balalaika.* She was by no means the only woman in the place. A sudden shriek, succeeded by high-pitched giggles and peals of laughter, emanated from the far reaches of the room, assuring us of others' presence, though I knew without seeing them, none compared to our interpreter.

Ruminsky himself proved an almost predictably Falstaffian personage, whose bald scalp was compensated by a white beard of considerable dimensions, within whose tendrils I detected what I took to be bits of food. This Father Christmas did not question or remark upon our unusual trio; a beautiful woman was its own justification in his eyes, that and the fact that our kopeks were genuine. He bit one to assure himself of this. Since supplementing our apparel at the souks in Odessa, we no longer quite stood out as foreigners. Mrs. Walling, in particular, blended in, wearing Uzbek peasant attire of a white blouse with red stitching and a colourful woolen shawl.

Vodka was new to Holmes. I had experienced the drink years before in Afghanistan, but we were both surprised by its strength.

"What is this?" he inquired, indicating a yellow ceramic pot on our table.

"Ground pepper," our guide explained. "Some take it in their drink. Go easy," Mrs. Walling cautioned, "or you'll be under the table before you know it."

I noticed with moody fascination, as the evening progressed, that the drink seemed to have no effect on her whatever.

Flourishing our copy of *Bessarabets,* Holmes put a question to her. "Can you ask our host if he is acquainted with Pavel Krushenev?"

After the briefest hesitation, she nodded. When Ruminsky next returned to top up our glasses — (I had begun discreetly tipping the contents of mine down the leg of my chair where it mercifully mingled on the wide floorboards with scraps of black bread and other debris) — she posed his query.

"Krushenev?" He shook his head. "That character. Always stirring up trouble about the Yids."

"You know him," his attractive guest pursued, smiling. There seemed no question in Ruminsky's mind his interlocutor was a Jewess, comparatively well-to-do in addition to radiant. He deferred to her accordingly, if grudgingly. Or was he perhaps intimidated by the presence of Holmes and myself?

"Not so much," the publican finally admitted. "I don't read, *devushka,** but I know he's always in trouble, that one." He gestured to our copy of *Bessarabets.* "He went broke, you know, had to sell the paper — but still he is the publisher and still lives above the print shop and writes most of the pieces himself, they say." He shook his head as if in wonder at this feat of legal legerdemain. *"Za vashe zdrovye!"*

*"Za vashe zdrovye!"* we chorused in return, having heard the shouted toast exchanged for the past hour.

Without bothering to ask, Ruminsky refilled our glasses.

"What sort of trouble?" Anna Walling inquired, tossing back her drink as readily

* Miss.

241

as he had replenished it.

"It grows late." The man grew uneasy, his manner less jovial.

Holmes reassured him by silently lining up several additional kopeks on the table, like pawns on a chessboard.

Shrugging unhappily, Saint Nicholas scooped them up.

"It was a long time ago," he began plaintively. "That boy, what was his name? Mikhail something, I can't think now. Wait, Rybachenko —, that was it! Mikhail Rybachenko. The constables found him with his head bashed in, and Krushenev got everyone worked up the Yids did it — called it Jew sacrifice or something. Blood libel! That was it! Next thing you know we're all at each other's throats — and then it turns out Igor Ivanovich was the killer. The lad's own cousin! For his share of the estate!" He shook his head once more. "I'm glad I can't read. All that news that made us wild and it turns out it wasn't true. These days how can we know what's true? Someone tried to kill him a while back." He gestured again to the newspaper, evidently referring to the publisher. "Probably a Yid. You couldn't blame him. We — many died," he amended. "Now he keeps Vladimir — that big Cossack — with him all the time, and his own chef! Worries about being poisoned. That's the rumor, anyway. Coming!"

He fled, pretending to answer a summons from the bar.

"Notice with what dexterity he rationalizes his part in the massacre," Holmes commented sourly. "It was 'a long time ago.' He was the victim of false information. Well done, Mrs. Walling," he added. "May I offer you a cigarette?"

"In Russia women do not smoke. Certainly not in public."

"Very like home," I mumbled through a haze of vodka. The decoction had released feelings of self-pity, loneliness, and longing for my sweet girl.

Holmes, his face flushed with the effects of the drink, took deliberate and elaborate care, lighting a cigarette of his own and blowing graceful smoke to join the blue haze of the room. His face now looked unfamiliar to me. Drink had transformed either his features or my vision. He sneezed, his eyes watering.

"Watson, you still have the Webley?"

This sudden change of topic gave me pause. I blinked in an effort to regain my senses.

"Yes, if it's not been taken from our rooms."

"And the bullets, I assume."

"Mr. Altmont, what are you suggesting?" Anna Walling remained sober.

"I think a visit to the publisher of *Bessarabets* may be in order."

Had I been sober, it might have occurred to me to caution "Manchester" in my friend's ear, but in my present condition, the proposition seemed eminently sensible.

Our rooms, as it happened, remained untouched. Having stumbled back to our lodgings from Ruminsky's in the cool night air, my heart was slightly clearer. I mean to say, head. Several vigorous shakes of my boot succeeded in disgorging my revolver.

Anna Walling's eyes widened at the sight.

"Dr. Watso— Colonel Morcar, what are you doing?"

"Boys will be boys," I returned, unrolling a pair of dark brown socks and spilling out a half dozen bullets, which I shakily managed to insert in the six empty chambers of the cylinder.

"Watson, are you ready?"

"Wait. Wait!" Anna Walling rushed to the door and stood before it, arms outspread, barring our way. "What on earth do you think you are doing?"

"Quite ready, Holmes."

"No. *No!*" Mrs. Walling cried. "We didn't

come here to kill the man. In God's name, I'm a pacifist!! Do you hear me? A pacifist!"

"Time is short, Mrs. Walling. If we are to prevent more pogroms, we are compelled to take extraordinary measures and take them quickly."

She stiffened, her back pressed against the door.

"The first man to raise a fist is the man who has run out of ideas!" It sounded as if she were quoting something, but before I could ask what, Holmes responded.

"I *have* an idea," he protested mildly, but to no avail. Her panic was now in full flood.

"No! Not this! It's the vodka talking."

"No. It's only me." He moved forward.

"If you do this, it is all over between —"

"And I need your help," Holmes hastily interposed with a sharp glance in my direction. "We must speak with Mr. Krushenev. And he must be made to answer."

This served to somewhat stem her alarm.

"Do you promise — ?"

"I need your help," the other repeated. "Please come now."

Gently, one might say tenderly, he edged her from the door and held it open. We followed him out.

There were few lights in the streets of Kishinev, and by this hour the few oil lamps boasted by homes in this vicinity had long since been extinguished.

My companion was unperturbed. "What is the one building whose lights always burn far into the night?" He answered his own question. "A newspaper!"

It didn't take long in this small place to locate a larger building, through the lighted lower-story windows of which we could see two compositors throwing letters into wooden page "fronts" almost faster than the eye could follow. I was surprised to find a woman loading the "make ready" forms. As it happens, I was not unfamiliar with such places. My years of chronicling Holmes's exploits for the *Strand* magazine had found me inside pressrooms on more than one occasion, arguing about my copy with intransigent editors. The *Bessarabets* press looked to be fifty years out of date but appeared nonetheless well maintained. It did boast rollers but was still hand cranked. When I reflected these letters were in fact Cyrillic and being loaded backward into the bargain, I could not help but admire the skill of these clever typesetting fellows, so at ease in a language that was entirely bewildering to me. The fact that the text they were so adroitly loading was just as likely to be filled with hateful bile and shameless falsehoods did not occur to me at the time. Compositors do not look different than other people.

The clattering of the lead type, audible from where we stood, made it unlikely our presence outside could be heard. Treading gingerly, Holmes motioned us to follow and led us around the building's exterior. There was an impressive entrance, above which large gilt wooden lettering proclaimed (I am assuming here) the name *Bessarabets.* Holmes eschewed this portal and continued his tour of inspection, discovering in the narrow lane behind the building — really more an alley — a smaller point of access.

Gently he prodded the narrow door, which appeared at first to be bolted. This would prove a setback, but he tried again, pressing more firmly now, and discovered the thing was merely warped and gave way with a mild squeak of protest.

We froze, listening for any reaction, but the clattering within continued apace, punctuated by talk and an occasional burst of laughter. And then luck favored us, for they commenced cranking the press, and its rhythmic clacking overlaid any sound we might inadvertently produce.

"Close it, but not tightly," Holmes whispered, gesturing to the door. "If we leave it ajar, they'll feel the cold air . . ."

I nodded. Anna Walling looked as if she were enacting the lead role in her own nightmare. She was by any measure a daring woman, but such an enterprise as this, to which she was, in addition, morally opposed, was quite beyond her experience and possibly her capacities. I was obliged to tug her forward inside the small entryway, wedging the door against, but not entirely into, its swollen jamb.

Inside, the odor of printer's ink mingled with the distinctive scent of the viscous paraffin oil printing presses require to keep them in working trim. Taking in our surroundings by the dim illumination, we spied a narrow staircase immediately to our left. Holmes gestured with an index finger, and we stole upwards behind him. There was a groan when he trod upon the fourth step. Again we stopped and listened. Again no one appeared to have been alerted to our presence over the furious rattle of the press. As we followed the detective, we made it our business to omit the treacherous stair. As we ascended, the sounds of work receded below.

Near the darkened top of the steps, a faint, intermittent *thwack* was now audible from above. This, too, was familiar to me. I recognized the fits and starts of a typist in search of just the right word or phrase. We stopped where we were and listened. It was hard not to imagine the rage behind that erratic pounding. I exchanged looks with Holmes, and we both understood we were listening to the imaginative outbursts of Pavel Krushenev. Sometimes the blows would cease for a minute altogether. Had the writer finished for the night? But no, soon inspiration returned, and his fingers pummeled the keys anew before a distant *ping!* announced the completion of another line of vicious text.

There were voices, too. At first only one, as though the writer were talking to himself, but then another, deeper, rumbled in return. I didn't have to be a lip reader to understand Holmes's mouth forming the word "Vladimir," referring to the editor's Cossack bodyguard, foretold by Ruminsky.

With his hand, he pantomimed his wish, and I produced the Webley.

Seeing the weapon, Mrs. Walling opened her mouth, but Holmes laid an emphatic index finger across his own. He inched up a step below the topmost, stood to one side, and then, with no warning whatever, deliberately and violently sneezed.

Instantly, conversation behind the door ceased. I looked at Holmes in dismay. His hand slid into the pocket of his own jacket.

The next instants were a blur. In less time than it takes to relate, the door was flung wide and an enormous figure, his shape defined by light from behind, appeared wielding a pistol whose proportions matched his own. But before he could discharge the weapon Sherlock Holmes had hurled two fistfuls of pepper in his face. The giant screamed, flinging away his weapon — which mercifully did not discharge — clawing madly at his eyes, sneezing convulsively (like the villain in *The Scarlet Pimpernel* I had disdained to believe), as Holmes smashed his legs from under him with a ferocious *baritsu* kick, followed by a nerve pinch to the neck and shoulder, peculiar to that Japanese form of combat.* The effect was instantaneous, forcing us to jump aside lest we be crushed by Vladimir's massive form as it barreled down the stairs like a human avalanche to the bottom, where he remained in a crumpled heap.

"Quick, Watson!"

Long experience had enabled the detective and myself to communicate in such

* Watson accounted Holmes a master of this Japanese mode of self-defense, introduced in England in 1899 by E. W. Barton-Wright.

circumstances with a kind of shorthand. Without pausing to determine whether our fracas had been overheard by the typesetters over the roar of the press below, we leapt like madmen into the upstairs office in time for me to train the Webley on the scrambling figure of Pavel Krushenev, who was in the act of throwing open the sash behind his desk, evidently attempting an escape through the window.

Seeing the barrel of my revolver leveled at his torso caused him to freeze in the act.

"Tell him to stand still," Holmes directed the ashen Mrs. Walling, "while I see to it Vladimir does not disturb us when he wakes." Woodenly, she obeyed. Before leaving the room, Holmes helped himself to the long muffler wound about Krushenev's neck, and on second thought appropriated as well the man's handkerchief to use as a gag.

I held the publisher at bay with my revolver, and we stared at one another, or rather, I stared at him and he gazed intently at the muzzle of my weapon, which he seemingly found of compelling interest. His glazed brown eyes, wide with alarm, put me altogether in mind of a twitching rodent's. His trick of constantly gnawing at the bottom of his impressive moustache added to this impression.

Pavel Krushenev was a smallish man of medium build with a bulbous nose and receding hairline. His chief distinction was a neatly trimmed beard, topped by the aforementioned moustache, whose artfully tapered and waxed tips in the style once called "Imperial" suggested a certain vanity. Later pondering these events, I noted a fleeting resemblance to that other wax-tipped-moustachioed scoundrel, Napoleon III. Given what we were to discover, this was certainly fitting. In England I would have set him down as impoverished gentry, which he more or less proved to be.

"Tell him to place his palms flat on the desk," I commanded.

He did as Mrs. Walling instructed.

"What now?" she inquired in a quavering voice quite unlike her own confident timbre.

"We wait."

And so we did for perhaps two minutes before Holmes returned, a trifle breathless but evidently satisfied.

"May I?" he asked, holding out his hand. I handed him the revolver, which he examined briefly.

"Now then." He turned to the writer. "I shall put some questions to you, and you will answer truthfully."

"*Nyet!* I shall say nothing!" Krushenev replied in a defiant tone when he understood Holmes's words.

The detective appeared both untroubled and unsurprised by this response. Studying the weapon in his hand, he appeared to give the matter impartial consideration.

"Do you enjoy games?" he addressed this question to the Russian but looked at Mrs. Walling, who hesitatingly repeated it in that language.

"Games?" the other responded in a tone of evident bewilderment. His rodent eyes shifted from one of us to the other and back again.

Holmes held up the revolver and snapped open the cylinder. As the editor watched with increasing apprehension, the detective tipped out five bullets into the palm of his hand, taking care to leave the sixth snug in its chamber.

"Games of chance." Holmes lined the five bullets upright like palisades on the man's desk. "Have you ever tried your luck in Monte Carlo?"

As we all watched in disbelief, Holmes spun the cylinder, then placed the barrel of the gun to his own forehead.

"Holmes!"

And pulled the trigger.

253

*Click.*

"A variation on roulette," he explained equably.

Mrs. Walling sank into a chair with a gasp. I felt my knees about to buckle and grasped at the table's edge for support.

"Holmes!"

Ignoring me, the detective smiled, lowered the gun from his temple, and spun the cylinder once more.

"I see you understand how the game is played," he told Krushenev in language and gestures which necessitated no help from Mrs. Walling, who was in any case, at this juncture, incapable of supplying any assistance. "Now then, my first question, this one merely a formality: Did you publish the Protocols of the Learned Elders of Zion?"

Before the quivering man could answer the translation, Holmes had put the gun to the publisher's sweat-soaked forehead and pulled the trigger.

*Click.*

*"Da!"*

"Very good." The detective patted him approvingly on the shoulder. "We understand one another. And you have beaten the odds. This time."

No translation was required.

"Sherlock, in God's name —"

"This will take but a moment," he assured our interpreter, spinning the cylinder yet again, this time nestling the barrel between Krushenev's eyes, slightly above the bridge of his nose. "Where did you obtain the Protocols? Mrs. Walling, if you please."

The question, when he understood it, appeared to puzzle the man. He looked about in confusion. Again, Holmes was not surprised.

"Let me rephrase the question. *Parlez-vous françcais?*"

*Click!*

*"Oui! Mais oui!"*

"Well done, Little Father. *Bien fait.* You have beaten the house again. Give him my congratulations," he ordered Mrs. Walling. Numbly, she conveyed them.

I heard a confusing noise, a dripping I could not at first identify, then realized the man had lost control. He screamed something at Holmes.

"You are insane," Mrs. Walling said. It wasn't clear whether she was speaking for herself or on behalf of the editor. Holmes remained impassive.

The cylinder was spun again.

*"Alors, dites-mois, donc, est-ce que vous connaissez l'ouevre de Monsieur Maurice Joly, écrivain français?"*

*Click!*

This time his answer tumbled from his mouth before the click was even complete.

*"Oui! Da, mon Dieu! Oui!"*

*"Quelle surprise,"* Holmes remarked acidly. "We're almost finished," he reassured us before turning back to Krushenev.

He now withdrew our copy of the Protocols from his breast pocket and placed them before the terrified man.

"You cannot explain where you obtained the Protocols because in fact you wrote them yourself. Is this not the case? Not only did you publish, you are in fact the actual author, creating the Protocols of whole cloth. Well, not entirely," the detective allowed. "You copied and adapted language from Monsieur Joly's *Dialogue aux enfers entre Machiavel et Montesquieu* for your own purposes?"

Mrs. Walling translated the question slowly so as to ensure it was comprehended in its entirety. Krushenev stared at the pages set before him. Though in English, the paragraphs separated by familiar numerals cast little doubt as to their contents, which served to convince the man we knew a good deal more than he'd supposed.

Holmes raised the Webley once more, but before he could place its barrel again —

*"Da. Da!"*

Heaving sobs; there could be no question the detective had broken his prisoner.

Holmes now opened his other hand to reveal the sixth bullet. The weapon had been empty the entire time. I had never in my life beheld or believed him capable of such behavior. Only his own fury could have accounted for his chosen means of interrogation.

Krushenev stared at the bullet with incredulity, then raised tear-filled eyes to Holmes. I shared his stupefaction. How had Holmes managed to extract the last bullet?

"Why do you so hate the Jews? What have they done to you?"

Hearing the question, the writer shot the detective a look of stubborn silence.

"Was it because of the girl?" Holmes asked quietly. He nodded, and Mrs. Walling, bewildered, rendered the question in Russian.

The explosive response was almost as surprising as the question itself.

"She has nothing to do with this!" Krushenev shrieked, leaping to his feet and trembling from head to foot. "The little baggage! Nothing, do you hear?" Foamy spittle flecked his lips. His mottled cheeks and beard were soaked with tears, the melted

257

waxed tips of his once impressive moustache now sagging. Curiously, now that the woman — whoever she was — had been mentioned, he could not abandon the topic. "Jew slut! I offered her everything! My name! I begged her to marry me, and she laughed! She laughed!"

Even now, in the midst of his collapse, the memory of his rejection pushed the present moment aside, unleashing his fury anew. "They must all die!"

Mrs. Walling flatly translated the appalling language. She was fully absorbed now, notwithstanding her principles.

"Including Theodor Herzl?"

"Who? Oh," Krushenev recollected with a sniff. "The Zionist. Why bother? He was going to lead them all to Africa or some-place."

Holmes considered this.

"Would that have contented you?"

The question was enough to set the maniac back on his hobbyhorse.

"Jew scum! Scum of the earth! Liars! Cheaters! Shysters! Usurers!" He had no interest in Herzl.

"Final question. Who commissioned the Protocols?" the detective inquired. Opening his silver case, he offered the man a cigarette, but Krushenev, still in the grip of his fever, ignored the gesture.

"Pharaoh should have pushed them all into the sea! Drowned them like the vermin they are!"

Shrugging, Holmes lit his own cigarette and had Mrs. Walling repeat the question.

"There is another way to play this game," he added, flicking open the gun under his victim's nose and letting Krushenev watch the lone bullet sliding into one of the chambers before snapping the cylinder into place. This time there would be no sleight of hand. Mrs. Walling and Krushenev flinched in unison at the sight, which appeared to focus the Russian's mind. He sagged into his chair, reminding me of nothing so much as a balloon with its hydrogen leaking out. Had he been capable of rational thought, the editor might have reasoned Holmes was again bluffing; were he killed, the detective would never learn the answer to his question, and a gunshot would certainly attract attention and capture. But the hypnotic stare with which the monster had followed the bullet's deliberate progress into a random chamber, and watched entranced as Holmes suggestively rolled the cylinder back and forth against his sleeve, assured me such logic was giving him no comfort. A quick glance in Anna Walling's direction likewise convinced me no such rationale had occurred to her.

Holmes raised the gun.

"Rachkovsky," Krushenev sighed. "Rachkovsky ordered it — to explain the pogrom."

"The pogrom you fomented with your tale about Jews and their human Passover sacrifice."

He nodded absently. "And to alarm the Tsar."

"Rachkovsky? Who is that?"

Krushenev eyed Holmes with a short laugh of disbelief. "You know nothing. You have no idea what your meddling has begun."

"Who is Rachkovsky?" Holmes repeated.

"Pyotr Ivanovich Rachkovsky, director general of the Okhrana. He was here after, immediately after the — immediately after. He gave the order in this room."

Holmes frowned and exchanged looks with us.

"Did he specify — ?"

"It was all left up to me. 'Give us a *casus belli,'* says he. May I have one of those now?" This last in a plaintive tone, accompanied by a feeble gesture that required nothing from Mrs. Walling.

Holmes lit a cigarette for him and placed it in his mouth. The Russian had barely the strength to suck at its glowing contents. What he inhaled prompted a coughing fit that doubled him over for a time. Holmes waited for his convulsions to end with the patient air of a man who had all the time in the world.

"And you knew about Joly," he resumed, tapping our pages when the coughing had ceased. Krushenev regarded them and gave an exhausted shrug.

"I studied in Paris. It was perfect. I didn't have to change very much."

"The Tsar's secret police commissioned a forgery to deceive the Tsar?" I asked. "What is the sense of that?"

He looked at me. "Many people wish to influence His Majesty. Justifying killing Jews and seizing their property —"

"Is easier than trying to modernize a country the size of Russia," Holmes finished for him. "Why translate the Protocols into French?" he added as an afterthought.

Krushenev favored him with a patronizing expression. "Because no one outside Russia can read Russian. All Europe understands French."*

The room fell silent. Daylight would

* The French translation of the Protocols from the Russian has subsequently been attributed to

261

shortly be upon us, and with it the risk of discovery. Holmes looked about the office.

"Where is your carbon paper?"

"What?"*

The response required no translation. The detective frowned at this but again appeared unsurprised. Looking about, he tore the typescript from the platen of Krushenev's cumbersome typing machine — its long keys looking like so many spider legs — and crumpled it, inserting in its place a sheet of blank paper. "Now then," he told the man. "You will write a full confession, including names, dates, and places. You will affix your signature to the bottom. And remember" — he displayed my Webley beneath Krushenev's running nose — "any hesitation, any omission, and we will resume the game with the difference of an actual bullet."

The man nodded dully, looking for his handkerchief, and then, remembering the detective had taken it, wiped his nose unceremoniously with the back of his sleeve

---

one Mathieu Golovinsky, a hack propagandist living in Paris, in the pay of the Okhrana.

* Carbon or "carbonic" paper was first invented around 1806, but its use was not fully popularized until the advent of the typewriter. Places such as rural Russia were unlikely to have any in 1905.

and sat before his typewriter.

"Begin with today's date. 'I, Pavel Krushenev, owner and editor of the broadsheet *Bessarabets,* do hereby confess that I alone forged and published the document known as the Protocols of the Elders of Zion. I did this at the direction of Pyotr Ivanovich Rachkovsky, director general of the Okhrana, for the purpose of inciting hatred against the Jewish race.' "

Holmes strode about the small room as he alternately dictated and waited while Mrs. Walling translated and Krushenev transcribed her words.

"I further state that to accomplish this, I plagiarized portions of Monsieur Maurice Joly's . . ."

There were fewer hesitations by the typist on this occasion. Krushenev had no need to search for words as Holmes was supplying them. The spider's long legs thwacked the paper in the otherwise silent room. When he had finished, Holmes presented the two pages to Mrs. Walling for her review.

She read carefully, silently mouthing the Russian words as we watched, then nodded without speaking, whereupon Holmes set the document before Krushenev and witnessed his signature. After the exhausted man reluctantly affixed his name to both pages, Holmes briskly retrieved and folded them before striking a match and setting fire to our copy of the Protocols, placing the smoldering ashes in a nearby dustbin. He then tapped the publisher forcefully on the shoulder, eyeing Mrs. Walling to translate his next words.

"And be sure, when next you see Director General Rachkovsky, to present the compliments of Professor James Moriarty."

"James Moriarty," he echoed her.

Holmes offered a cigarette to Mrs. Walling, and this time she accepted.

for the next few days until the train return.

"They will be scouring the country for us
endlessly," I remarked gloomily.

"You may rest easy, Watson; it is a very
big country, and that for so large they will
be immediate—

"Wait—say—or—

"because, my dear fellow, I think it how."

# 10.
## UNFORESEEN

"It is now a race to escape this country with
ourselves and the proof intact," Sherlock
Holmes informed Mrs. Walling and myself,
while traveling at a crawl atop an ox-drawn
hayrick as we struggled to make our way
three hundred miles back to Odessa. Our
present mode of transportation did not
provide cause for optimism. Such convey-
ances were the norm in this backward part
of the world, and our recourse to the phleg-
matic peasant who negligently guided the
animal and his wagon was by no means
unusual. I had suggested sharing a barge on
the River Bic as arguably faster, but Mrs.
Walling cautioned that the river was where
our pursuers would look first. Holmes
deferred to her reasoning but reminded us,
"We are booked aboard the Orient Express,
departing the second of February from
Varna. If we miss that connection we are
stranded next door to Russia and exposed

for the next ten days until the train's return."

"They will be scouring the country for us regardless," I remarked gloomily.

"You said it yourself, Watson, it is a very big country, and I'm not so sure they will be immediately on the *qui vive.*"

"Why on earth not?"

"Because, my dear fellow, I think it possible that Pavel Krushenev may be reluctant to report our encounter to the authorities. It will almost certainly prove awkward for him."

"The same may not be true of Vladimir," I insisted. The look of pure fury with which the Cossack favored us as we stepped over his massive, trussed-up form during our flight was one I shall not soon forget. "Should that man lay eyes on us again, I would not wager a brass farthing on our odds of survival."

"Vladimir will do as he's told. Such men always do," Holmes reasoned. "But assuming, with Falstaff, the better part of valor to be discretion, let us give your scenario the benefit of the doubt, Watson. They have unleashed the hounds. But for whom are they baying? Not Colonel Morcar. Nor Gideon Altmont. Not even for Sherlock Holmes and Dr. Watson, but" — and here he could scarcely suppress a chortle of satisfaction — "for a Professor Moriarty. They are searching a haystack for a nonexistent needle."

"A haystack is where we happen to be," I reminded him.

Throughout this exchange, Mrs. Walling remained studiously silent, seemingly lost in her own thoughts. I could see that an alteration had taken place in her relations with the detective. It was clear to me that while she rejoiced in our success and indeed had contributed to it, she was deeply troubled by the methods he had employed to achieve it.

Presently, in an effort to narrow the gap between them, I attempted to make conversation.

"Holmes, where did the pepper come from?"

"In Ruminsky's, while you were busily disposing of your vodka supply on the floor, I was helping myself to the contents of that ceramic pot on the table. Incidentally, I've revised my opinion of *The Scarlet Pimpernel* entirely."

It seems Holmes hadn't left the theatre that night but had witnessed the end of the play. I had to own I now agreed with him completely.

"And however did you learn about the girl?"

"The girl?" I knew by his expression he was thinking of Rivka Nussbaum, the wool merchant's catatonic daughter, but as he understood my question, his physiognomy reassumed its accustomed configuration.

"Oh, that girl." He cast a sideways look at Anna Walling. "The Jewess who broke Krushenev's heart and turned him into a goader of rapists? That was a long shot, I confess. What you would call 'a guess,' Doctor. I merely took a leaf from our Viennese friend."

"What Viennese friend?" Mrs. Walling abruptly demanded, joining our talk at last. Holmes and I exchanged glances. He was, I think, eager to reestablish a connection with her.

"A certain physician with whom I became acquainted some years ago in Austria. Beyond question a genius, though he holds some outlandish views, many of which, I suspect, may prove to be mistaken."

The paradox drew her in.

"How can he lay claim to genius if his views are mistaken?"

Holmes lay back and stared at the sky, his hands clasped behind his head.

"He is by way of being a cartographer."

"Cartographer?" I could not help repeating. I had not thought of our friend in this fashion and never heard Holmes so describe him.

My companion shrugged where he nestled on his bed of straw. "A mapmaker of sorts, yes. To my knowledge he is the first non-artist to discover and set foot on a hitherto unknown and unexplored continent."

Mrs. Walling frowned. "Which continent?"

Holmes continued to gaze with dreamy abstraction at the cerulean canopy above. All was silent save the creaking of cart wheels, punctuated now and again by gaggles of what I took to be Russian geese honking in formation overhead.

"The Land of the Unconscious."

"The Un— ?"

"— conscious. And if his subsequent maps of that strange place should subsequently be proved in error, does anyone still remember or care that Columbus thought he was in India? The error pales to insignificance compared to the discovery itself. At all events," the detective resumed before his argument could be addressed, "our friend has altered the way in which I find myself thinking about people and their motives. Working backward from Krushenev's hatred of Jews, I wondered if there mightn't be

269

some personal origin for his foaming animus. Yes, I grant you, a lucky guess."

Mrs. Walling said nothing to this. Holmes stuck a piece of straw in his mouth and continued to study the sky as silence reigned. I had begun to suppose him asleep when he spoke again.

"We must change wagons and avoid inns and public places until we reach Odessa, where the population will absorb us. Sleeping in barns may be preferable to stopping at inns. Speaking of which, Doctor, your new hat is a sight and will attract notice. And what is worse, Mrs. Watson will never forgive you for so neglecting her gift. Give it here."

I removed my grey homburg and handed it to my friend, who spent some minutes plucking off bits of hay and brushing the felt with his sleeve before returning it.

"Better," he declared, and went back to gazing upwards.

"Anything else?" Mrs. Walling asked without regarding him.

"Yes. Traveling as a trio is conspicuous. We must separate."

Now it was Mrs. Walling and I who exchanged glances.

"Separate?" she repeated.

"Before we reach Odessa. It's much the

safest course. You and Dr. Watson will journey together as man and — together," he amended. "Two is far less remarkable than three, especially if one is a woman. I will continue alone, as I am carrying and must be responsible for Krushenev's confession." He tapped his breast pocket. "Our tickets have already been purchased; it only remains to specify and confirm dates. We will board the Orient Express at Varna on the second, but travel in separate cars. Once in Paris, it should be safe to reunite for the final portion of our journey."

"You seem quite sure of yourself," Mrs. Walling observed, still without looking at him.

Holmes had the decency to blush.

"I may *seem* sure," was the best he could manage.

**29 January.** This indeed was the plan we followed. It cannot be said that spending three successive nights in as many barns was particularly edifying, but at least, as old campaigners, Holmes and I might claim to be accustomed to such experiences. The same could not be said for Mrs. Walling, who nevertheless endured the deprivation of proper shelter or comfort without a murmur of complaint.

**31 January.** In this fashion, festooned with straw bits and pieces clinging to our well-worn clothing, we entered Odessa. The last sight I had of Holmes was that of a rail-thin, unshaven individual, slinking off into a souk near the City Garden, carrying a small, battered valise. Odessa had begun to regain its *laissez-faire* character as life returned to normal in the weeks following the suppression of its ill-fated insurrection. Civil authority had been allowed to reassert itself. This was probably a pragmatic as well as strategic consideration on the government's part, though I was not to learn the reason 'til Varna: with the latest Russian defeat at Mukden by the Japanese, and martial law still in effect in St. Petersburg itself, troops could not long be spared in provincial capitals.

Where Holmes stayed in Odessa, I had no way of knowing. Mrs. Walling and I registered under the names on our passports at the overcrowded Hotel Esplanade, where we were obliged to share a single room. The detective had been correct, foreseeing a couple would attract less notice than a trio. The management offered no demur. Assuming Holmes would make his own arrangements, I employed the services of the obliging concierge to confirm places for Colonel Morcar and Miss Sophie Hunter on the Orient Express from Varna to Paris on the second of February.

Sharing a room with Mrs. Walling cannot be described as less than awkward. We stood silent in the tiny lift as the bellman, carrying what remained of our luggage, escorted us to something like a garret on the fourth floor with not even an ocean view to commend it. We did our best to preserve decorum, but, having spent three nights in as many barns, we had by this time few secrets from one another. Mrs. Walling's first order of business was a hot soak, procured by means of a procession of bellmen pouring the contents of steaming kettles into a large copper hipbath located improbably in the middle of our room. I stood with my back to this procedure for what seemed the longest time, listening to a succession of sensuous sighs as Mrs. Walling took her well-deserved ease. Later, all too aware of her proximity, I gave myself a clumsy sponge wash. Poor Juliet! Pork sandwiches were then brought up to the room as a collation, but we both declined the offer of a vodka accompaniment. Afterwards I insisted Mrs. Walling take the bed and undertook to sleep on the settee. She more sensibly pointed out that her smaller frame was better suited to that place, insisting I occupy the bed, as my bulk would never fit comfortably anywhere else. Considerably embarrassed by these mechanical considerations and the circumstances which prompted them, we confined our conversation to perfunctory monosyllables and averted eyes until we were both decently under the covers (I using the coverlet and she the bedding), and the lights extinguished. In the darkness, each knew the other was awake.

"You have been with Sherlock Holmes for a very long time." Her voice came softly in the gloom. We were situated across the room from each other, but in the dark she sounded close by. Her sentence was neither a statement nor a question.

"You make it sound as though I were his factotum," I responded more tartly than I'd intended.

"Sorry. I only meant that you know each other very well," she said in the same quiet voice.

"That is so."

There was another silence. But I knew the conversation wasn't over.

"Do you approve of what he did?"

"To what are you ref— ?"

"You know perfectly well. I'm speaking of Kishinev. He tortured that man."

"I wouldn't call it that."

"What would you call it?"

To my consternation, I found myself unable to answer. Holmes's actions had shocked us both.

"My friend is the best and wisest man I have ever known," I replied at length. "But every man has his limits, and our encounter with Rivka Nussbaum surpassed them. If he did what he did, it was because he couldn't think of anything else. It was imperative we obtain that confession."

"What confession obtained under duress can be relied upon?" she demanded. "People will say anything in fear of their lives."

Again, I had no answer for that line of reasoning and fell back on what I knew instead of addressing it. "So much depends upon the hoax of the Protocols being exposed. Many, many lives may hang in the balance. You better than I know what took place two years ago in Kishinev. Nussbaum and his family were but one example." And though I knew better than to mention it, Manya Lippman was another.

In the darkness, I sensed her considering my logic.

"So," said she at length, "the ends justify

the means."

Like many of her sentences this night, it was hard to tell if it was a statement or a question.

"If the ends don't justify the means," was all I could think to reply, "what the devil does? Can you truly state with confidence Holmes did the wrong thing?"

She could not. Once more silence descended like a curtain between us. What next popped out of my mouth I cannot explain, but neither can I deny I said it.

"What happened between you and Sherlock Holmes?"

I heard something like a sharp intake of breath that was in turn succeeded by another pause before she responded quietly:

"Nothing, really."

**2 February.** Following the bone-crushing journey on the desiccated milk train from Odessa, I heaved a sigh of relief when we alighted at Varna, having crossed into Romania with little interest and no impediment at the frontier. Whether Krushenev had or had not sounded the alarm, the Okhrana was nowhere in evidence.

"Don't be overconfident," Anna Walling cautioned me. "Borders and customs of all kinds are permeable hereabouts, and we've already established that agents of the Russian secret police operate freely in other countries. We are not yet out of harm's way. I wonder if we ever will be," I heard her add under her breath.

At the telegraph we both sent wires couched in euphemisms, mine to London, hers to New York. "All's well that ends well," ran mine. How I longed to see my own dear girl again.

And with what joy that afternoon did we reboard the sumptuous Orient Express, relishing every inch of her polished Italian walnut paneling, her inlaid marquetry, her gleaming Sheffield cutlery, Waterford tableware, and smartly uniformed attendants, all poised to cater to our every whim! It is a routine trip the train makes every ten days, an ordinary undertaking perhaps from her point of view, but from ours, nothing less than a luxurious voyage to freedom.

It is a fact known to soldiers that during the crisis we hold ourselves together. Duty prompts us to feats of endurance, heroism even, of which we might normally prove incapable. It is only when the crisis has passed, when we have risen above and stretched ourselves beyond what we would have believed possible, that we feel free to collapse. I am no longer a young man, and the time spent on the run on foreign soil, in imminent danger of capture under circumstances where my own people would not deign to lift a finger on my behalf (not to mention other complications I had witnessed), and the continued deprivation of a uxorious existence to which habit and inclination now disposed me — all these, I say, combined to exhaust me. Even the confined space of our compartment — (and the urbane staff of the Orient Express did not lift an eyebrow at our joint occupation of same) — failed to trouble either of us.

Though still daylight, we requested Jean-Claude (the porter whom I remembered from our previous trip and who gratifyingly recalled me in return) to convert our cushions into sleeping berths. Mrs. Walling, having long since perceived my leg injury, offered me the more accessible lower berth, but I now gallantly insisted on allotting her the more comfortable place. It was a decision I would come to regret.*

"I shall nap 'til supper, if you've no objection," I told her, contriving to hoist myself aloft.

"*Nyet.* Perhaps I do same, but not sure I sleep." Her thick Slavic accent was return-

---

* This sentence appears to have been added later.

ing. I suspected it was some sort of instinctive camouflage.

As the sun set before us, turning the sky rose-pink through our window, I clambered between those sweet-smelling, crisp, ironed white sheets and slept like a dead man. My last conscious thought was wondering where on the train Holmes was. Even a distant thudding failed to rouse me.

When I awakened, Anna Strunsky Walling was nowhere to be seen.

At first I had no idea where I was and looked stupidly around trying to remember, startled to find a ceiling so close above my head. In my hazy state I was tempted simply to drift back to sleep, but it was slowly borne in upon me that I was on a train and that we were slowing. Craning my neck, I peered out the window, blinking at the dim light — for all I knew it was dawn and I'd slept the night through. I thought abruptly to consult my watch, according to which I realized, with some relief, we must be pulling into Bucharest, having traveled less than a hundred and fifty miles from Varna. I had been asleep little more than two hours and did not yet realize anything amiss.

"Mrs. Walling?"

There was no response from the lower berth, which, when I craned down to look, proved to be empty, as were the lavatory and shower, when I knocked on and then tried the swinging open door. The colourful woolen shawl my traveling companion had worn since purchasing it in the souk at Odessa was nowhere in evidence. Perplexed but not yet alarmed, I splashed some water on my face from the pewter basin, then brushed and adjusted my clothing, with the intention of making my way to the nearest dining car. Perhaps she was taking tea. And perhaps I'd see her there with Holmes, though we had agreed to ignore one another.

I found the porter at the end of the car, head down, having presumably nodded off.

"Jean-Claude, have you seen Miss Hunter?"

The man who looked up was not Jean-Claude.

"Jean-Claude is off duty," the unfamiliar porter explained. The name "Miss Hunter" and my description meant nothing to him. He had not seen any woman since coming on duty over an hour ago.

"Perhaps she's having supper," I said.

He considered this.

"The dining cars do not open 'til after Bucharest."

Frowning, I grunted something by way of

reply and continued backward to the next car, where one compartment, whose shades were drawn, proved to be occupied by an amorous honeymoon couple. At least I assumed they were honeymooners.

In another, whose shades were raised, I saw a lone gentleman of perhaps forty absorbed in a game of patience. He, too, shook his head when I slid open his door and inquired about Sophie Hunter.

"Nope," was the distinctly American reply. "Can't say I have, 'cause I haven't." With which he resumed his game and I my inventory.

Many of the compartments I passed were as yet unoccupied. Varna, where the train originated, was not the most popular destination. I knew the train would accumulate passengers as we headed west, just as we had shed them during our earlier transit in the opposite direction.

The business car held four typists busily at work, but was otherwise underused at this hour. None of the clacking typists had seen the woman I described.

As I lurched rearward, the train squealed into Bucharest's palatial Filaret terminus, with the customary wheezing of smoke and steam, as if to demonstrate to all and sundry the enormous effort involved in the task.

The nearest dining car, a cherrywood-paneled affair, was indeed empty when I reached it, unless one counted two Greek Orthodox monks seated side by side, hands on their open missals, eyes closed in either sleep or mute prayer, just as I had marveled at them in St. Basil's.

"Meditation," one of the stewards informed me in a confidential tone over my shoulder. "They never speak," the other added with a shrug.

The stewards were meticulously inserting fresh roses and sprigs of white baby's breath into the Lalique vase on every table, each table in turn draped in gleaming, starched damask linen with serviettes of matching purity.

I was now fully awake and distinctly uneasy. As the train idled, I stepped onto the platform for the benefit of an unobstructed view, but saw nothing to arouse my suspicions. As the left side of the train faced a high wall of brick, I did not worry about disembarkations from that side. Abruptly mindful of Mycroft's warning regarding Bucharest, I clapped my hands over my pockets even though I saw no sign of the street urchins he had mentioned.

I had no idea what I was looking for, only a vague concern that for whatever reason, and from whatever place of concealment, Mrs. Walling might choose to disembark without my knowing it.

Or had she done so while I was quizzing our dining car? This struck me as improbable. But when I slept? This thought made still less sense. I may have been sound asleep, but had we stopped, I surely would have waked. Merely slackening our speed had served to rouse me.

The fact that I had not found Holmes either set off a disquieting train of thought,* one that I tried to banish as it arose, namely, that the two might be somewhere together. Had both somehow contrived to leave the train? I realized that after our encounter with Rivka Nussbaum and her father in the hovel in Kishinev, Holmes was no longer the man I had known for almost twenty years. The episode with my Webley had shown me I could no longer be confident of his actions.

And then I recalled the thudding I had ignored as I slept. On the heels of that recollection a still more disturbing idea occurred, one that involved a struggle right beneath my berth.

* Watson, the diarist, appears to have been unaware of this pun.

*Don't be overconfident,* Mrs. Walling had warned me.

She and Holmes had gone nowhere. Rather, I had slept through her abduction.

It then followed, I told myself, that if Anna Walling had been abducted, surely the next order of business would be to spirit her off the train — and Bucharest was the first plausible opportunity to do so.

In fact I saw no one leaving the train, but several individuals and couples now climbed aboard as friends and relatives clamored their *adieux.* Behind the second-class carriages were the baggage and mail cars, and it was here that I observed an unnerving sight: two oblong pine boxes were being wheeled up and loaded with some little difficulty onto the train. They were evidently heavy, for the porters were obliged to struggle with them. As I drew nearer I suddenly understood: the boxes were coffins.

I spied the conductor, also unfamiliar to me, about to blow his whistle and caught him by the sleeve.

"What are those coffins doing aboard the train?"

He looked at me, stroking the bottom of his large grey moustache suspiciously with his knuckles. "You are the family?"

"No. What has happened?"

He shook his head. "Tragedy. Hungarian couple. Holiday in Carpathia." He made a swift downward swipe with his hand. "Avalanche. Now they go home to Pest."

"Pest?" What irritant was he referring to?

"Two cities as one — Buda and Pest. Since thirty years now. The river separates them."

I had forgotten or never learned this fact.

Shaking his head once more, the fellow again made to blow his whistle and bellow tidings of our imminent departure.

"One moment, please. How many miles to Budapest?"

"Eight hundred and twenty-five kilometers, *monsieur.* All aboard!!" He brushed past, blowing his shrill whistle. There was nothing for it but to climb back on the train.

As the engine gathered speed, commencing its corkscrew route through the Transylvanian Alps, I resolved to continue my search to the rear of our dining car, where second-class passengers enjoyed less luxurious accommodations. With some hasty calculations scratched on my shirt cuff, I understood the conductor to say we had roughly four hundred miles before us. Given the speed at which we were moving, I estimated a journey of approximately seven hours that would put us in the Hungarian capital by dawn. This being the case, it was plausible to assume both Holmes and Anna Walling, wherever each of them might be, must both remain on the train 'til Budapest.

Our dining car was now open, and I spoke with Benoit, the *maître d'hôtel*. He had not seen Miss Hunter, though he claimed to remember her from our journey east. Kissing the tips of his fingers, he said, "One does not soon forget such a woman," but otherwise could offer no information or guidance.

The car had by now filled with diners, and he pointed them out, one by one. Like any good hotelier, Benoit made it his business to know his passengers.

"That one is Professor Cherniss of Heidelberg, yes, he knows the ancient Greek. Also his wife, *italienne, je crois.* Across from them by herself, Miss Fram. *Elle est mignonne, mais non?* Those blue eyes! A governess, I think she goes back to England. Traveling unaccompanied, *mon Dieu.* That one, Colonel Esterhazy, he calls himself. *Prends garde* — he is a professional gambler." He pantomimed gestures with cards dealt from the bottom of the deck and made a *comme çi, comme ça* gesture typical of his race.

"And the couple by the window?"

"Countess Agneska de Maio and her

husband, his name I forget. Then the American, MacDonald, who sells the guns . . ."

"Yes, I spoke with him. What guns?"

Benoit scowled briefly. "Colt," he remembered, then gestured, tossing his head behind us. "Mr. and Mrs. Spottiswoode, just married . . ."

"So I heard." It seemed tactful not to elaborate. "And that one?"

I indicated a devilishly handsome youth who didn't care who knew it. Muscular and not yet twenty-five, he looked more a trapeze artiste than anything else — slicked dark hair, flashing Latin eyes, and dusky skin set off by his white twill suit, from whose confines his massive chest threatened to burst.

"You don't know? Everybody knows. Erik von Hentzau! Argentine. He plays the polo. We have eight of his ponies with the luggage."

"With the coffins?"

"Coffins?" He shot me a brief look of incomprehension before his countenance cleared. "*Ah, les cercueils! Dommage. Si jeune.*"

"I see the monks have gone."

"*Les frères?* Ah, yes. They never speak." He raised an eyebrow. "But they eat *toujours cordon bleu.*"

"Which compartment?"

He scowled again, consulting his encyclopedic memory. "*Numero quinze, wagon-lit Ione.*"

There being nothing for it, I chose to continue my inspection, beginning with the other two dining cars, then knocking on every compartment door, regardless of whether the green aisle shades were invitingly raised or forbiddingly lowered. Our mountainous route had now so many curves I was continually obliged to clutch at walls and bulkheads for balance.

The honeymoon couple was presently engaged in acrimonious argument as furious as their earlier encounter had been amicable. They ignored me entirely. In the bar car, the arms dealer, MacDonald, appeared to be in his cups and had resumed his patience with a bottle of Glenfiddich single malt for company; across the aisle, Colonel Esterhazy invited me to sit in on a game of faro, which included von Hentzau, the Argentine polo player. I politely declined. In compartment fifteen in the car dubbed Ione, the two monks were engaged, as always, in mute recitations, paying no attention either to me or to one another. Countess de Maio and her husband with the forgettable name regarded me with silent condescension, she over the tops of her reading glasses, he in the act of trimming his beard, catching a piece of my reflection in the mirror above twin wood-paneled wash basins.

A score of times my gambit was repeated: "Forgive the intrusion, but" — stealing a look at their surroundings — "I'm searching for a young lady . . ."

The business car now boasted only one typist, at work on a German machine. Intent on her task, she shook her head without looking up when I asked yet again if she had seen anyone matching Anna Walling's description.

Sometimes my search was humoured by folk doing their best to be helpful while at others doors were slid in my face. Passengers smiled or shouted at me. Once I was pushed.

Miss Fram, with wide blue eyes, seemed moved by my dilemma and heard me out, but had seen nothing of the woman I described. "I'm so sorry. I do hope you manage to find her."

"Fram. Do I have your name right?"

"Yes. Rhymes with jam," she added, still smiling.

One compartment with its shades lowered refused to respond at all. My calls and knocks were resolutely ignored, and when, desperate, I tried the door, I found it locked.

"What can I do?" the conductor protested when I explained the situation. "I have no authority to authorize the forced entry of one of our *première classe* passengers, *mon colonel.*"

"Devil take it!" I expostulated. "A woman has been abducted aboard this train —"

"A woman only you have seen, *monsieur,*" the cheeky fellow saw fit to remind me.

"Jean-Claude saw her!"

"Jean-Claude left the train in Bucharest. He was feeling unwell."

"Damn it, man! Take me to the baggage cars! Take me or I shall make a scene! Would your precious passengers care for that? I doubt it!"

With something between a sigh and a shrug, the conductor led me to the rear of the train. In one car were strapped two motorcars — a Mercedes and a Daimler — and several crates of homing pigeons, cooing raucously. The second baggage car proved likewise unexceptional unless one counted Erik von Hentzau's string of eight polo ponies. The flooring, deliberately slanted so it could be hosed clean, didn't make matters easy for the poor animals struggling for purchase as the train twisted to and fro. There were several sacks of mail. Though locked at the necks, they appeared to contain nothing but paper that crinkled and crunched when I prodded them. There were various trunks and crates of food and merchandise, one of which I insisted on prying open with a crowbar (kept in the car for use by customs officials), only to find it filled with Biedermeier chairs.

"That is enough!" the conductor commanded, scandalized by my temerity. "Touch one more item and I shall have you removed from the train. I shall deposit you in the middle of nowhere by the locomotive cistern! And" — following my gaze — "do not dream of committing sacrilege!" Meaning the two coffins.

I knew enough of human nature to understand the man had reached his limits. Reclaiming my coat, which I had doffed when working the crowbar, I followed him forward. He deposited me back at my compartment, where I repeated a fruitless inspection of the lower berth, but achieved little except to confirm my impression that a struggle had taken place there. I then realized that in addition to her shawl, all Mrs. Walling's clothes and her suitcase had also been removed, doubtless while I slept my hideous sleep. With a jolt to my stomach, I realized that, as the conductor had pointed out, there was now no evidence the woman had ever existed.

Pacing within the confined space availed nothing, and staying put was impossible. I returned to our now half-full dining car, where I sat and ordered a cognac neat.

"You might prefer to enjoy it in the parlour car," Benoit offered. He was, I knew, concealing his impatience to clear the supper detritus so as to set up for breakfast in the morning, but I was in no mood to accommodate him, or indeed anyone else. Other diners were dawdling over their puddings and brandies; why should I not enjoy the same privilege?

"Cognac, neat," I repeated, and sat sullenly staring at the tablecloth as I sipped the honey-coloured liqueur.

"May I join you?"

Before I could respond, the tall stranger of military bearing had answered his own question and seated himself opposite me. There was something familiar about him that I was for the moment unable to place.

"Colonel Morcar, is it?" His English was embellished by traces of a foreign accent.

"I don't believe I've had the —"

"Or perhaps I should say, Dr. Baskerville?" His slate eyes glittered like ice chips.

With a chill to match their temperature, I now recognized him, but he cut me off.

"Or is it not rather Dr. John H. Watson, M.D., late of the army medical department, Fifth Northumberland Fusiliers, and chronicler of the doings of Sherlock Holmes?"

"Cedric West!"

The man opposite me offered a smile that manifested neither mirth nor warmth.

"Ah, yes," he said, like one fondly reminiscing. "Cedric West. I'll have the same," he ordered the *garçon,* jutting a confident forefinger in the direction of my snifter, never taking his eyes from mine.

"But that's not who you are, is it?" I countered, as the waiter departed, gathering my wits in a lightning flash of comprehension.

"No?" His tone was silkily mocking, like a cat toying at its leisure with a mouse.

"No. You are in fact General Pyotr Ivanovich Rachkovsky —"

"Director General Rachkovsky."

"Director General Rachkovsky," I amended, "of the Okhrana."

"Very good, Doctor."

He regarded me, motionless as a cobra poised to strike, so very unlike the amiable stockbroker who had offered jovially to share his taxi outside the British Museum. I returned his look with a steadfast regard of my own. In this fashion we passed the better half of a minute, each gauging the measure of the other. I was right to have set him down from the first as erstwhile military; I had merely picked the wrong army.

"Why are you here?" I demanded after I judged we had enjoyed sufficient silent communion.

"Come, come, Doctor." His head cocked to one side in a gesture I took to be one of impatience. "You have something we want; I have something you want."

"Your English is excellent," I noted, in a bid to buy time.

"I read history at Camford,"* he assured me, looking around. "Where is Sherlock Holmes?"

"I have not the slightest idea. Where is Sophie Hunter?"

"Anna Strunsky," he corrected me, carefully enunciating her Russian maiden name. "Ah yes, that is what you wish to know."

"Anna Walling," I persisted, "is an American citizen. She is married to —"

* If the Russian is speaking truthfully, he attended the same university as Holmes. Though they appear roughly the same age, it would be too improbable to discover they were classmates.

294

"Possession is nine-tenths of the law," he bluntly interrupted.

"Then you do have her."

"Do I?"

"Let us not play games, Director General."

"She is no longer on the train."

"The train has not stopped. There have been no stations."

"The train pauses occasionally to take on coal and water. We did so at Teregova."

I remembered the irate conductor threatening to put me off the train at one such "cistern." I tried not to let the scoundrel across the table see any change in my expression.

"What do you want with her?"

His meticulously trimmed eyebrows arched in surprise. "With her? Nothing at all. She is merely what you would call a bargaining chip."

Reaching into his breast pocket, he withdrew a newspaper, spreading it on the table between our snifters. I recognized the language in the typeface as German, as well as words in the headline that caused the blood to stand still in my veins.

"Behold the first German-language edition of the Protocols of the Elders of Zion, Doctor."

"No reputable paper has printed this trash."

Rachkovsky employed his own silver toothpick with evident satisfaction.

"It makes no difference. The Protocols are now spreading like a virus. And a virus must spread," he added with what doubtless was intended as clinical detachment, as if conferring with another physician. "Or it dies."

"The Protocols are fake," I responded.

He smiled. "Fake is in the eye of the beholder, Doctor."

"Holmes has the full confession of their creator. Once it is revealed, your hoax collapses."

The scoundrel slid his toothpick into an ivory scabbard, meditatively swirling the cognac in his snifter with deft wrist movements before swallowing some. His favorable expression informed me he was a connoisseur.

"Ah. So now we come to the nub of the matter. You want what we have; we want what you have."

It took several seconds for his meaning to sink in.

"Krushenev's confession."

"Nothing escapes you, Doctor."

"Or else?"

"Anna Strunsky's —"

"Walling —"

He shrugged to indicate a distinction without a difference. "Under any name, her body will never be found. You perceive the transaction is a simple one."

I stared at the man in amazement. "The confession will do you no good. We have copies."

"That is untrue," he responded without rancor. "But even if it were, copies are unpersuasive. It could always be argued they were forgeries, and a carbon signature, I hazard, would be viewed as inadmissible in most courts. No, Doctor, only the signed original will suffice."

For some reason, I found myself thinking of Holmes's shattered Stradivarius.

"Why is it so important to you? Why is it worth a woman's life to preserve this nauseating falsehood? Two women's lives," I now felt compelled to add. "For you have already taken Manya Lippman's. It was you, wasn't it?"

He regarded me thoughtfully with a blank expression before snapping back the last of his drink.

"Alas, Doctor, soon we will be in Budapest, and I don't have time to explain the intricacies of Russian politics or the machinations of Count Witte,* who is trying to turn our beloved Tsar into a progressive. This we cannot allow."

"Cannot allow? Do you work for Nicholas Romanov, or does he work for you?"

This was greeted with a cynical shrug.

"There are many ways to express loyalty. His Imperial Majesty tends to be swayed by the last voice in his ear. It is necessary — for his own good, you understand — for us, patriotic Russians, to be that last and loudest voice. Russia is losing the war with those little Nips. Someone must take the blame. You understand."

He stood. "I am in the closed compartment you banged on earlier and found to be locked. Anna Strunsky is not inside it. You have until Budapest, Doctor."

"I tell you I've no idea where Sherlock Holmes is!"

"Then I suggest you find him, Doctor. Find him at once. Or Anna Strunsky will share Manya Lippman's fate."

---

* Sergius Yulyevich Witte (1849–1915) became Russia's prime minister in 1905 and designed Russia's first constitution. He was loathed by the Okhrana.

# 11.
## Budavari Siklo

Ten years or so before these events, a piece in *The Lancet* introduced the world to the concept and reality of adrenaline, a secretion of the adrenal gland in times of excitement, responsible for several physical sensations affecting the heart, blood pressure, respiration, etcetera. I was familiar with these symptoms long before they had a physiological designation. I had experienced them on the battlefield in Afghanistan, later on a police steam launch chasing Jonathan Small and his Horrible Companion down the Thames, and later still on the marshes of Dartmoor, confronted by a gigantic spectral hound.

So there was now no question in my mind what was overtaking me physically as once more I raced through the train, trying not to succumb to debilitating panic.

*Where was Holmes?*

Between the parlour and business cars yet

again, and realizing I was starting to hyper-
ventilate, I forced myself to stop moving,
lean up against one of the trembling pan-
eled bulkheads, and think. Sweat was trick-
ling in rivulets from my scalp down the
length of my body.

*When you eliminate the impossible, what-
ever remains must be the truth* had long been
a dictum of the detective's, and I racked my
mind now to eliminate all that was impossible.

I had searched the entire train by this
point, including the galleys, dining, parlour
and business cars, the coal tender, and the
baggage cars. The mysteriously locked
compartment I now knew contained only
Director General Rachkovsky and possibly
other members of the Okhrana, not the
detective, whom they wished to see as
eagerly as I, nor Mrs. Walling, whom they
had spirited off the train during a momentary water stop. I was missing something
obvious.

At which point, in one of those bizarre
moments of unexpected, intuitive clarity —
no doubt also a by-product of my adrenaline
jolt — I knew.

The two monks were precisely where I had
last seen them, side by side in their second-
class compartment, pantomiming their

familiar supplication, *Lord Jesus, have mercy upon me.* My heart leapt to see only one was seated with a missal in his lap. The other held what looked to be a volume that had been torn apart.

"Holmes!" I fairly shouted.

The monk looked up and smiled when he beheld me.

"This is the most wonderful book ever written, Watson. Notwithstanding all those Russian names, *War and Peace* is the nearest thing to the *Iliad* that was ever —"

"Holmes, she's gone!" I slid the door shut behind me and tugged down the shades.

"Mrs. Walling?" He appeared thunderstruck. Clearly the detective knew nothing of what was happening.

"The Russians have her."

The blood drained from his face.

"Tell me everything."

He was already tugging off the strands of his false beard and stepping out of his cassock. All this commotion produced absolutely no effect on his fellow congregant, who, eyes closed, continued his silent chanting.

"Very obliging," Holmes remarked, following my look. "I simply attached myself, and he appears neither to have noticed nor offered the least objection. Go on, man."

"There's not a lot to tell," I responded, but related with mortification all that had followed after I'd awakened from my stuporous slumber.

He heard me out in gloomy silence as he adjusted his clothing.

"They want you, and they want the confession."

He nodded. "Me they may have, the confession they may not."

"But how will you — ?"

"Come, Watson, let us hasten to where these gentlemen are to be found."

He slid open the door and led me backward to where our porter, having bedded down all the passengers in our car for the night, was once again enjoying a nap in his chair.

At his feet rested a bull's-eye for emergency use. Holmes delicately extracted the lantern without disturbing its owner and led me still further rearward to the baggage car, which we examined anew, this time with no conductor to intervene.

Erik von Hentzau's polo ponies nickered nervously at the bull's-eye's beam.

Immediately the detective focused his attention on the two caskets, shining the lantern slowly along their lengths.

"Hullo," he exclaimed, kneeling closer.

"How often does one see a coffin with air holes?"

I knelt beside him, able to confirm his observation. Someone had indeed used a brace and bit to auger six apertures on either side of the pine box at the widened portion meant to accommodate the cadaver's shoulders. Holmes nudged the casket, which moved easily. It took no great intelligence to understand it was empty.

"This is where they concealed her until the water stop," the detective reasoned. Using the crowbar I'd employed to open what proved to be a crate of furniture, Holmes prised the lid to confirm the coffin was indeed empty. A fragment of red cloth caught on a pine splinter within, which I recognized as belonging to the shawl Anna Walling had been wearing, served to confirm his deduction.

Behind the box, almost lost in the shadows, I now spied a pile of stones. This was what the porters had labored to carry. We levered the lid off the second casket and found it weighted with more of the same.

Behind us, the horses whinnied. Holmes and I looked at one another.

"Why two coffins?" I wondered.

"The second may have been for you, Doctor. Had one kidnapping not served to motivate me."

Before I had the chance to digest this prospect and its implications, we were interrupted.

"Sherlock Holmes, I presume." Swiveling the bull's-eye, we beheld in its feeble light the director general of the dreaded Okhrana flanked by two silent henchmen.

"Yes, I've been waiting for you," the detective responded.

"You put my men to a great deal of inconvenience in Odessa."

"They were clumsy and deserved what they got."

Holmes offered the Russian a cigarette, which he declined.

"You know what I have to say," Rachkovsky offered.

"You also know my answer," the detective returned.

"Let me spell it out, so there can be no misunderstanding." Rachkovsky seated himself on the other coffin. "I want Krushenev's confession."

"I do not have it."

The Russian was first to blink.

"Where is it?"

"I posted it in Varna."

The other considered this gambit for several moments, then dismissed it, smirking confidently. "That is a lie. You would not dare entrust such a precious document to the mails, not in this part of the world."

"Nevertheless, I do not have it. You are welcome to search me and such belongings as I currently possess."

With a suddenness that sent the detective reeling across the undulating floor, Rachkovsky smote Holmes across the face with the back of his hand, a blow so fierce that, enhanced by the pronged ring on his third finger, it served to open a vivid gash on his right cheek and send Erik von Hentzau's polo ponies into a neighing frenzy of prancing hooves.

"You have no idea with whom you are dealing," the Russian exclaimed.

Holmes coolly retrieved his cigarette, dabbing at his cheek with a handkerchief. "On the contrary, you have just convinced me — if your scurrilous Protocols had not already done so — precisely with whom I am dealing. In addition, Rivka Nussbaum had entirely persuaded me days ago."

"Who?"

"And you poisoned Theodor Herzl."

"Would I admit it if I had?"

"True. Invite the world to speculate as to his cause of death."

The other inclined his head to concede

the point. "I might."

"Let us leave it at this," Holmes concluded, seating himself insouciantly on the coffin opposite and blowing smoke. "My friend here has a revolver aimed at your heart. Move an inch and he will shoot you dead."

I produced my weapon, its chambers full, trigger cocked. Rachkovsky was not a man who was often surprised.

For several moments only the *clickety-clack* of the train was to be heard. Doubtless his own minions were armed; it was a question of who would shoot first, and I could see in the chief's eyes that the game was not presently worth the candle.

"If you shoot me, you will never see the girl again."

"If your men return fire, you will never obtain the confession, but others will."

The last thing Rachkovsky wanted was an incident involving gunplay aboard the Orient Express. Even assuming he and his cohorts managed by some chance to emerge unscathed, such publicity as would inevitably accrue would shine a ruinous light on people best suited to conducting their endeavors in the dark.

As if to confirm my intuition, one of Rachkovsky's men leaned over, displaying his watch and whispering. The Okhrana chief nodded, then smiled at Holmes.

"Very well. We approach the Austro-Hungarian border, where I must leave you. When you reach Budapest, we will contact you regarding the arrangements."

"Those arrangements must include Sophie Hunter's passport and visas as well as her unharmed person," Holmes stipulated.

"Well thought on," the other conceded with a thin smile.

"How will you know where we are?" I asked.

"We will know."

So saying, and careful not to make any sudden movements, the three Russians withdrew, leaving Holmes and myself alone with the horses and mail as the Orient Express slowed for the frontier.

We knew that customs officials would shortly be asking for our papers and inspecting our possessions.

"Holmes, where is the letter?"

"Where they'll never find it."

"Yes, but —"

"May I trouble you for your homburg, Doctor?"

Wondering, I handed over my hat. Running his finger around the inside of the headband, he deftly extracted the folded paper from its place of concealment.

"Do you mean to say I had it the entire time?"

"Yes, my dear fellow. I knew if they discovered me, I would be searched until they found it."

"But you never warned —"

He smiled a trifle sadly, I thought, and lit another cigarette, offering me one, which I accepted.

"I thought it might be best if you didn't know."

"You mean my innocence would be more convincing."

He shrugged. It was typical of the man that he was at times capable of such a cold-blooded calculation. It was also true, I realized, that I had grown accustomed to my role as a packhorse in carrying out his sometimes labyrinthine schemes.

"What are you going to do?"

"That is indeed the question. Our cards are not very promising."

"It's either the woman or the Protocols. And he's already murdered another."

"You are very blunt."

"Very honest." More honest than you have been, I was tempted to add, but hadn't the heart.

He nodded. "I know, Watson. I know."

We smoked for several moments in silence while the distant hissing of steam told us the boiler was taking on water. The Emperor Franz Josef's civil servants would shortly be seeking to stamp our passports.

"I expect we've little choice except to proceed to Budapest and learn their plan," Holmes said, more or less thinking out loud. "Perhaps some flaw in their arrangements will inspire us."

I tried to take comfort from this idea, but didn't get very far. It seemed the Okhrana had been ahead of us almost every step of the way. Why should they not remain so?

We returned to my compartment, where those same civil servants did indeed give our papers a cursory examination before stamping them with more Hapsburg double eagles and, upon their exit, emphatically slamming our sliding door as if to demonstrate their unimpeachable authority. In the darkness they either failed to notice or did not care about the detective's slashed cheek, now embellished with dried blood. Dueling scars were not their purview.

The berths still being in place, Holmes with awkward movements began to clamber to the topmost.

"You ought to clean that gash."

He made no answer, and I had to content myself by stretching my own weary frame on the lower berth. Holmes had not uttered a word since we put out our cigarettes in the baggage car. There seemed little enough to say at this juncture, and the rhythmic noise of the train lulled one into silence as we wound through mountains we could not see.

"Transylvania," I remarked, at last, "home of vampires."

After a silence, Holmes responded in a hollow voice.

"Not exclusively Transylvania." I knew what he meant. There seemed now to be vampires everywhere.

"It's a very pretty problem, as you would say."

Another silence.

"Not that pretty."

With a pang I found myself recalling the overconfident telegram I'd sent Juliet from Varna, *All's well that ends well.*

"Holmes, even assuming we agree to whatever it is they propose, how can we be sure they will keep their end of the bargain?"

"We can't," he reflected, "but they have every motive for doing so. As you reported his conversation, 'the girl,' as Rachkovsky terms her, is nothing but his means to an end. To kill her is to risk the wrath of the British and American governments. But they must be *willing* to kill her," he added bitterly. "Never make a threat you are not prepared to carry out."

"They might kill her simply to insure she does not expose her own abduction and the reasons behind it."

Another silence.

"They might."

"Her tale of being buried alive in a pine coffin might not endear Russia to the world at large."

"Watson," said he very softly. Meaning, I knew, *Enough.*

The train barreled through the night, as we lay silent, each aware we were fast approaching a moral cul-de-sac. Though my mind continued racing in fruitless circles, I was on the point of sleep, when I became aware of Holmes noiselessly descending the ladder.

"Holmes?"

"I'm going for some air, Watson."

"Would you like company?"

More silence as he considered my offer.

"Thank you, no. If you've no objection."

"Of course not."

Throwing on his ulster, he slid open the door and left.

Fully awake now, I lay contemplating the truly awful choice that was only the detective's to make. But no matter how I turned the conundrum over in my mind, it was unclear what that choice would or should be.

Holmes was gone for a surprisingly long time. Waiting for his return, it was as if someone had dropped a single shoe. I had assumed he would come back within fifteen or twenty minutes, but in this I was mistaken. I must have entirely lost track of time when I was awakened by the soft sliding of our compartment door and the stealthy return of the detective.

"I'm so sorry, old man." He shook his head like a pugilist who has absorbed one too many punches. "I seem to have made off with your hat instead of mine." He hung it up next to his own on the brass hook.

"Did the air do you any good?"

"Who knows? Who knows? What a mystery life is, Watson. What a damnable mystery. Do I mean mystery or misery?" he added, under his breath.

I thought it best to say nothing. Holmes would see through any effort of false cheer on my part. He sat on the berth by my feet, hunched below the upper bed, and stared out the window at the coming dawn, peering at or oblivious to his own chiseled features reflected in the glass, motionless as a statue as the darkened landscape flitted behind it.

**5 February.** The weather was indisputably winter by the time the Orient Express crawled into Budapest. We trundled past the enormous, red-domed capitol and bone-white parliament building on the western bank of the Danube (the city formerly designated as Pest), before turning east and creeping to a stop at Keleti station, among the most modern in all Europe.

I was unacquainted with Budapest and unprepared for the opulence of Hungary's capital, still less for its indecipherable tongue.

"They say it most resembles Finnish," Holmes remarked, which made still less sense to me and helped neither of us. Hailing a taxi that skidded to a stop where we stood on bustling Rakoczi Avenue, Holmes simply said, "Hotel." Taking his cue from this single noun, our driver wove expertly through snow-clogged traffic in this prosperous and animated metropolis. He took it upon himself to bring us over the Emperor Franz Josef Bridge to the Palace Hotel, doubtless one of the costliest in the city.

There we registered in conformity with our passports as Mr. Gideon Altmont and Colonel Rupert Morcar.

"What will Mycroft say?" I wondered, as we ogled the gold-flecked foyer. Mycroft's idea of accommodations, I knew, was the shoebox Hotel Esmeralda.

"Mycroft is the least of our problems."

Rachkovsky had said he would find us and instruct us regarding "arrangements." But who knew what portion of the truth the Russian Machiavelli was speaking? Had he made some alternative plan regarding Anna Walling? Was she already dead, her body, as he threatened, floating in the Danube, anonymous as Manya Lippman's, or cached elsewhere, never to be found?

After depositing my bag in a room large enough to house a family of five, I strode down the wide carpeted hall and knocked on Holmes's door. He didn't answer at first, and when he finally did, his customary pallor had now metamorphosed into a sallow grey. He stared briefly, then admitted me without comment. As I passed him, I distinctly smelled cognac on his breath. Indeed, he presently extended a snifter in my direction. I had never known him to be incapacitated by drink and could only be grateful his syringe and its lethal contents were nowhere to hand.

"Thank you, no. Holmes, I think Mrs. Walling would be better served if you were sober."

He considered this, passing a hand across his forehead in a familiar gesture, then nodded, seemingly incapable of either conversation or movement.

I rang for room service and ordered coffee, another noun that arguably required no Hungarian, and held up two fingers before the bellman that I hoped would be understood to indicate two cups. When they arrived, I coaxed Holmes into taking his black.

"How many hours has it been?" he demanded, not yet drinking.

"Almost three since we arrived."

"What are they planning? Are they planning anything? What have they done to her?"

"They've done nothing! Holmes, remember your own irrefutable logic. They have every interest in getting hold of Krushenev's confession. To do that, they must be able to produce Mrs. Walling."

"Yes, yes, to be sure," he acknowledged woodenly, finally raising the dark liquid to his lips.

Passivity did not suit Sherlock Holmes at the best of times; on the chase, he found it insupportable. It was foreign to his nature

315

to wait in circumstances such as these, and yet his hands were tied no less securely than had they been bound with hoops of steel. On former occasions, he might have endured such stress with recourse to his violin or (a lifetime ago) cocaine; now he had neither. He paced. He sat. He smoked and sipped at his cold, unleavened coffee.

I saw the envelope first when it was slid under the door, but when I pointed it out the detective fell upon it like a tiger.

"It's addressed to Professor James Moriarty," he observed ruefully. "How they must enjoy their pound of flesh."

"Not the association I think you want on this case," I commented.

He looked up from the envelope. "This isn't a case. It never was."

"I wonder how they found us."

"Elementary. They sent the taxi that so conveniently fetched us at the station. The driver's instructions were no doubt clear. Had I said not a word, he still would have brought us to this place." He handed me the envelope. "Here. Read it to me. There's a good fellow."

He closed his eyes as I slid open the flap and extracted a single sheet of paper, typed all in capitals: "ACROSS FROM YOUR HOTEL IS THE CHAIN BRIDGE. AT

PRECISELY FOUR-THIRTY, YOU WILL BOTH CROSS IT ON FOOT. ON THE FARTHER SIDE AT 'ADAM SQUARE PARK' YOU WILL BE MET AT THE BOTTOM OF BUDAVARI SIKLO. FURTHER INSTRUCTIONS WILL BE ISSUED AT THAT TIME. YOU WILL BRING THE DOCUMENT. WE ASSUME COLONEL MORCAR WILL BE ARMED. AS WILL WE."

I looked at my watch.

"Ten past four," I informed Holmes. "Whatever it is, they are cutting it fine."

"Deliberately. They do not wish to provide us with time to maneuver."

Holmes stared out the window. The bridge in question was directly before our hotel, spanning the Danube and leading to the hilly portion of the city formerly known as Buda on the opposite bank, atop which sat its imposing eponymous castle.

I reread the note. "Budavari Siklo. I wonder what that could be."

On the far side of the bridge, we beheld a funicular railway, whose two alternating cars passed each other carrying passengers up and down the steep hill below the impressive fortress.

"I think I know," said the detective with mounting excitement. "Ingenious," he murmured. Then, abruptly springing to life, in an instant the Holmes of yore, he threw on his coat. "Quick, Watson, there is no time to be lost. Let us fetch your warm things and our passports. And remember your revolver — and your hat!" he added almost as an afterthought as he dashed past me to the door.

"You are going through with this, then?"

He turned and regarded me, his grey eyes clouded with pain. "What would you have me do?"

"I only wish to point out that you went to considerable lengths to obtain Krushenev's signed confession."

His eyes closed briefly, as though he were remembering just what lengths had been involved. Then he opened them again and gazed frankly into mine.

"She went through much more, Watson."

Of whom was he speaking? Anna Walling? Manya Lippman or Rivka Nussbaum? Perhaps all three.

It was bitterly cold and growing dark as we made our way across the windswept stone and iron suspension bridge. I judged the span to be about a thousand feet. At either end the structure was guarded by two stone lions that put one in mind of Landseer's enormous sculptures in Trafalgar Square. The Danube that divided the city in two was far from its fabled blue; it rushed past below us as a muddy, icy torrent. As we passed one of the huge stone towers, a plaque informed the curious that the bridge had been constructed in 1849 by one Adam Clark.

Clearly the square on the farther side, alluded to in the note, with its non-Hungarian designation, had been named for the bridge's architect. And at the end of that square at the base of an enormous incline was a sign above a small building — *Budavari Siklo** — indicating the lower terminus of the twin funicular railways to the top. Waiting for us was one of Rachkovsky's minions whom I recognized from the baggage car of the Orient Express. The fellow evidently spoke no English but handed Holmes a second envelope, the contents of which he now read aloud to me:

"YOU WILL ACCOMPANY IVAN TO THE BOTTOM CABIN NAMED 'MARGIT,' WHICH IS HELD FOR YOUR

* The funicular opened in 1870 and was in continuous operation until bombed by the Allies in World War II. It was restored after the war and continues to function.

USE. YOUR WEAPON WILL GUARANTEE YOUR OWN SAFETY. THE OBJECT OF YOUR INTEREST AND I WILL BE AT THE TOPMOST CABIN, NAMED 'GELLERT.' AT MY SIGNAL, BOTH CARS WILL MOVE. AS WE PASS, THE EXCHANGE WILL BE MADE. IVAN WILL THEN COVER YOU UNTIL I SIGNAL I AM SATISFIED. IF THAT PROVES THE CASE, YOU WILL BE FREE TO GO." There is no signature.

"Ingenious," I was forced to acknowledge, producing my revolver so that Ivan could see it. There would be no forcing us to deliver Krushenev's confession prematurely.

The man nodded and motioned us to follow him to the lower housing, where inside we boarded the waiting cabin, whose name, *Margit,* was painted in gold above us. Ivan nudged the detective into position at the open left-hand doorway. Holmes held out his hand, and I removed my hat and gave it to him, whereupon, with slow, deliberate movements, he allowed Ivan to see him remove the folded paper from my headband.

Opening it, he displayed the confession out of Ivan's reach, but Krushenev's signature was visible by the light of the lone bulb above us in the roof of the cabin.

Ivan nodded, satisfied, grunted and

opened his bull's-eye, flashing a beam up the steep hill, which I judged to be at least forty degrees.

After a pause, perhaps three hundred feet above us, there came an answering beam, then a whistle, following which both cabins began to grind towards one another. Holmes refolded the papers and extended them in his left hand, leaving his right free to grab hold of Anna Strunsky Walling. What would happen should he fail? Would the woman fall between the tracks? Rachkovsky I knew for a cold-blooded murderer. Would he let her slide from his grasp to her death as if by accident? The possibility was so unthinkable my mind refused it admittance.

Gears grinding, the cars moved slowly in opposite directions, theirs descending, and ours, *Margit,* climbing, guided by the cogs beneath them and the unifying cables that ensured an identical rate of progress. Our cabin was empty save for we three, and I assumed a similar configuration in the car that was nearing us. As it approached and gained in size, I suffered the optical illusion it was moving faster. Its painted name, I could now see, was *Gellert.* How Rachkovsky secured the exclusive service of the funicular for this occasion I could not guess, but Holmes read my mind.

"The device can be hired for weddings," he surmised.

The clanking sound of the descending cabin added to our own, besides which my heart was now pounding like a pneumatic drill as the adrenaline once more coursed through my veins. What if Holmes should miss? I looked down to behold the parallel railroad ties blurring hypnotically past beneath me with vertiginous speed. What if, by the slightest miscalculation on his part, the courageous woman should fall to her death?

"Watson! Don't look down!" Holmes's stern command obliterated this terrifying prospect. I looked up in time to see the cars passing one another. In a flash, Rachkovsky's hand shot out and reached the detective's to snatch the precious paper, even as Holmes's right arm encircled her waist and pulled Anna Walling across the distance of two feet, clutching her in an iron embrace.

She remained clasped to him, her eyes shut.

"Your travel papers?"

She nodded, eyes still closed.

In the next instant, the cabins parted, continuing their journeys in opposite directions without hindrance, *Margit* nearing the top and Rachkovsky's *Gellert* approaching the terminal housing at the bottom of the hill. Holmes and Anna Walling never took their eyes from one another. I was unsure where to look, but could not help noticing their hands almost touching. Ivan was in no such confusion. He kept his revolver trained on us as we bumped to the end of our journey and then peered down the incline.

For the longest, agonizing time, there was nothing, but finally a bull's-eye beam assured us Rachkovsky was satisfied the bargain had been kept. With a grunt, Ivan signaled we were free.

"Quickly!" Holmes yelled. "Find a taxi!"

At the top of the hill, near Buda Castle, there was no shortage of motorcars, and one of these was easily ordered to take us to Keleti station, which was, in fact, not far from the upper terminus of the funicular. There was no thought of returning for our belongings at the hotel.

"Are you all right?" Holmes asked Mrs. Walling, as the taxi slewed across melting snow, making its way to the station.

Mrs. Walling, pale in a way I could not have believed possible given her colouring, could only nod. We rode in silence, each preoccupied with our own reflections.

"You should not have rescued me," said she finally, her Slavic accent fully returned.

# 12.
## JOURNEY'S END

"Where do ideas come from?" Sherlock Holmes wondered, as our train for Vienna wound out of Keleti station with the three of us seated in rudimentary third class, carrying only the clothes on our backs. Holmes had stubbornly put off all our questions until we were under way. Finally he deigned to address them.

"There I was in Watson's upper berth, seemingly at my wits' end, torn between Scylla and Charybdis —"

"Which one am I?" Anna Walling inquired mildly.

"Between a rock and a hard place," the detective translated, without answering her question. It was obvious he was intent on relating her rescue in his own way. "Surrendering Krushenev's confession and allowing the hoax of the Protocols to flourish was unthinkable. I had seen the mischief they enable."

" 'Mischief' doesn't seem to quite cover Rivka Nussbaum and her family," I remarked sourly. "Nor does it do justice to —"

"Granted, Watson, granted," Holmes allowed hastily. "On the other hand, neither could I allow anything to happen to Mrs. Walling. And yet, my mind refused to function. I lay there, staring at the ceiling eight inches from my nose, when out of nowhere I remembered something. As I said, where do ideas come from?"

"What did you remember?" Mrs. Walling and I demanded as one. I knew Holmes savored his dramatic touches, but we were exhausted and at the end of our patience.

"I remembered the business car."

"What are you talking about?" Anna Walling demanded with more than a touch of asperity. Her manner seemed strange, given that it was only thanks to Sherlock Holmes she was alive at all, but I began to sense what the detective was getting at.

Realizing we occupied a carriage with open (albeit cushioned) seating, I lowered my voice. "Ah yes, the business car on the Orient Express with all the typists —"

"What typists?" Mrs. Walling began, her impatience mounting.

"Precisely, Watson! In desperation, it occurred to me there was likely a Russian typist and typewriter aboard the train. I told you I was going for some air, then raced to that selfsame business car, which, as you might expect, was virtually unoccupied at that hour, save for an Italian typist with a stack of material awaiting attention and her reddened eyes barely open, poor woman. I am not sure whether you observed, Watson, but the typewriter used by Krushenev in his office was in fact of German manufacture, a Blickensderfer. Examining the machines on the train, each keyboard calibrated in a different language, you may imagine how overjoyed I was to find a Cyrillic Blickensderfer. I rang for the porter and explained I had urgent need of the Russian typist. The man went casually off on my errand and, after what seemed an eternity, returned with Miss Ludmilla Ogareff, as she introduced herself, blinking sleep from her eyes but doing her best to appear cheerful, as advertised. I presented her with the confession and asked her to retype it, word for word. She slipped on a pince-nez and went to work. I worried the text might arouse her suspicions, but I imagine by now these ladies are accustomed to every sort of document, and at this hour Miss Ogareff was not disposed to do anything but get the job over with and go back to sleep.

"I peered over her shoulder as she worked. Though, as you know, I can neither read nor speak Russian, yet I was perfectly capable of comparing the original to what she typed and ensuring that each letter was identical to its source. Several times she made mistakes, and I was obliged to ask her to begin again, which she did, though shaking her head and allowing me to crumple and pocket her previous attempt. At other times, she instinctively corrected typographical errors made by Krushenev and appeared more than a little put out when I insisted these be replicated. Certainly the hour did nothing to encourage precision on either of our parts, so I was careful to proceed at a glacial pace, my pockets slowly bulging with rejected efforts.

"When at last the two pages were complete, I thanked her and pressed a gratuity into her hand, which I think surprised her and sent her off to dreamland in restored good humor. I now had a complete and identical —"

"But the signature!" I exclaimed. "You didn't have Krushenev's signature!"

"Quite right, old chap. That indeed I lacked. But I'd already worked that part of the problem out in my mind. The business car being empty save for the Italian typist, who took no notice of me, I held Krushenev's pages against the window, where the coming daylight easily illumined the man's signature. I had then only to place my copies on top and trace his name on them with my own pen. It was tricky," the detective added with evident satisfaction, "as the unsteady motion of the car made the work more difficult, but again I resolved to take my time. In addition, I have always found when forging signatures that copying the originals upside down makes for a freer, more spontaneous-appearing result. In this case, I also had the advantage of knowing that when Rachkovsky scrutinized the writing, he would remember Krushenev had appended his name under terrifying circumstances. I am certain that in attempting to exonerate his role in the business when relating our encounter, the editor had surely emphasized the duress under which he'd produced the document. Any shakiness in the signature might well be the result. Afterwards, I tore the rejected pages to bits and flung them off the train, where the elements will make short work of whatever is left."

The detective sat back with the evident intention of lighting a cigarette, only to find his case empty. "Rats," he mumbled.

There did not appear to be much more to say, but my admiration for my singular friend at that moment knew no bounds. He was clearly functioning at the height of his powers.

"They will realize mistake," Anna Walling predicted in the silence. Holmes shrugged.

"Perhaps. Maybe the difference in paper will call attention to itself — that is certainly a possibility — but we are far from Russia now. In less than two hours, we will be in Vienna, farther still. The Emperor Franz Josef and the Tsar are not, as I understand it, presently working in harness. After that" — he sighed — "we'll be off to Munich, then Paris, then the boat train to London. From there Romeo Watson will rapturously rejoin his Clarendon Street Juliet, and at long last Mrs. Walling, with our undying gratitude for all the hardships she has undergone, will travel to Southampton, thence to follow her husband's footsteps to New York."

I was sure I saw Anna Walling wince at this.

"If you will excuse me," was all she said. We rose automatically as she left the compartment.

After a moment, Holmes rose again without comment and followed her.

I sat where I was, trying not to let my imagination run off in all directions.

Some minutes later, Holmes returned, resumed his seat by the window, and stared at the countryside, still without a word. I thought it wiser not to speak.

**6 February.** The rest of our journey continued in this vein. While we scoured the Vienna *bahnhof* for another train heading west, Holmes drew funds from Rothschild's and purchased sandwiches, as well as cigarettes and such necessaries as he could procure for Mrs. Walling. These included a blue muffler obtained from a shop across the road.

"Thank you" was Mrs. Walling's only murmur when he offered it to her.

While our improvised trains and accommodations were not on a par with the Orient Express, neither were they as problematic as the unforgiving benches on the "Odessa Flyer." We took turns sleeping against the window, Holmes proffering his coat for Mrs. Walling's use as a pillow. I don't believe she acknowledged this kindness on his part.

"I don't understand this gloom," I said as we later left Munich, finally in a compartment of our own, bound for Paris. "We should be celebrating. Holmes, you have pulled off what will prove the triumph of your career!"

"You will write about this?" Anna Walling inquired dully.

"Of course he will not," the detective hastily replied.

I saw no reason to make mention of these notes.

**10 February.** It all fell out as Holmes prophesied. Four days later, my own best beloved met me on the platform at Victoria, where I stumbled into her arms like a drowning man grasping at a life raft. As such, I did not witness the parting of Sherlock Holmes and Anna Strunsky Walling. Perhaps it would be more truthful to say I did not dare to witness it. What passed between them on that occasion I have no way of knowing.

"John!"

"Juliet!"

We stood there motionless for I don't know how long and then, arm in arm, floated from the place and hailed a taxi from the rank.

"You must tell me everything. John, I was so worried."

I promised her I would but explained there was a meeting I had to attend first.

"A meeting? So soon? At the hospital? You've only just got back. John!"

"Not the hospital, dearest. It can't wait." I patted her hand, and she understood.

The Diogenes was much the same as on my last visit. Harcourt, the blue-liveried steward, ushered me into the Strangers' Room, where I found Holmes already seated. Even the dust appeared unchanged.

"Watson," said he with a faint smile. "Good old reliable Watson."

Whatever carapace he had shed during our exploit, I now perceived, with a mixture of emotions growing back in its accustomed shape, altered only by the addition of a faint white scar on his right cheek.

"Holmes."

"All is well?"

"That ends well." There was a pause. "Mrs. Walling?"

"Sails this afternoon from Southampton." He occupied himself intently packing his pipe. The awkwardness ended when Mycroft joined us.

"Sherlock, well done!" He shook his brother's hand with jovial energy, as if he meant to prime a pump. "And you, Doctor.

Splendid. Really, brilliantly brought off."

"Mycroft —"

"No, truly. I think I may tell you — in confidence, of course — that you are both due for formal recognition."

"Oh?"

"Yes, a private investiture will take place at St. James's Palace in a fortnight's time. I'm afraid you will not be able to wear your decorations. They must be returned at the end of the ceremony."

"Naturally." I saw the faintest hint of a smile on the detective's face.

"And now," Mycroft said, seating himself in his long-suffering armchair, which wheezed air as he compressed it, "tell me everything."

We then proceeded to do so. More precisely, we told him a great deal, not, in fact, all, but enough for Mycroft to utter a running commentary of exclamations and surprise; also to raise toasts in our direction with what he averred was an outstanding lemon squash.

Holmes delivered Krushenev's confession. "A trifle worn," he admitted, handing over the much folded and wrinkled pages.

"But the signature legible nonetheless. I'll have one of our Russians go over it."

"Not Mrs. Garnett?" I chided.

"Not this time." He patted my arm in a fashion that seemed unusual. It was only when he withdrew his hand that I saw the word "Remain" on a slip of paper torn from a familiar source.

Holmes, it must be said, appeared distracted throughout our conversation and disposed to leave as soon as he felt he could without exciting curiosity or comment. "A new case," he murmured. "Most suggestive. Demands my full attention. Watson?"

"I believe I'll have a lemon squash before I make my way."

"As you please. Mycroft."

"Congratulations again, my dear Sherlock." The big man walked his incongruously slender brother — a giraffe and a grizzly bear, or perhaps tortoise and hare? — to the door and waited a decent interval, until certain the detective had left the premises, before turning to me.

"Thank you for staying, Doctor."

"Why have you asked me to do so?"

He sniffed, took a turn about the room, bringing a large hand down the back of his head, as though to smooth the remaining hairs there. I realized abruptly that he was melancholy.

"I'm not quite sure how to begin."

"The Caterpillar tells Alice to begin at the

beginning and when you get to the end, stop."

"Yes." He smiled. "I seem to recall Alice being invoked in this room before."

I waited, passing the interval by lighting a pipe of my own.

"You once wrote, and I recently had occasion to cite your observation, that my brother's knowledge of politics was — how did you describe it? — 'feeble.' "

"I daresay it is less so than formerly."

"I daresay less than formerly." He cocked his massive head, a man not entirely convinced. "But still . . ." He stole a glance in my direction and seemingly determined on another tack. "We live in strange times, Doctor."

What ailed the man? I rose to my feet.

"What are you endeavoring to tell me, Mycroft?"

He turned and faced me directly at last.

"I'm endeavoring to tell you that my brother has failed. That Sherlock Holmes has failed."

I don't know what I thought he was about to say, but this was certainly the farthest thing from my mind.

"Failed? How?" I protested. "Your brother went to Russia, ingeniously obtained a full confession from the perpetrator behind the nauseating hoax known as the Protocols of the Elders of Zion, and managed to keep hold of it despite the most urgent personal promptings to surrender it."

"The problem is it doesn't make any difference."

"Doesn't make any difference," I dumbly repeated.

"The damned Protocols of the Elders of Zion have taken root in the popular imagination; confessions be damned, they are disbelieved. Worse, the confessor, this Krushenev creature, has recanted."

"Recanted?" All I seemed able to do was echo every final word.

"Mr. Krushenev declares the confession to have been coerced, and if I understand what transpired, he is in fact telling the truth."

He waited, peering at me closely.

"He is," I found myself admitting. "But I was there! I tell you his confession was genuine."

"It makes no difference, alas. Those people who are determined to hate and fear the Jewish race have fastened onto it in half a dozen languages already. Of course we have contacted the newspapers," he went on, anticipating my next remark. "There will be the inevitable retractions, articles, and

337

exposés." He shook his massive head again. "But people believe what they want to believe."

"I think I expressed that idea in this very room not so long ago."

"What they *need* to believe — and no facts will convince them otherwise," he went on, speaking as much to himself as me. "They will not be accepted as facts. They will produce alternative facts. Sherlock was naïve to think otherwise. We all were."

Now it was my turn to subside heavily into a chair as the realization sank in.

"Then everything we went through, everything she went through —"

"Mrs. Walling?"

"Rivka Nussbaum. And Manya Lippman. What they all went through. It was all for nothing."

Mycroft didn't reply. There was, I suddenly understood, nothing he could say.

"What will you tell Sherlock?"

This question he had at least anticipated.

"I shall tell him nothing. And I suspect he will not ask," he added before I could object. "He will not ask because I imagine that somewhere he has already understood. There will always be a war between light and darkness, between science and superstition, between education and ignorance.

Ignorance is easier. It requires no study. Faith is the enemy of thought," he added, mordantly pleased with his aphorism.

I now recalled Holmes's prescient question at the start of this entire misbegotten affair. He had asked me if I thought it better were the Protocols bona fide or fraudulent. I had unhesitatingly chosen the latter, but now I perceived my error. Authentic, the Protocols could be halted in their tracks, their nefarious perpetrators — Jewish or otherwise — found and dealt with. But how to stop a lie from spreading?

"You paint a gloomy picture of our new century."

"I'm afraid I do."

He saw my expression change. "What are you thinking?"

"I was just remembering — it was only weeks ago. Holmes, Sherlock, I mean, and I were celebrating his birthday. He was bemoaning the lack of criminal ingenuity and talking of retirement . . ." I trailed off.

"And later?"

"Later he said the crimes were getting bigger. He spoke of Dr. Pavlov and his conditioned reflex as applied to people."

"He understands more than I gave him credit for." Mycroft Holmes loved his brother.

My pipe had gone out. Or perhaps I'd entirely forgotten to light it.

Shortly thereafter, I left the Diogenes Club and walked for some time before boarding the Underground. Juliet knew me well enough by this time to comprehend my moods. Supper was waiting, and Maria was happy to welcome me back with mutton, dressed as I preferred, with mint sauce, parsley, and new potatoes. I did the best I could by way of enthusiastic conversation, but there was so much I could not tell Juliet, much that would only distress and confuse her.

I did see Holmes once again, not two but three weeks later at St. James's Palace, where, in a small ceremony attended by Mycroft, and no one else so far as I was able to determine, we were duly decorated by His Majesty King Edward VII. In fact, this is not strictly speaking, accurate. Before our investiture, His Majesty solemnly affixed a decoration we could not see to the lapel of a young boy whom I judged to be roughly thirteen years of age, telling him something I could not make out. The lad was accompanied by an older woman of perhaps sixty. Both were dressed in black and left directly the King shook their hands. My sense was that Edward VII had a heavy schedule that day, for after pinning OBEs on our lapels and mumbling perfunctory salutations on behalf of a grateful nation, His Majesty took himself off at a brisk pace, surrounded by his bevy of attendants, leaving his equerry to gracefully repossess the blue *fleur-de-lis* crucifixes and purple-ribboned honors we could never display, for services that would remain forever secret. For some reason the whole exchange put me in mind of a trip to the dentist, a mere detour out of one's normal day. Afterwards, in the open air on Kensington Gore, I could inhale the first inklings of spring.

"Come, Doctor, we have a visit to make."

I did not need to ask where. The Highgate Cemetery was already quite green, and we threaded our way in silence through its pleasant leafy pathways without speaking. We found the sexton, who directed us to Manya Lippman's simple headstone. According to the dates, the woman had been only thirty-four years of age. Beneath her name, and dates of birth and death, was engraved a startling postscript:

*Beloved Mother of Boaz.*

With a shock of recognition, I now realized who the young boy was whose investiture had preceded our own.

"Perhaps the lad will be allowed to retain

his medal," Holmes murmured, reading my thoughts.

"Small enough recompense" was my only comment. I wondered, without saying so aloud, if the woman known as Manya Lippman had also been awarded a medal. Come to that, had she possibly been buried with it?

We stood by the grave for some moments, each wrapped in our own thoughts. And then left her as we had abandoned her in the London City Morgue.

**March 15.** Our old, comforting routines — Juliet's and mine — soon reasserted themselves. "A kingdom for an appendectomy!" I laughed, and soon our mad chase back and forth across the Continent receded from immediate memory. Time passed, and I heard little from my remarkable friend. There was a short note on our wedding anniversary in which he alluded again to the possibility of retirement. I read the line with a twinge and wrote back asking if he had replaced the Stradivarius. Its destruction, I was convinced, had taken a toll on him that music might redress — that remedy had worked wonders before — but he did not answer.

Juliet and her friend Edith Ayrton — aka Mrs. Israel Zangwill — continued their efforts on behalf of women's suffrage. After my experiences with Anna Strunsky Walling, the idea struck me as increasingly sensible, if not inevitable.

I did not confide my reasoning to Juliet, but now and again, when my schedule permitted, I found I was marching, banner in hand, for the cause.*

The following Christmas I was agreeably surprised to receive a note from Mrs. Walling, wishing me the season's greetings and relating the progress she and her husband were making spearheading their brainchild, the National Association for the Advancement of Coloured People.

Nowhere did she mention Holmes.

And I doubt the detective, his carapace fully reformed, will ever again allude to her.

As years passed, the Protocols of the Elders of Zion intermittently resurfaced, usually in hate sheets and always rebutted in *The Times of London* and other reputable publications.

But sometimes, fast asleep, I would dream of Rivka Nussbaum and wake weeping.

THIS IS WHERE WATSON'S
NOTEBOOK ENDS.

---

* Women in England did not get the vote until 1918; in the United States they got it in 1920.

343

# EPILOGUE

Watson's notes were made contemporaneously with the events he describes. The reader may be interested to learn what followed.

In 1905, in Portsmouth, New Hampshire, President Theodore Roosevelt helped negotiate an end to the ruinous Russo-Japanese War. For his contribution, he was awarded the Nobel Peace Prize, the first president to receive one.

Pyotr Ivanovich Rachkovsky, head of the Okhrana, the man who commissioned the Protocols of the Elders of Zion, sometimes referred to as the Protocols of the Learned Elders of Zion, died in 1910 at the age of fifty-seven. (The actor Michael Bryant portrayed him on television in *Fall of Eagles*.)

In 1917 Foreign Secretary and former prime minister Arthur Balfour made a declaration that His Majesty's Government would look "with favour" on a national Jewish homeland in Palestine.

Israel Zangwill lived until 1926. Many of his works were staged or filmed, including an unsuccessful musical based on his book, *The King of Schnorrers.*

The abortive Russian revolution of 1905 merely postponed the inevitable collapse of the Romanov dynasty, which the catastrophic losses of World War I brought about in 1917. The Tsar was forced to abdicate. The following year, Nicholas, his wife and children, including his hemophiliac son the Tsarevitch, were all shot to death in a cellar. If you compare their photographs, cousins Tsar Nicholas II and King George V (who ascended to the throne in 1910) look like identical twins.

The death of the charismatic Zionist Theodor Herzl was put down to heart failure.

Anna and William English Walling remained married until 1917. The marriage foundered in part when Walling resigned from the Republican Party (he had also been a Socialist), in protest because of its opposition to participation in the war in Europe, which he felt America was morally obligated to join. Anna, a lifelong pacifist, could not accept this. Walling died in 1936; Anna lived until 1964. A prime mover in the movement for women's rights, she was also a novelist.

Constance Clara Garnett, translator of Tolstoy, Dostoyevsky, Turgenev, and Chekov, died in 1946.

In 1949, chemist Chaim (Charles) Weizmann became the first president of Israel.

In 1919, copies of the Protocols of the Learned Elders of Zion were distributed by White Russians to delegates at the Versailles Peace Conference. The Protocols were first exposed as fraudulent by *The Times of London,* but printings continue to flourish. They were translated into Polish in 1920 and were published intermittently but in their entirety also in 1920 by Henry Ford in his newspaper, *The Dearborn Independent.* (After a lawsuit charging him with libel ended in a mistrial, Ford issued a public apology and closed his newspaper in 1927.) The Protocols appeared in Arabic and Italian in 1921, by which time they had been translated into sixteen languages and sold half a million copies in America alone. In 1925, the Protocols were endorsed as authentic by Hitler in his book *Mein Kampf.*

In 1964, Senators Dodd and Keating wrote a report for Congress that denounced the Protocols as "a fabricated 'historic' document," but in 1972, a second Spanish edition appeared to explain and justify certain reforms by the Vatican. That same year, the Protocols were published in Egypt. In 1974 they appeared in India under the title "International Conspiracy Against Indians." In 1977, the Protocols were republished in the United States, and in 1978, they reappeared in England. In 1987, the first Japanese edition appeared, and in 1988, they were published by Hamas. Some Catholic schools in Mexico made the Protocols required reading in 1992, the same year they reappeared in Russia.

In 1993, a Russian court labeled the documents "an anti-Semitic forgery."

In 1999, the French newspaper *L'Express* "definitively" identified the propagandist hack Mathieu Golovinsky as the author of the Protocols. Others have attributed them to Sergius Nilus, and still others to Pavel Krushenev.

In 2000, the Protocols were published in Louisiana. They appeared in Lebanon the same year.

In 2001, they turned up in San Diego, California.

In 2002, Arab TV broadcast the series *Knight Without a Horse,* derived from the Protocols. Egyptian state TV praised the series, stating the Protocols were a reflec-

# ACKNOWLEDGMENTS

The work, talent, and time of many people helped make this book. Credit must always go first to Sir Arthur Conan Doyle, creator of Sherlock Holmes and Dr. Watson, those quixotic adventurers whose perils and characters continue to delight millions of readers around the world. Minus Holmes and Watson, the world is without form and void.

In writing *The Adventure of the Peculiar Protocols,* I found inspiration and information in many books about the year 1905, and the Protocols of the Elders of Zion in particular. I am indebted to *The Plot: The Secret Story of the Protocols of the Elders of Zion,* a graphic novel by the late Will Eisner, and to *Pogrom: Kishinev and the Tilt of History,* by Professor Steven J. Zipperstein. I returned again and again to *Photographs for The Tsar: The Pioneering Color Photography* of Sergei Mikhailovich Prokudin-Gorskii; his pictures must be seen to be believed (and even then, it's tough — they look like outtakes from *Dr. Zhivago,* but they're not).

For Edwardian period detail and European geopolitics, *The Proud Tower,* by Barbara Tuchman, proved indispensable, and for the Orient Express, Shirley Sherwood's beautiful and comprehensive history of that remarkable train was a delight. I hope train buffs will forgive my rearranging a few details and adding one carriage that never existed.

For Sherlockiana, the list is endless, but I consulted *Sherlock Holmes's London,* by Tsukasa Kobayashi, Akane Higashiyama, and Masaharu Uemura, as well as Michael Harrison's classic Holmes guides (*In the Footsteps of Sherlock Holmes,* etc.) and *Good Old Index,* compiled by Thomas W. Ross.

I have played fast and loose and mushed around several dates during the year 1905. I hope the Bloomsbury crowd and 1905 buffs will forgive me. And Alfred Hitchcock, for his *chef d'oeuvre, The Lady Vanishes,* to which I helped myself.

Lastly, I must thank the many friends who, while doubtless having better things to do, nonetheless stopped to read — and in many cases reread — the novel's various iterations, after which they were generous with criticisms and suggestions from which I eagerly benefited. These folks include but are not limited to Gerry Abrams, Tom Barad, John Collee, Barbara Fisher, Leslie Fram, Alan Gasmer, Cole Haddon, Steven-Charles Jaffe, Keith Kahla, Susan Kinsolving, William Kinsolving, Les Klinger, Gary Lucchesi, Juliana Maio, Constance Meyer, Dylan Meyer, Madeline Meyer, Paula Namer, Michael Phillips, Greg Prickman (who turns out to be real), Terry Rioux, David Robb, Ron Roose, David Shaw, Charlotte Sheedy, Roger Spottiswoode, Tatiana Spottiswoode, and Robert Wallace.

To all of them, my profound gratitude.

# ABOUT THE AUTHOR

**Nicholas Meyer** is the author three previous Sherlock Holmes novels, including *The Seven-Per-Cent Solution,* which was on the *New York Times* bestseller list for a year. He's a screen-writer and film director, responsible for *The Day After, Time After Time,* as well as *Star Trek II: The Wrath of Khan, Star Trek IV: The Voyage Home,* and *Star Trek VI: The Undiscovered Country* among many others. A native of New York City, he lives in Santa Monica, California.